EAGLE
AGAINST
THE STARS

DISCARD

STEVE WHITE

BAEN

EAGLE AGAINST THE STARS

This is a work of fiction. All the characters and events portrayed in this book are fictional, and any resemblance to real people or incidents is purely coincidental.

A Baen Books Original

Baen Publishing Enterprises
P.O. Box 1403
Riverdale, NY 10471

ISBN: 0-671-57846-4

Cover art by Stephen Hickman

First printing, January 2000

Distributed by Simon & Schuster
1230 Avenue of the Americas
New York, NY 10020

Typeset by Windhaven Press, Auburn, NH
Printed in the United States of America

KNOCK KNOCK . . .

The swarm of gigantic spacecraft were in visual range, although their daunting massiveness was reduced to the dimensions of iron filings by the distance. We turned our backs on the universe. But the universe didn't take the hint.

"Colonel? It's Cheyenne Mountain, sir. Top security."

"Of course," Roark sighed. *So soon? I'd hoped to have a little longer.*

He turned to the comm screen. General Harris looked out from it, as haggard as Roark felt.

"Colonel," Harris said heavily, "the Lokaron demands have been reviewed at the highest level. The decision has been made to implement Case Gamma, effective immediately."

"General, we have Dr. Kazin here. I respectfully request a delay so that we can send him down."

Another uniformed figure pushed Harris out of the pickup. The new image had only one star—but he was the Orbital Command's resident political officer. "Doctor Kazin is a member of the Earth First Party," he snapped. "He—unlike, it seems, certain others—will recognize the necessity for this action, Colonel. Do I make myself clear?" With a final sneer, he turned away.

Harris moved back into the pickup. "Carry out your orders, Colonel," he said firmly. Then, with a sideways glance as though to make certain he was alone, he spoke in a different voice. "Good-bye, Mike."

To Sandy, more than ever.

PROLOGUE

The sun broke over the edge of Earth, bringing with it a slender blue-white sickle of dawn that encroached on the expanse of darkness that was the planet's nightside as seen from low orbit. The Orbital Command-and-Control Station's viewport polarized against the glare.

But, thought Colonel Michael Roark, there was still plenty of light to see despair by. The swarm of spacecraft that had no business being there were in visual range, although their daunting massiveness was reduced to the dimensions of iron filings by the distance, and the sun glinted on them.

He shifted uncomfortably in his pressure suit. They'd all been wearing the things, rather than the usual blue jumpsuits with U.S. Air Force Orbital Command shoulder flashes, for almost twenty-four hours. That was how long it had been since those impossible ships had appeared, effortlessly matching orbits with OCCS, and they'd gone to Red Alert status. Since then the uncharacteristically rigid military routine had been armor for their sanity in the new world of unreality they'd abruptly entered. Still, eyes constantly wandered toward the viewport, and Roark wasn't inclined to reprimand anyone for it.

At least the aliens—*Lokaron*, they called themselves—hadn't kept them in suspense. They'd responded to the Station's hails at once, with a lengthy message to be transmitted to the U.S. government. Roark had patched them into the satellite net as requested—a process which had given him access to the message. He hadn't shared it with his personnel, for they would be just as able as he was to foresee the goverent's response . . . and the likely consequences for themselves.

Roark shifted position, moving with the ease of one long-practiced in the art of walking in zero gravity on a metal deck with magnetic soles. Drugs counteracted the effects of long-term weightlessness on the human skeleton and immune system, but nothing could prevent the loss of muscle tone. *I'll be weak as a kitten down there at first,* he thought . . . then laughed silently at himself. Unless he was very wrong about his probable future, he didn't need to worry about anything pertaining to his return to Earth.

There was a sound of awkward movement by his side. Sidney Kazin, PhD, wore the same USAF issue as everyone else on the station, but he couldn't conceivably have been mistaken for any kind of military man, even on the Orbital Command's relaxed standards. He lacked zero-gee experience, and had been miserably uncomfortable since a shuttle had brought him up to run tests on some quirky new instrumentation. That discomfort had been forgotten the moment the strange craft had appeared, as had everything else.

"Anything new, Colonel?"

"No, Doctor." *Not in the last five minutes,* Roark didn't add. "Our latest word from Cheyenne Mountain is to sit tight and await further orders. And the . . . Lokaron still haven't been inclined to chat with us."

"But they've told us quite a lot, you know . . . just by the way they arrived." Kazin's eyes glowed behind his Coke-bottle glasses, and his frizzy hair and beard formed a weightless aureole. Roark smiled at him, and wondered what the ecstasy of scientific curiosity was like. "In the first place, their message was in English. They've obviously been around a while for their computers to have cracked the language."

"But maybe not as long as we might imagine," Roark demurred. "After all, we don't know the capabilities of *their* computers. Besides, nobody's seen them conducting any studies."

"Come on, Colonel! Remember how they just appeared out of nowhere, without being tracked until they were practically entering orbit?" Kazin laughed nervously. "Big surprise! We're dealing with a technology that can beat the lightspeed limit and send a major expedition—not just some half-assed little robot probe—across interstellar distances! Unless they *want* us to detect them, we *won't* detect them."

"Funny the UFO cultists in the last century, with all their alleged photos and radar sightings, didn't think of that," Roark mused. "But why do you assume they came here faster than light? Granted, interstellar travel slower than that would take a long time. But it doesn't violate any physical laws, which faster-than-light travel does."

"Oh, I'm not saying they can actually break through the lightspeed barrier. You're right, that's a

mathematical absurdity. But they must be able to get
around it in some way." Kazin pointed out the
viewport. "Those are too small to be STL interstellar
ships."

"Small? You call those things *small*?"

"Colonel, anything designed to keep a crew alive
that long would have to be *humongous*! I don't care
what it's using for propulsion. And that's another
thing," Kazin went on, words practically tripping over
themselves. "What *does* make those suckers move?
They didn't perform any magic feats while matching
orbits with us—they've obviously got to play by the
rules of inertia. But they've got nothing that could
possibly be exhaust nozzles or anything like that.
They have something that isn't a reaction drive—
something Newton didn't allow for. Something we
can't even theorize." An uncontrollable shiver ran
through the young scientist, and he hugged himself
to contain the trembling. "Dear God! The things we'll
be able to learn from them!"

Roark felt a wave of sadness wash over him. He
knew the type. Kazin was considered politically
harmless, or else he wouldn't have been sent up
here. Indeed, he was a member of the Earth First
Party . . . under constant suspicion, and as blissfully
unaware of that suspicion as he was of the philosophical contradictions between his work and the
Party's antiscience doctrines. It wouldn't last forever,
of course. Sooner or later, he'd be told he couldn't
publish something because his findings were ideologically unacceptable. Like the innocent he was,
he would voice his indignation openly . . . and
there'd be yet another mysterious disappearance,
officially blamed on "reactionary elements" and used
as an excuse for still further encroachments on the
civil liberties Americans would once have missed.

Presently, Kazin went below to his tiny cubicle. It was no accident he was staying at OCCS; it was the only manned installation in orbit. The Orbital Command's weaponry—and most especially the fusion-pumped X-ray lasers that waited to die that they might yield up ultrahigh-energy pulses at the moment of death—were unmanned. All the rest of the Command's personnel were dirtside. Only Roark and a few others were actually in orbit to oversee America's remote-controlled defenders. *Defenders against what?* he wondered in prudent silence. *The continent-sized slum that is Russia? Or whatever generalissimo is currently top snake in the snake pit that used to be China?* Nobody else was in space at all.

Roark's eyes strayed to the bone-white crescent of Luna. Men had set foot there, more than fifty years ago. The science-fiction writers of his grandparents' generation had imagined a lot of things in connection with the first moon landing . . . but not that humans would attain that ancient dream and then simply drop the ball. Such idiocy had been beyond even their powers of imagination.

We turned our backs on the universe. Roark's gaze swung back to the alien ships. *But the universe didn't take the hint.*

"Colonel?" The comm technician's voice, charged with an odd mixture of diffidence and tension, broke into his thoughts. "It's Cheyenne Mountain, sir. Top security."

"Of course," Roark sighed. *So soon? I'd hoped to have a little longer.* He turned to the comm console, where General Harris' face looked out of the screen, as haggard as Roark felt. The image, like the sound, was carried on waves that were scrambled into meaninglessness and reconstituted only at this console, with no appreciable delay. The Lokaron wouldn't be able to intercept anything useful.

"Colonel," Harris said heavily, "the Lokaron demands have been reviewed at the highest level. The decision has been made to implement Case Gamma, effective immediately."

Roark heard the muttering around him in the cramped spaces. Everyone present knew what that meant. He ignored it. "General, you realize of course—"

"Those are my orders, Colonel—and yours!" Harris' voice cracked.

In a detached sort of way, Roark wondered at his own despair. This was, after all, merely what he'd expected. "General, we have a civilian here—Doctor Kazin. I feel uncomfortable about putting him at risk. I respectfully request a delay so that we can send him down. A shuttle can be made ready in—"

Another Air Force-uniformed figure pushed Harris out of the pickup. The new image in the screen had only one star to Harris' two. But that didn't matter—Roark recognized him as the Orbital Command's resident political officer. "Doctor Kazin is a member of the Earth First Party, Colonel," he snapped. "As such, he—unlike, it seems, certain others—will recognize the necessity for this action. He will be glad to place himself in the front line of defense—a defense of everything America has achieved in the last two decades under the Party's progressive, enlightened guidance! Everyone's behavior in this crisis will be subject to later scrutiny. *Everyone's*, Colonel. Do I make myself clear?" With a final sneer, he turned away.

Harris moved back into the pickup. "Carry out your orders, Colonel," he said firmly. Then, with a sideways glance as though to make certain he was alone, he spoke in a different voice. "Good-bye, Mike."

"Good-bye, sir," Roark replied . . . but to a blank screen, for astonishment had rendered him speechless until after the general had cut the connection.

He set to work briskly, allowing himself to think of nothing save the series of orders he needed to give. Those orders went out, and at various points in various orbits, weapons began to ponderously realign themselves on a single target, or rather a cluster of targets. The personnel of OCCS moved just as mechanically, performing a task about which they dared not brood.

That task was about done when Kazin's head appeared in the hatchway, wearing an expression brewed from alarm and disbelief. Roark smiled. The rumor mill worked quickly in a small, enclosed environment like this.

"Colonel, what's going on? I've got clearance, you know. What are you doing?"

Roark heard a robot speaking for him. "You have the requisite clearance, Doctor Kazin, but not the need to know. I must ask you to go below, as you are a civilian and we are about to enter a war footing."

The scientist's expression took on a new element: desperation. "So it's true! You're going to *attack* them! But you *can't*! I mean—"

"It's hardly my decision, Doctor. I'm acting under orders."

"But . . . but. . . . " Kazin clambered up to face Roark, and tried to speak calmly. "Colonel, this is crazy. Do you have any idea what you're dealing with? Just imagine . . . well, no offense, but imagine a bunch of Civil War guys going up against the U.S. Air Force!"

"I repeat, Doctor, it's not exactly my idea. However, I have no choice but to follow orders."

"In a pig's ass you don't! We're all going to *die* here, Colonel! And for absolutely nothing. Can't you understand that? You've got to tell those shitheads down there that—"

"Doctor Kazin!" The bullwhip crack of command in Roark's voice stopped the scientist's rising hysteria dead. "This is an Air Force installation, and you are under military jurisdiction. You will control yourself, or I will order you placed under restraint." He leaned forward into the stunned silence and spoke in a murmur only Kazin could here. "Come on, Sidney. Nothing I could tell them would make any difference. You know that."

Kazin's lower lip trembled, and his eyes grew red. "But . . . *why*? Why are they doing this? I don't understand."

He really doesn't understand, Roark realized. *But why should he? The only reason he's an Earth First Party member is because he has to be to get funding.* "You saw the Lokaron message, Sidney. I shouldn't have shown it to you, but I did. They're demanding trade concessions. They want to sell us advanced technology. Stuff beyond anything we've got. And the Party can't allow that. It rode the antitechnology hysteria of the late twentieth century to power. It's committed to freezing even our 'dehumanizing' homegrown stuff at an arbitrary level. How do you expect them to react to this?"

Kazin didn't collapse—people generally didn't in zero-gee. Instead he hung, a limp vessel of despair attached to the deck by his magnetic soles, as Roark turned away and murmured a query to the comm technician.

"Affirmative, Colonel," was the reply. "All targeting solutions are locked in. And the groundside system's prepared to coordinate with us on a time-on-target basis."

"Very good." Roark straightened up. He glanced out the viewport at the sunlit slivers of the alien ships, here within visual range, with OCCS under whatever they used for guns. "Commence countdown."

From behind him came Kazin's broken voice. "It won't even matter, you know. After they've brushed off whatever you can do, they'll go ahead and get their trade concessions anyway. So what's the point, Colonel?"

Good question, Roark admitted silently. *But you wouldn't understand the answer, Sidney. I'm obeying these stupid, futile orders from a government which publicly despises me and everybody else in uniform because if I don't obey them my life will have meant nothing.*

I'm not even sure I understand it.

It was, he thought with a touch of guilt, relatively easy for him. Unmarried, with his parents both dead, he had no immediate family that he'd never see again. No family at all, really . . . except his younger cousin, Ben Roark. Even at this moment, his lips twitched upward in a smile at the thought of the ribbings he'd given Ben, now in his early thirties, over his career choice. A *spook,* for God's sake. What a disgrace!

The smile died aborning. Kazin was probably right. Ben would live in a world where the Lokaron would be a fact of life—something new under Earth's sun. *What will that world be like?*

The countdown ticked on.

CHAPTER ONE

The recent hurricane had left Grand Cayman even flatter than usual. But by some miracle the Buccaneer Inn, near the center of Seven-Mile Beach, had been spared, and its bar was already back in business. So Ben Roark could sit in the sea breeze at one of the few authentic beachside bars left, and toast the dispensation of nature which had left him his favorite watering hole. It was as good a thing as any to toast.

He sat with his back to the hotel pool and the agreeably seedy buildings behind it, looking out Caribbean-ward at the setting sun behind the array of bottles. Behind him and to the left, the pinochle game was in full swing at the little table where, he was assured, it had been going on for at least two generations, since the 1970s. Roark didn't know about that, but he could testify that it had been in progress since he'd started frequenting the Buccaneer. The players changed, one Caymanian taking over another's hand as the other shuffled off to do whatever it was Caymanians did, but the game lived on. He wondered

what would have happened if Hurricane Sergei had
blown this place away. Would they have set the table
back up, lonely on the beach, and resumed the game
in splendid isolation with only the seabirds for spectators? Probably not. They would have found another
hotel bar.

Roark shifted position on the stool, careful to keep
his back in its practiced anti-interruption arch. It was
how he always presented his back to the tourists—
mostly tipsy on the foo-foo rum drinks with little
paper parasols that provided the bar's profit margin—
who shot curious glances at the white man who
obviously wasn't one of them. He had no desire to
be drawn into any conversation but the one he was
already having with Marlowe, who occupied the stool
to his left.

The Jamaican dropped into the Buccaneer whenever he was in the Caymans on his obscure business
trips. (Drugs, of course, though Roark had never
been boorish enough to ask him.) They'd been
talking about Jamaica, and Roark was just through
telling Marlowe what he wanted to hear: that Jamaica
had an *identity*, it was a *nation*, not just an offshore
U.S. beach like the Caymans.

"Dis mon speaks nothin' but de truth!" Marlowe
announced to everyone in earshot, thumping the bar
for emphasis. "Bring him another of what he drinkin',"
he added imperiously, in the general direction of the
bartender.

It was, Roark thought, good to know that some
things never changed—like the way the Jamaicans
had of lording it over the blacks from the other
ex-British colonies in the West Indies. The bartender produced an Appleton's straight up with
wordless dignity, darting Roark a look of disapproval
for bullshitting Marlowe out of free drinks.

What the hell, Roark thought, *it's only justice. This way, at least some of the money he's made selling drugs to Americans finds its way back home.* He instantly regretted the thought. The fact was, he genuinely liked Marlowe—and most Jamaicans, come to that. It wasn't their fault that Americans were determined to destroy their brains. Given a demand like that, somebody was bound to supply it. Jamaican drug dealers—and Mexicans, and Colombians, and the up-and-coming Haitians—had never *forced* a single American to use their wares. Pointing out that fact was a one-way road to total unpopularity in the U.S., whose national symbol should have been the scapegoat rather than the eagle. Roark could attest to that.

Marlowe took a swig of his Red Stripe beer and gave Roark an appraising look. "So how you holdin' up, mon?"

"Can't complain." That was another thing he liked about Marlowe: the Jamaican had always reciprocated his own disinclination to ask detailed occupational questions. "I'm sort of semiretired, you know. A freelancer."

"Uh-huh." Marlowe nodded. "Been doin' much freelancin' lately?"

"Well, business is kind of slow. . . . "

"Uh-huh," Marlowe repeated, and gave his head a shake of commiseration. "It de times, mon. Terrible times all over. So many changes." He took another gulp of Red Stripe and looked around at the sea, the beach and the palm trees as though in search of something immutable. It was a mistake, for as his gaze swung around to the left he saw what had been in Roark's line of sight all along.

The Cayman Islands had maintained—indeed, cemented—their position as the Switzerland of the western hemisphere, and George Town had recently seen a building boom. The new edifices the banks had put up were visible from here, for they soared to a height their slender lines seemed incapable of supporting. *Lokaron structural materials,* Roark thought. He recalled long-ago briefings: metals of a perfect, molecularly aligned crystalline structure, produced in zero gravity. . . .

"Yeah," he agreed. "Awful goddamned times." He looked away from those hateful towers, then glanced to his right, where he heard someone settling onto the neighboring stool. His eyes met those of the new arrival . . . and froze.

Henry Havelock gave his patented lift of one gray eyebrow. "Why, Ben!" he exclaimed, smoothly counterfeiting surprise.

Well, I was searching for things that never change, Roark told himself. One such thing was the way Americans expected high-level government operatives to look. Havelock had that look in spades: a vigorously spare man in his well-preserved sixties, lean keen face tanned red-brown, gray mustache clipped to mathematically perfect neatness, unconscious military bearing even in the touristy getup he was now wearing. In every generation, that look seemed to carry a reassurance that the men of an earlier, more solid America were still quietly running things. *Total bullshit, of course,* Roark reflected. *Especially in Havelock's case.*

"You a friend of Ben's, mon?" Marlowe asked, extending a hand.

Roark performed curt introductions. Havelock gave the Jamaican a level blue regard (yes, he had blue eyes, too) and briefly took the proffered hand. "So I am," he said, sparing Roark the need to lie. "Ben and I go back a long way. In fact, I was hoping I'd run into him here. He and I need to talk a little business." He gave another eyebrow lift to place emphasis on the last sentence.

Marlowe looked at Roark quizzically. Roark briefly considered his options, then smiled at the Jamaican. "Yeah. Henry and I have some things to discuss. I'll catch you later."

"Sure, mon. Sure. Nice meetin' you, Mr. Havelock." Marlowe chugged the last of his beer, stood up, and ambled over to study the pinochle game.

"Interesting class of friends you've acquired down here," Havelock observed.

"It's called social climbing. Now what the hell are you doing here and what the hell do you want?"

"I have a little job that needs doing. I thought you might be interested."

"Go fuck yourself. I'm retired."

"No, you're not retired. You're unemployed . . . unless one counts as employment your full-time occupation of drinking yourself to death." Havelock raised a restraining hand as Roark started to angrily open his mouth. "Yes, I know: you'd saved some money before you left the Company in a snit. And the dump you're leasing can't be costing you much. But sooner or later you'll drink up the last of it, and then you'll just be another dying beach lush."

"Sweet of you to care."

"I suppose I shouldn't. It's a fairly typical way for burned-out ex-Company types to wind up. But in your case I hate to see it, because I hate waste. You were the best, and I feel I ought to—"

"I've never yet been so drunk I couldn't recognize the smell of bullshit. And I never *will* be so hard up that I'll work for you and the fucking Company again. I'll be damned and roasting in hell before I let myself be set up like . . . like . . . "

"Katy knew the risks," Havelock said quietly. "She understood—"

"No! She didn't understand squat! In particular, she didn't understand the kind of lying, backstabbing son of a bitch you are. You set her up! And now she's dead. And you can take your job, smear Vaseline on it, and—"

"Suit yourself." Havelock stood up, looking bored. "I just thought you might find this operation interesting because it targets the Lokaron. *Directly*."

It was a tribute to the product of Appleton Estate, Parish of St. Elizabeth, Jamaica, that Havelock's words took a full heartbeat to register on Roark's alcohol-misted mind. Then he shook his head several times, partly to clear it and partly as a gesture of incredulity. "But . . . but *how*?"

Havelock smiled the smile of a fisherman who'd felt a tug on his line, and settled back onto his bar stool. "Oh come now, Ben. You know the drill. I can't tell you any details until you've signed on, and accepted all the usual security restrictions and conditions. In fact, I shouldn't even have revealed as much as I have. For now, you'll just have to take my word that you'll be doing the Lokaron one in the eye."

"But that's *impossible*!"

Roark's bewildered exclamation merely stated what had been axiomatic since the day, a decade earlier, when Lokaron ships had appeared in Earth's skies, putting an end to the long debate about extraterrestrial life and presenting demands for trade concessions to the United States government. (The aliens hadn't concerned themselves with the pathetic, vestigial legal fiction that was the United Nations, and that was the last anyone had heard of it. Roark sometimes wondered if it still met, unnoticed, in New York, performing rituals as remote from contemporary concerns as those of the monks of Mount Athos.) The ruling Earth First Party, which had turned its back on the universe beyond low Earth orbit, had been called on to accept as a trade medium the kind of advanced technology its zero-growth ideology anathematized. It had ordered the destruction of the intruders. The U.S. Air Force's Orbital Command—including Roark's idolized older cousin Mike—had done its best. That best hadn't even scratched the Lokaron ships' paint. In fact—infuriatingly, humiliatingly—it hadn't even made them *angry*. With an almost audible yawn at having gotten a tedious bit of routine out of the way, they'd repeated their demands . . . not even jacking them up, as though what had occurred had been too inconsequential to require reparations. There had been no further nonsense about resisting those demands.

"It's impossible," Roark repeated mulishly. "No direct attack on the Lokaron can succeed. Everybody knows that. It's just pissing into the wind."

"Whatever you may think of me, you know I've never been given to jousting with windmills." Taking advantage of Roark's sudden thoughtful silence, Havelock pressed on. "Of course we're not talking about a full-dress military assault. It's your kind of covert operation. And I'm not the only one who thinks it can succeed. It has support at high levels. *Very* high levels."

"Oh, wow!" Roark sneered. "I'm *so* impressed! I'll bet you're going to reel off the important-sounding titles of all sorts of palace eunuchs who didn't even need the surgery."

Havelock ignored the boozy sarcasm. He leaned forward and murmured three words: "The Central Committee."

The remaining alcohol fumes seeped out of Roark's brain, leaving a chill.

Havelock spoke briskly. "I've said far more than I should have. Now, you have to make up your mind. Are you in or out?"

Roark took a gulp of his rum. It hit the pit of his stomach hard, as is often the case after an overly rapid sobering-up. "All right, count me in. I owe the Lokaron one."

"So you do. In fact, feeling the way you do about them, I'm surprised you never joined . . . " Instead of finishing his sentence, Havelock gave an airy wave to indicate the music wafting from the pool area. It had switched from reggae to the current North American top forty. The refrain that reached their ears held the unsubtle message that much popular music did these days:

> *"Soaring on high,*
> *Bring down the sky,*
> *Eagle against the stars. . . . "*

Roark snorted. "*Those* jerk-offs? Oh, sure, all the bullshit about their daring exploits makes the teenagers cream in their jeans. But I outgrew pimples a long time ago."

Official disapproval had been powerless to prevent the Eaglemen from becoming underground pop-culture heroes. Drawing the core of its membership from among the junior officers of the humiliated U.S. military, the secret organization had two goals: expel the aliens, and restore the United States government to its old constitutional form, as they conceived it. So far, their most notable exploit had been the assassination of Secretary of State Wainwright, who had signed the treaty with the Lokaron. But for a society whose deeply buried discontents were openly voiced only at the risk of one's health, they were figures of romantic heroism: high-tech Robin Hoods, new-wave Zorros, Scarlet Pimpernels with caseless minimacs instead of rapiers. . . .

"Ever notice," Roark went on, "that for some odd reason they're vague about the details of just how they're going to kick the Lokaron off Earth? And as for going back to some idealized fantasy of the good old days when there were two parties—the Republicrats and the Democritans, or whatever they called themselves . . . Shit, the only change is that now the U.S. *admits* it's a one-party system!"

"My, aren't we cynical? But I remember you used to be interested in that sort of thing, back in the days when you *had* interests that didn't come bottled. Speaking of which, you might want to finish that drink before we leave. It's the last one you're going to be having for a while."

"*What?* You mean we're leaving *now*? And . . . what was that about drinks?"

"You heard me. You're on the wagon for the duration, my friend. Starting now."

"But . . . but look, I can handle it! I never drink too much at once—you get sloppy that way. No, it's just *maintenance* drinking. You know, just enough to keep my edge . . . keep me humming at exactly the right level."

The sun had set into the Caribbean, but even in the dusk Havelock's eyes could be seen to harden. "There was a time when you would have been the first to recognize the line of crap you're spouting for what it is. Not that recognizing it is any great accomplishment. Every drunk says the same thing, practically verbatim. Well, I'm not going to let you jeopardize the success of this operation. If you want in, you're off the stuff. That's the condition. If you can't live with it, say so now, and I'll waste no more of your time or mine."

"All right, all right." Roark finished the rum, storing the taste away in his memory. Then he stood up and looked around. Marlowe had already gone. "Gotta go to my place and—"

"Don't worry about it. Your lease will be taken care of. And you won't need any personal effects; everything will be provided. Now let's go. My plane is waiting."

Havelock's car had been supplied by a Company front in George Town. The driver and another equally uncommunicative character in the front seat said nothing as they drove toward the airfield—not the commercial one, but a little private strip Roark already knew about.

"Well," Roark ventured as they pulled up on the apron, close to a twin-engined tilt-rotor, "maybe you'll at least be able to give me some details while we're in the air."

"We won't be traveling together that long," Havelock said as they got out. "Just to Miami. Then we part company. I have business in Washington. You're going to Area 51."

Roark smiled. The ultrahigh-security installation in the Nevada desert dated back a couple of generations, to the height of the "flying saucer" craze. In those days it had figured in the UFO mythos as the place where the U.S. government carried on a secret study of extraterrestrials. Nowadays, ironically, that old wet-dream had become sober fact.

They proceeded toward the plane, with the two strong, silent types falling in at their flanks and looking watchful.

"Hey, mon!" came a familiar voice from off to the right, where a smaller, less prepossessing plane—the field's only other occupant—was being fueled. "You leavin' tonight too? Guess the freelancin' business lookin' up!" Marlowe stepped out of the darkness, his grin white against his dark face. Then he looked at Roark's three companions, and the grin faded. "Everything okay, mon?" he asked quietly.

"Yeah, fine," Roark assured. "Something's come up. My friends here are just—"

The little control shack exploded.

The light that flooded the scene gave them only a tiny fraction of a second's warning. But Roark was already on his way to the deck as the shock wave and the ear-bruising roar hit them, dragging Marlowe down with him. Old training took command of his reflexes, and he looked around. The two guards, also flat on the tarmac, already had handguns out and were firing at four approaching figures. Havelock was fumbling for something inside his jacket. The attackers returned fire, and a tracery of automatic fire ran over one of Havelock's men, whose body jerked convulsively and then sprawled motionless. His companion continued to fire at the approaching figures. Something hit the fuel truck beside Marlowe's plane; it, and the plane, went up in a roaring gout of flame. Against that bright background, Roark saw one of the attackers stagger from a hit. But staggering was all he did. Those guys were wearing battle dress, fashioned from one of Kevlar's successors. It could stop assault-rifle rounds at point-blank range, which was why the trend in infantry weapons was now away from the assault-rifle philosophy and back toward higher calibers and lower rates of fire. Unless he scored a lucky head hit, the guard might as well have been shooting a water pistol at them.

Then Havelock finally brought his right hand up into firing position. What that hand held didn't fully register on Roark at first. Then, with a *crack!* of air rushing in to fill a narrow tunnel of vacuum that had been burned through it, a line of glimmering ionized air instantaneously speared one of the attackers, who fell backwards and lay still.

Experimental weapon-grade lasers dated back to the 1980s: energy hogs that had filled a helicopter or an APC and proven less deadly than a light machine gun. The things had gotten better, of course. Big ones had been the mainstay of the late lamented U.S. Air Force Orbital Command. You could even build a man-portable one, if you didn't mind lugging around a backpack-sized battery-*cum*-capacitor and were willing to accept degraded performance in fog or smoke. Not that anyone did build them. It was precisely the kind of technology the Earth First Party had long suppressed.

But the Lokaron, unsurprisingly, could do better. Their little superconductor-loop energy cells could handle the rapid energy discharge a laser weapon required. And their lasers automatically shifted wavelengths up and down the spectrum to compensate for atmospheric conditions. With their technology, you could even engineer that old science-fiction staple, the laser *pistol.* . . .

Like the one Havelock now pointed at the three remaining attackers, one after another in rapid succession. Three flashing spears of light impaled them in as many seconds. And all was quiet, save the roaring flames of the shack and Marlowe's plane.

Roark got slowly to his feet. Beside him, Marlowe did the same—silently, eyes wide. Havelock turned to face them. Roark pointed a shaky finger at the thing in the older man's hand, started to ask a question. . . .

As abruptly as a striking rattlesnake, Havelock brought his hand up. The laser flashed.

Before Roark had time to react, or even to think, Marlowe was toppling over.

Roark whirled and stared. The Jamaican was lying on his back. Smoke was curling up from the neat hole just above the bridge of his nose. There was no blood. Those who die instantly do not bleed, to speak of.

Roark turned, and advanced slowly—or so it seemed in the state of protracted time he currently inhabited—toward Havelock. The hand holding the laser pistol rose very slightly. Roark stopped dead.

"You murdering bastard," he croaked. "Why—?"

"He saw this weapon, Ben," Havelock explained patiently. "More to the point, he saw *me* with it. As we all know, there are a certain number of illegal Lokaron weapons in circulation on Earth. But I can't be seen to have one—not by living witnesses. And he's certainly no loss."

Out of the corner of his eye, Roark saw that the surviving guard had gotten up and was covering him. Even if he could avoid Havelock's weapon, which struck at the speed of light, that second man would get him. He forced himself to relax, one muscle at a time. He even managed a smile. "Aren't you worried about leaving him, and the others, lying around here to be found?"

"Not really. A laser burn isn't like a bullet, you know. It can't possibly be traced to a particular weapon. These things are going to be a boon to the criminal element, when they become generally available."

"That's an odd thing to hear, coming from a man who works for a government committed to keeping stuff like that out of circulation." The Earth First

Party had sought to minimize the impact of Lokaron technology by restricting to the government the purchase of all the weapons and other forbidden import items the treaties required Earth to accept. They were then destroyed—or so the taxpayers who underwrote the arrangement were assured. Now Roark wasn't so sure.

"Oh, we mean to keep it in the right hands," Havelock assured him. "But we have to be realistic. There are too many independent Lokaron merchants who're willing to make a sale anywhere they can. And there are too many independent states on Earth willing to buy. So far, the Lokaron authorities are willing to deal exclusively with the U.S. and abide by the treaties. But we've been getting indications that they have multiple . . . jurisdictions, or factions, or whatever, and they may not all follow that same policy forever. Even if they do, they can't permanently control all their entrepreneurs; and we can't permanently keep the rest of this planet bullied. That brings us to the operation you're going to be participating in."

"Huh?"

"Think about it. You don't seriously imagine the Lokaron sell their state-of-the-art stuff to primitives like us, do you? We need their *real* technology—tightly controlled by the government, of course—if we're ever going to be respected by them enough to get a better deal than the humiliating treaties that were forced on us. And, just incidentally, we also need it if we expect to stay in the driver's seat here on Earth when the trade-goods-level stuff becomes widespread."

"You mean—?"

"Oh, I think you can figure it out for yourself. Someone else obviously did." Havelock indicated the scattered corpses of their attackers. "I'd love to know who. But of course they won't have anything on them that would identify their employer." With a decisive motion, Havelock put away the laser pistol. "And now, we need to get out of here before the local constabulary arrives. You'll be told all you need to know at Area 51."

Roark gave Marlowe a last look. Then he raised his eyes to the fires . . . but without really seeing them. Instead, his memory's eyes were focused on another night that had exploded into flame. What had been burning that night had been a depot for one of the Lokaron's human distributors. . . .

"Let's get the fuck out of here!" Mike Hodges had screamed into his ear, trying to make himself heard above the gunfire from the security guards. "The operation's blown! They were waiting for us. We can still get out if—"

"Not yet!" Roark had barked, just before a blast had made them both duck back around the corner of the building. As soon as the tinkle of grenade fragments had ceased, he'd swung back around, M-72A minimac leveled, and snapped off a burst down the alley. "Not without Katy."

Hodges had grabbed his shoulder. "Get real, Sir Galahad! They're coming from the direction she was headed toward. She's dead or captured—like we will be if we don't get the lead out!"

"She'd never let herself be captured." It was one of the things that had been drummed into all of them. There could be no prisoners to be interrogated by whatever unimaginable means the Lokaron used, lest the Company's link with this operation be compromised.

"Bingo! She's given her life for the glorious cause

of plausible deniability." A lull in the firing had
allowed Hodges to speak in a softer voice. "Look,
Ben, I'm sorry. I know about you and her. But you
can't change the facts. Now let's go, for God's sake!"

He'd allowed himself to be led to the manhole
they'd used. Their pursuers could follow them into
the sewer system, of course, but they'd known routes
that weren't on the official maps. Hodges had gone
down first, and Roark had started to lower himself. . . .

"Ben! Wait!"

He'd whirled around toward the unexpected voice
from the equally unexpected direction, consciousness
emptied of all save the reddish glint the light of the
flames had awoken in Katy Doyle's hair even in the
night.

"I circled around," she'd gasped in answer to his
question before he could ask it. "I couldn't contact you,
of course." Nothing but static had come from their
earplug-phones since this cluster-fuck had commenced;
the Lokaron must have been blanketing the area with
some kind of ultrahigh-tech interference.

"Come on!" he'd snapped, not pausing for anything as suicidally stupid as an embrace. He'd started
to lower himself the rest of the way so he could help
her down.

A renewed burst of firing had shattered the night.

"Come on!" he'd repeated, reaching for her. Their
hands had clasped. . . .

A burst of automatic fire had slashed across her,
throwing her sideways, pulling their hands brutally
apart, violating her obscenely with a row of holes
from which blood had gouted, spattering his face.
She'd fallen to the pavement just barely too far away
for him to reach her and pull her in after him.

But he had been able to see her eyes. They'd met

his, in what must have been her last moments of consciousness. Her lips had moved, but he hadn't been able to make out her words.

He'd tried, though, wiping the blood—her blood—out of his eyes. He'd tried so hard that he hadn't even noticed that part of him was dying with her.

A skirmish line of figures had approached through the flame-riven gloom. Among the humans had loomed the tall, slender, somehow wrong figure of a Lokar. The sight of that figure had stopped Roark from firing on Katy's killers. The rules of engagement had been inflexible: under no circumstances were any Lokaron to be killed, not even in direct self-defense, much less for vengeance. The possible consequences of such a thing were incalculable.

So he had let Hodges pull him down into the sewers.

They had eluded pursuit . . . almost. Hodges had died of sheer cockiness when they'd thought themselves home free. Only Roark had gotten away, carrying with him the knowledge that had haunted his every waking moment ever since: only Henry Havelock had known enough about the mission to betray it.

Havelock's testy voice brought Roark back to the here and now. "Come on, we haven't time for any more conversation. At any rate, I'll see you at Area 51 in a few weeks."

Roark turned an absolutely expressionless face toward him. "Yes. I'll be seeing you again. Oh, yes, I definitely will."

Their eyes met for a moment that lasted so long the guard grew fidgety. Then Havelock abruptly motioned them toward the plane. The little airstrip was left to the dead.

CHAPTER TWO

Autumn might be hurricane season in the tropics he'd just left, Henry Havelock thought as he gazed out the car window at the fall foliage, but it was the single decent time of year in Washington. Last time he'd been here, summer had been at its stupefying worst.

The climate was one thing about this town that hadn't changed. Another was the name. At one time, it had seemed that would have to go. The Fifty-seventh Amendment had decreed that no public monuments, institutions, installations, schools, cities or anything else could be named after slaveholders. It had caused consternation at first, as the realization had dawned that quite a few things were named after Washington, Jefferson, Madison, Monroe, Jackson and others. Then the Fifty-*eighth* Amendment had saved the day, with its requirement that at least fifty percent of such entities had to be named after women. So the name had been kept, with careful explanations to everyone who'd listen that the capital city was really named after *Martha* Washington.

But very little else was still the same, Havelock recalled as the car passed the Ellipse and he looked north at the White House. It had been enlarged in accordance with a plan dating back to the late-nineteenth-century presidency of Grover Cleveland. Two new wings had more than tripled the total floor space without sacrificing the building's integrity—an almost aberrational lapse into good architectural taste. So the grandeur of the President's residence had waxed even as his political power had waned. But the palatial edifice seemed an appropriate adornment for the city that was in effect the global capital.

The collapse of the Soviet Union four decades before had only been the beginning. Japan's economic doldrums of the late 1990s had proven permanent, and the island nation had gone from economic superpower status to a chronically depressed equivalent of the old "rust belt," with silicon substituting for steel. For a while, China had seemed to loom like a thundercloud on the future's horizon. But the PRC had gone the way of the USSR, only worse, and the country had reverted to warlordism. By default, America's position as the world's sole superpower had become unassailable.

It had proven unfortunate for the world and for America.

As the car proceeded eastward along Constitution Avenue, past Capitol Hill and beyond into what had been residential areas and were now an array of new government buildings, Havelock reflected—not for the first time—on the way a holiday from history brought out Americans' worst political instincts: isolationism, technophobia, coercive utopianism, and the politics of envy. There was nothing new in any of these impulses. But the newly consolidated Earth First Party had exploited them with unprecedented skill after the turn of the century. Neither the cynical power-junkies who'd led the party nor the zealots who'd followed them had been hampered by any concern for constitutional values. And they'd commanded the unanimous support of the media, which the *lumpen* electorate had become conditioned to obey. The Forty-fifth Amendment, restricting office-holding to EFP members, had merely legalized an accomplished fact.

Afterwards, not nearly as much had changed as might have been expected, or had been promised. Every four years, with farcical solemnity, a President was elected—always the EFP's officially sanctioned candidate, though any Party member could run. Senators and Congressmen were also elected on the same basis. In fact, the whole governmental structure was still in place, though its only function was to implement the commands of the all-powerful EFP Central Committee. And those commands, for all the pro-environment, anti-multinational corporations rhetoric in which they were couched, had never done anything to improve the former or suppress the latter. This had come as a surprise to the true believers, who'd never grasped a simple truth about government that George Orwell had once distilled into six words: "The purpose of power is power." Those true believers who'd been too vocal with their disappointment had tended to drop from sight, confirming another early-twentieth-century aphorism, widely (but inaccurately) attributed to Trotsky: "The revolution always ends by eating its own."

In one respect, though, the EFP had been as good as its word. It had frozen technological innovation, to the rapturous cheers of the upper-middle-class intellectuals who were the party's backbone, and who'd had no wish to see their comfortable status quo disturbed. The need to pressure the rest of the world into abiding by the same technological strictures had overcome those intellectuals' antimilitary reflex. Even orbital military platforms had suddenly seemed a good idea after all.

And then, nine years ago, the Lokaron had arrived. . . .

The large, gratuitously ugly hulk of Company headquarters came into sight, putting an end to Havelock's musings. He entered, passing through layers of security: palmprint and retina scanners in the outer areas (Havelock wondered how useful they still were) and, as he worked his way inward, illegal Lokaron ranged genetic scanners. Then he was in the one office he was absolutely certain wasn't bugged—except, of course, by its occupant, who glared at him from across a deceptively old-fashioned desk.

"What the devil happened down there?" the Director demanded without preamble, in the unmistakable regional accent.

"Unknown. I can't be certain who they were working for, although I can think of several possibilities."

"Couldn't you have taken one of them alive, for questioning?"

"That might have been awkward. Are you certain you would have *wanted* to uncover something that might have been impossible to ignore? Any action you'd have had to take in response would have been an unplanned variable, with unpredictable consequences. We hardly need that now, when our operation is about to commence."

The Director still didn't look happy, but she subsided back into her chair.

Colleen Kinsella's surname was that of her late husband. For a married woman to *not* keep her maiden name was mildly eccentric nowadays, but she had her reasons. She was an EFP member, of course—otherwise she wouldn't have held this or any other office. But she sprang from a dynasty which had been closely identified with one of the two old political parties—Havelock could never remember which one, it was so hard to keep them straight. That family's name was one to conjure with, and had been ever since a President who'd borne it had placed himself beyond criticism by being assassinated. It was a name she would have been ill-advised to flaunt, given the dim view the EFP took of connections with the old political order. So she went by her married name, and kept quiet about her ambition to reassert her blood's political dominance.

Havelock was one of the few who were privy to that secret agenda. And he had to smile at the irony. A woman was now the standard-bearer of a dynasty whose founding patriarch (a bootlegging Nazi sympathizer) and his sons had been noted for treating women like Kleenex.

Now she ran a nervous hand through her graying chestnut hair. "I'm taking an awful risk. You know that."

"To the contrary, Director. This is a win-win situation. Your arguments for the operation were perfectly valid—so much so that they persuaded the majority of the Central Committee to approve it. Anyone but a cretin or an old-line EFP wheelhorse can see that we need state-of-the-art Lokaron technology—kept under strict controls, of course, and restricted to government use—if we're to deal with these aliens other than as supplicants. So the obvious course of action is to infiltrate the Enclave." The Lokaron, with an air of humoring the EFP's desire to minimize contacts between themselves and the citizenry, had agreed to restrict their presence on Earth's surface to a closed extraterritorial settlement. "Their use of human employees provides the opening we need to get our people in: a combination of technical specialists and experienced covert operatives. It all makes perfect sense. In fact, it would redound to your credit even if—contrary to our plans—it actually *worked*."

Kinsella smiled briefly at the reminder of their real intentions, but then worry closed over her features again. "Yes, and it will be even better if matters go according to plan and the operation fails. It will embarrass the Central Committee and drive a wedge between the government and the Lokaron. But what if we make the Lokaron *too* angry?"

"So much the better, Director. The more thoroughly discredited the present leadership is, the more complete the turnover will be. There'll be a whole new Central Committee. If you play your cards right, you'll be on it—maybe even chairing it."

"Yes, yes . . . but what if we provoke the Lokaron into an open break?"

"Better still. It would strengthen still further your position with the President. The position you've created so astutely."

Kinsella acknowledged the flattery with a brief smile, even though she knew as well as Havelock did that her position was largely a gift from her enemies on the Central Committee. Unable to get rid of her outright, they'd searched for an office outside the little world of intra-EFP politics—the only world they really knew or cared about. The Directorship of the Company had seemed made to order. Its principal predecessor, the old CIA, had always been a favorite whipping boy among the electoral elements to which the early EFP had appealed. After coming to power, the Party's behavior had been characteristic: it had changed the agency's name, combined it with some others, put it into a new building, and announced it had abolished it. The official name was now an unwieldy bit of euphemism; even the alphabet soup was inconveniently lengthy. So nobody ever called it anything but "the Company," a carryover from the older outfit.

Such was the venue Colleen Kinsella's enemies had chosen for her political exile. But they'd overlooked one thing. The Director, by tradition, had automatic access to the President.

That official's position was a curious one these days. Politically powerless, the President still embodied the nation in the eyes of the people, who knew little of the actual power structure and had little liking for what they did know, although most were too prudent to say so aloud. If anything, the symbolic stature of the office had grown now that its occupant really was "above politics"—once a pious wish, now fact. The EFP had encouraged this tendency, seeking to maximize the Presidency's usefulness as legitimizer of the power the party wielded.

Occasionally, though, the Party had reason to have second thoughts. There was little that could be done when a President actually spoke his or her mind in public—as the previous incumbent had, in opposition to signing the Lokaron treaties. That President had been one of the old hard-liners of a party whose name, originally an environmentalist slogan, had come to have a second meaning: doctrinaire opposition to all space exploration. To her and others like her, the notion of the stars coming to Earth had been no more palatable than its reverse. The Central Committee had gotten rid of her at the next "election" and installed John Morrison, now a year into his second term. He'd kept his mouth shut as was expected of him . . . until recently. Then he'd let it be known that he shared his predecessor's views on the Lokaron treaties. He'd done so on the clandestine advice of his chief intelligence advisor, acting in turn on the advice of the man now sitting across the desk from her.

"It wasn't hard," she allowed. "Sitting in that damned ivory tower of his"—she gestured vaguely in the direction of the White House— "he can afford to ignore the reality of our military helplessness. But the Central Committee can't—and neither can I! Those goddamned inhuman freaks own our orbital space!"

"Military strength and weakness are relative concepts, Director. It is possible for the stronger side to place itself in a position of vulnerability . . . as the Lokaron have by putting their personnel into the Enclave here on the surface, where overwhelming numbers could outweigh technological superiority."

For a space, Kinsella seemed incapable of speech. "What are you saying?" she finally asked, very quietly.

"I'm merely suggesting that you command considerable paramilitary forces." This was true; the Company had been given the capability to respond directly to foreign infringements of the ban on "dangerous" technologies. "And additional support could be arranged. A sudden attack, made without regard to losses, could sweep the Enclave into oblivion before the Lokaron could react."

"And then what? Where would that leave us? Up shit creek without a paddle, that's where! Jesus Christ, have you gone mad? They could retaliate from orbit. We don't even know what they've got up there—nukes may be the least of it. They could burn this planet down to bedrock, and there's not a damned thing we could do about it!"

"Ah, but would they? They've made it clear that they're here to make a profit. They couldn't trade with a radioactive desert. And evidently trading is a more economical proposition for them than outright conquest and enslavement would be. The expense of a military occupation might well eat up any profits they could hope to make. No, I think they'd be amenable to an apology . . . and a scapegoat."

Curiosity overcame Kinsella's rage. "What are you hinting at now?"

Havelock's reply was oblique, as his replies often were. "A few minutes ago, when we were discussing the attack on me in the Caymans, I mentioned I had some theories as to who may have been behind it. Actually, I have a leading suspect: the Eaglemen."

There was silence, but Kinsella's expression couldn't have made her feelings much clearer. To high-ranking government officials, the Eaglemen were trouble-making terrorists. To the upper military brass, they were all of that and also insubordinate puppies, idolized by scruffy popular musicians and their even scruffier fans. The latter aspect especially worried the EFP hierarchy, whose predecessors had used the popular culture as a tool to subvert the old American system. More than most, they appreciated the truth of the old saying that poets are the unacknowledged legislators of the world.

But it was difficult to act too decisively against the secret organization. Officials who did so had a way of being assassinated.

"What would their motive have been?" Kinsella demanded. "And what does this have to do with . . . what we were discussing?" Even in her sanctum, the

Director shrank from speaking aloud the possibility Havelock had voiced.

"To the first question, the answer is, 'I don't know.' And as for the second . . . it occurs to me that these pipsqueaks could be useful to us. Properly infiltrated—and I already have an operation in the works to do precisely that—they might be manipulated into believing that the attack I've suggested is their own idea, and that they're leading it. Matters could be arranged in such a way that most of them would die even if the attack succeeded. Thus, we could kill two birds with one stone: drive a *serious* wedge between the Lokaron and the present Central Committee, and destroy the Eaglemen. Afterwards, a new Central Committee dominated by you could renegotiate the treaties."

Like a biologist observing the activities of a specimen, Havelock watched the struggle of greed and fear reflected in Kinsella's face—the face he'd always been so adept at reading. As though in search of support from her ancestors, her eyes strayed to the wall. The direction they strayed was perhaps ominous, for the portrait they settled on was hardly the most inspiring one: her great-uncle, a shapeless mound of alcohol-saturated fat who'd been the Senator for life from the family's home-state fiefdom in the last quarter of the twentieth century.

But, Havelock philosophized, perhaps she saw it differently. After all, it had been her life's work to dredge the family up out of the sewer of degeneracy into which it had fallen in that era. It had to be the reason she kept that particular portrait on her wall; Havelock could think of no other.

He decided a little encouragement was in order. "So you see, Director, whether the operation succeeds or fails, you're presented with another win-win situation."

Kinsella glowered at him. "You use that expression a lot. It worries me, sometimes." Havelock presented a poker face to her, while reminding himself that she wasn't stupid—merely obsessional, which could sometimes have the same effect. After a moment, she resumed. "All right. Continue preparations for infiltrating your people into the Enclave. Also, continue your efforts to penetrate the Eaglemen organization. Keep me abreast of both operations. As for . . . the other thing, I'll reserve judgment until we have some definite reports on how the other two matters are progressing."

"Very wise, Director." Havelock departed.

He proceeded to the residential hotel on Massachusetts Avenue where he had permanent quarters, to be used whenever he was in Washington. (At no cost to the Company's discretionary funds; the management owed it a favor, in exchange for not being prosecuted for certain national security violations.) He settled into his room in a perfectly normal way. He could have scanned the premises for listening devices, but that would have been bad form. After all, the advantage of knowing Kinsella had him under surveillance (of which he was pretty sure, anyway) would have been canceled by her knowing that he knew it. So he simply went to the bar and ordered a Scotch and soda, as per his established behavior patterns, and waited for the woman who was also part of those behavior patterns.

He didn't have long to wait. He didn't even have to look at the neighboring bar stool to know it was her. The sound of her movements—swift and decisive and economical, beneath the song of sliding nylon—identified her. He turned and smiled, as was expected, at the Hispanic face—predominantly Castilian, but with a certain Native American sharpness to the cheekbones and African duskiness to the skin—under the unfashionably short bristle of black hair. She smiled back, and leaned forward in a way that, with the outfit she was wearing, couldn't help but be provocative. He occasionally wondered what it would be like to actually have sex with her.

He also leaned forward, and whispered into her ear. "Is everyone present?"

"Yes, sir."

"Good." They spent a few more moments miming the expected byplay, then she led the way toward the elevators. Following her, Havelock frowned with worry. The bimbo getup only revealed her lithe muscularity. Surely, he fretted, not even Kinsella's stupidest surveillance monitors could be fooled. But she was the only available woman of the type he'd spent years establishing—falsely—as his preference.

They reached the elevators, and went to one in particular—one that never seemed to come for anyone else. The bar was on the street level, with nothing below. After they got in and the elevator door slid shut, the lights above that door blinked through floor after floor, stopping at the fourteenth, where a couple who strongly resembled them got out of what was to all appearances an elevator car, and proceeded to a room.

In the meantime, the genuine elevator car descended through levels that only a very few people knew existed.

As they emerged, the woman fell into a military stride that seemed natural to her, however little it accorded with her clothing. They walked along a dimly lit corridor of rough concrete walls, to an equally unprepossessing room. Half a dozen young men sat around a table. All had short military haircuts, but all wore civilian clothes—none as glaringly incongruous as those of the woman, who took one of the two vacant seats. Havelock took the other, at the head of the table, and spoke without preamble.

"All right, why did they fail?"

They all came to a kind of seated position of attention at the whipcrack in his voice. One of them, slightly older than the others and the cell leader, cleared his throat and spoke. "We're not sure, sir. But statements by the local Caymanian cops—before they clamped the lid down—indicated that there may have been a laser weapon involved."

A kind of angry gloom settled over the room.

The woman spoke up, with what might have been taken for asperity had she been addressing anyone else. "We were hoping *you* could shed some light on it, sir. Weren't you down there in the same area at the time?"

"If I knew, Captain Rivera, I wouldn't be asking you, would I?"

Captain Ada Rivera, U.S. Army Special Forces, swallowed. "Of course not, sir," she admitted in an uncharacteristically small voice.

"Actually," Havelock went on, "I was in Cuba, on other business. I'm not sure who it was Kinsella sent to the Caymans to recruit Roark. But the laser fits. We know Kinsella has gotten hold of some illegal Lokaron weaponry, and sometimes uses it. This time, she used it on our people."

Now the anger that pervaded the room intensified into audible form, a low collective rumble of uncomplicated fury. *How easy they are to manipulate,* Havelock reflected, with a touch of genuine sadness.

"Yes," spat Rivera, always the fiery one in the

councils of the Eaglemen. (*Must do something about that name,* Havelock made a mental note.) "And now the bitch is out to get more alien technology, to use for her own filthy ends . . . which will just make her more dependent on them. And the more power she accumulates—"

"I'm not altogether unfamiliar with this line of argument," Havelock said dryly.

"Sorry, sir," Rivera murmured. "It was only through your access to Kinsella that we knew about her plot."

"But can't she *see*?" The outburst came from the youngest-looking member of the group. "The more we use Lokaron technology, the more we become *addicted* to it. . . . " The boy's fair skin was flushed, and he seemed on the verge of tears. "We'll *never* get rid of them!"

"Kinsella doesn't want to get rid of them, Jens," Rivera snarled. "All she wants is to get a better deal out of them."

"And," Havelock said quietly, "we'll never restore the governmental system the framers of the Constitution intended. Kinsella isn't interested in that either. She has no objection to the present system, as long as she's in charge of it. That's the limit of her vision." He let the depression in the room's air thicken for a heartbeat or two, then resumed briskly. "So as usual it's up to us. We have to be prepared to act . . . against the Lokaron themselves, if necessary."

After a moment, the cell leader hesitantly broke the stunned silence. "Sir, you don't mean—?"

"I know, Major Kovac. It's an old idea of ours— an old dream, actually, because we've always ended up regretfully consigning it to the dustbin of the impractical, especially since our contact inside the Enclave, who provided us with the layout of the place, stopped reporting. But now there's a new factor in the equation. We'll have inside help . . . thanks to Kinsella and her infiltration project!"

An excited hubbub began. Havelock raised a hand to quell it and hurried on. "I've been able to persuade Kinsella that direct action against the Enclave may become necessary. If it happens, I'll have a hand in choosing the personnel. Which means some of you, and the members of the cells you control, will be involved. You'll be in a perfect position to obtain state-of-the-art Lokaron hardware, as Kinsella plans . . . but obtain it for *us!*"

The blond young officer seemed to have passed beyond bewilderment. "But, sir—"

"Think about it, Lieutenant Jensen, and all the rest of you. Kinsella is right about one thing: we need Lokaron technology. We need it if we're ever going to expel them from this planet . . . and resume humanity's own conquest of space!"

Havelock watched their eyes ignite. The Eaglemen's determination to get rid of the aliens and the humiliating treaties they'd imposed didn't imply agreement with the EFP's return-to-the-womb policy of banning space exploration and redirecting the funds into "socially useful" patronage. Most of these young officers burned with a desire to recommence the space program of the previous century. Knowing he had them, Havelock continued. "Kinsella's mistake—aside from wanting to use the technology only for her own self-aggrandizement—is that she thinks only in terms of stealing or buying what the Lokaron make. As all of us here realize, that will just make us an economic dependency of theirs. What we need isn't the hardware but the *knowledge*. We have to learn the principles, the techniques, and then manufacture the hardware ourselves. Then we'll be able to order them off Earth. And we'll go out into the universe, rather than submit passively as it comes to us!"

He let them babble their excitement for a few moments, smiling and revealing no hint of the thoughts behind that smile. *They really are splendid young people. Rather a pity that they'll all have to die.*

Finally he got their attention and resumed. "The chief obstacle at present is Kinsella's caution. So, before any of this can occur, it will be necessary for us to force matters. . . ."

CHAPTER THREE

Looking north from Lookout Mountain, the Front Range of the Rockies extended into infinity, curving away into the distant haze. To the right, the Great Plains stretched eastward into the same haze, which was thicker where Denver lay under its characteristic smog. But to the left, the remoter ranges climbed into realms of crystalline clarity, range piled atop snow-capped range into the uttermost west.

Svyatog'Korth liked this view for its sheer exoticism. His homeworld of Harath-Asor was older and more geologically mature than this one. It had ceased to have scenery like this long before his colonizing ancestors had arrived. Its worn-down mountains were lower than this, despite its lesser gravity, and their foothills merged insensibly into the lowland plains with their sluggishly flowing rivers.

But it was time to stop sightseeing. Svyatog gave the low whistling that was the equivalent of a human sigh and severed the connection which was feeding these sensory impressions directly into his brain. He removed the headpiece of open latticework and was

45

back in the physical actuality of his office, gazing through the transparency at a quite different landscape.

No question about it, this eastern part of the continent had a more homelike aspect, for all the oddness of its vegetation, whose green lacked the proper bluish undertone. At the present season of the planet's year, the coloration was even odder: reddish or golden browns which had caused the first Lokaron observers to wonder if the local plant life was infected with some disease. Westward, ghostly bluish in the distance, rose the gently rounded mountains of the Shenandoah National Park, whose northernmost end overlooked this political subdivision called Fauquier County, Virginia. (Svyatog prided himself on his ability to remember all this unpronounceable native gibberish without calling on the database implanted in his skull, which could have fed the names directly to his optic nerve as visible symbols.)

Had the local rulers had their way, the Enclave would have been located in the region Svyatog had just been virtually touring, or one even more remote from the continent's population centers. Gev-Tizath, whose explorers had first happened onto this system, probably would have gone along; the Tizathon, while basically fine fellows, tended to be altogether too accommodating. But Gev-Harath (Svyatog unconsciously swelled a bit with pride in belonging to the richest, most powerful *gevah* of them all) had more experience in dealing with natives, and understood the necessity of firmness. Its representatives had insisted on a location close to the capital city. But they'd permitted a face-saving concession. There would be no intrusive alien presence among the teeming urban multitudes. Rather, the Enclave would be in a rural area, a short air-car hop from the capital yet out of sight of all but a few. Thus the corrupting effect on the common people's belief systems would be minimized. (Natives were funny that way.)

A message appeared, the angular characters seemingly floating in midair a few inches in front of his face. Yes, it was time. He stood up and left his office, proceeding along an airy, sunlit passageway past occasional others who worked here in the Hov-Korth building. He could have resumed the light openwork helmet and entered into a shared virtual-reality hookup with Huruva'Strigak. But it wasn't far, and the Harathon government's resident commissioner was something of a traditionalist. That traditionalism was reflected in his office's appointments, and in the courtesy with which he rose to greet the new arrival.

As well he might, Svyatog told himself. As chief factor of Hov-Korth—the preeminent *hovah*, or merchant house, operating on this entire segment of the wave front of Lokaron expansion—Svyatog was as important as Huruva, despite the latter's official status. *After all,* he thought, *it's the hovahon—especially Hov-Korth—that provide the revenue which pays the government's expenses . . . including Huruva's salary.* It was no accident that the commissioner's office was here in this tower, where Hov-Korth had graciously placed a suite at his disposal.

Nevertheless, Svyatog reciprocated the administrator's courtesy. Huruva and his like were indispensable, if only as mediators among the hovahon. Industrial feudalism had been tried. . . . Svyatog's mind recoiled in distaste from what he'd once learned in history classes.

"Thank you for coming, Factor," Huruva said as they settled into their loungers. "May I offer you refreshment? Some coffee, perhaps? With a drop of something to give it an edge."

"With pleasure." Like most Lokaron, Svyatog had taken to the mildly stimulating local beverage; it had become a profitable item of the luxury trade. But, also like most, he preferred it with a slug of *voleg*. (Alcohol, like caffeine, affected Lokaron and human nervous systems similarly.) Some insisted the native brandy served just as well as voleg. The Rogovon were especially vocal on that point . . . but what could one expect of barbarians like them?

Huruva touched a signaling device, and a steward entered with a tray. The servitor was a Tharthacharon, standing slenderly erect on four legs but with an upright torso whose shoulders provided leverage for the two arms. The top of its head rose to a height shorter than the human average and therefore considerably shorter than the Lokaron. It was covered with thin brownish fur, in which feature it resembled this planet's higher animals but which made it even more exotic in Lokaron eyes. Huruva had brought it from his last posting, which had been on its homeworld. Traditionalism again. The commissioner was old money, and regarded the use of robotic devices for domestic service as . . . as . . . The useful local word *tacky* came to mind.

Svyatog had been both amazed and amused by some of the imaginary aliens that populated this planet's science fiction. The humans were sophisticated enough to realize life might arise on other worlds by nonsupernatural evolutionary processes. But they hadn't grasped the corollary that evolution tended toward similar basic shapes for life-forms occupying similar ecological niches. For excellent reasons, most higher animals were bilaterally symmetrical quadrupeds; hexapods like the Tharthacharon ancestors were a distinct minority. And there was only one logical way to liberate one of a quadruped's pairs of limbs for tool using. So the Lokaron, like humans, were erect bipeds, not many-tentacled blobs. Some humans had been bitterly disappointed.

The servant withdrew, and Svyatog and Huruva sipped in pleasurable silence for a few moments. Then the commissioner set his cup down with an air of getting to business. "Now, then, Svyatog, I asked you to come here today because I need your advice. Not just as the representative of Hov-Korth, but also as a friend—a friend whose counsel has always proven sagacious."

"I do what I can," Svyatog said graciously. He actually did like Huruva, for all the latter's tendency toward stuffiness. And promoting the success of a commissioner representing Gev-Harath's present governing coalition, in which Hov-Korth was the dominant member, was part of his job. "How can I be of assistance?"

"I need your advice," Huruva repeated, "on how best to forestall a potentially grave development. You see, it's come to my attention that there is a danger of the natives learning that we are not a single, monolithic political entity."

Svyatog had been expecting some question involving interhovah protocol, or some minor personnel matter. So Huruva's words caught him flat-footed. They implied a breach of a principle so fundamental to the Lokaron interaction with this planet's natives that any departure from it had become unthinkable.

When the explorers from Gev-Tizath had turned up this system, they'd realized at once that they had something special on their hands. Tool-using non-Lokaron races were no great novelty. But bronze-working had represented the highest technology, and city-states the highest sociopolitical organization, yet encountered . . . unless one counted the occasional crumbling ruins on certain planets where something more advanced had once existed. Here was a living civilization—admittedly not in the best of health at present—whose attainments bore comparison with those of the Lokaron homeworld merely a century or so before it had achieved interstellar flight. A civilization that could provide a market for Lokaron technology and offer more than curios and rare minerals in exchange.

But the Tizathon had known better than to hope they could keep the discovery to themselves. Their *gevah*—young and relatively unimportant, for all its brash expansionism—was a minor player even in this region. The great powers had begun to gather, like *hzuthon* circling around a lesser predator and its kill. So the Tizathon had proposed that the marvelously promising new system be open to all four of the powers active in the region: themselves, Gev-Lokarath, Gev-Rogov and, of course, ubiquitous Gev-Harath. They'd also proposed that all four present a united front, not even revealing to the natives that they were separate sovereignties. The others had agreed, partly because the arrangement defused a potential bombshell of intergevah rivalry, and partly because nobody wanted to see the natives bargaining the prices of Lokaron goods downward by soliciting competing bids from competing gevahon. (The humans weren't as stupid as they looked.) And there was enough potential business here for everybody, wasn't there?

So Svyatog's response was the natural one. "Commissioner, I must have misunderstood you—"

"No, you didn't," Huruva cut in with uncharacteristic bluntness.

"But, Commissioner," Svyatog temporized, "surely

there can't be any danger of the natives seeing through the deception. After all, it's one which they're predisposed to believe. Their science fiction *always* portrays technologically advanced aliens as being politically unified. And it's only natural that they should think this way." Svyatog belatedly recalled that Huruva did not share his own in-depth knowledge of the local history, so he elaborated, carefully skirting the edges of being patronizing. "A hundred-and-twenty-odd local years ago, when their 'First World War' broke out, the natives began to experience warfare at the levels of intensity the Industrial Revolution permitted. At the same time, they displayed a truly awe-inspiring incompetence at managing the violence they'd suddenly acquired an unprecedented capacity for inflicting on themselves. The results were as one might expect. They've never really gotten over it. So they've come to think any higher civilization *must* have a unitary state, capable of enforcing peace, or else it would have destroyed itself. We've merely been telling them what they want to hear . . . or, more accurately, what they *expect* to hear. Even if they stumbled onto evidence of the actual state of affairs, they'd rationalize it away."

"No doubt," Huruva agreed. "But the danger of which I speak isn't the natives ferreting out the truth by their own efforts. Rather, I have reason to believe that . . . certain parties among us may be leaking the information to their native contacts."

"Gev-Rogov," Svyatog stated rather than asked.

Huruva said nothing, shrinking from undiplomatic bluntness. But his expression was answer enough.

As he looked across the desk at Huruva, Svyatog suddenly saw the commissioner in a different light: not simply as a Lokar with certain individual characteristics (average height, distinguished looking if a little out of shape) and the basic features they all shared in common (a crestlike ridge running from back to front of the head, ending just above the practically lipless mouth, where it formed the equivalent of a human's nasal bridge; large, elaborately convoluted ears; upward-slanted brow ridges over slit-pupiled eyes that ranged from amber to pale yellow), but as a fellow member of Gev-Harath. One normally took one's own ethnic characteristics for granted. But the thought of the Rogovon brought them into focus. Huruva's hairless skin was a good Harathon shade of blue, and he had the right kind of slender body build, and. . .

While browsing among this world's scientific speculations, Svyatog had encountered the concept of terraforming. The Lokaron had never for a moment considered such a hideously expensive idea as altering a world for colonization, given the relatively trivial cost of altering the colonists themselves. Out of the genetically engineered subspecies planted on various worlds, the gevahon of today had grown. And Lokaron expansion had entered a second phase, for many of the gevahon were forging outward from the worlds they'd settled, seeking still newer frontiers as outlets for their tradition of pioneering. The now-variegated Lokaron species was pushing outward in all directions, filling a sphere of space that was now becoming oblate as its top and bottom came up against the limits of the galactic disc.. The expansionist gevahon jostled for advantage, sometimes warring with each other. But all were conscious of their common Lokaron heritage, of belonging to the only known race ever to have discovered the secret of interstellar flight.

Still . . . as Svyatog thought of the Rogovon, a single emotional reaction rose uppermost in his mind: *ugly!*

He forced the feeling down. *Think with your*

brain, not with your gut, he ordered himself. "Commissioner, I'll grant you that the Rogovon resent Gev-Harath's primacy, and are constantly scheming to undermine us—"

"They *are* rather tiresome about it," Huruva put in.

"—but I can't believe they'd do anything that might cause our united front to come unraveled. It benefits everybody's business."

"Ordinarily, your point would be well taken," Huruva conceded in his ponderous way. "Unfortunately, I have reason to believe that Gev-Rogov is no longer interested in the ordinary conduct of business."

A grim silence fell. What the commissioner was referring to had always been a possibility, the Rogovon being what they were. But Svyatog had hoped it could be avoided. *Everything's been going so well,* his rather plaintive thought ran. *Why would anyone want to spoil it?*

But, then, foreigners will *be foreigners.*

He was about to speak when Huruva's communicator buzzed for attention. The commissioner activated it and spoke irritably. "I gave instructions I was not to be disturbed except for an emergency."

His confidential secretary—Lokaron, of course—looked out of the screen, apologetic but unabashed. "I'm afraid this falls into that category, sir. A trade delegation in the local city of New York has been attacked. A Harathon delegate was killed."

Svyatog leaned hastily forward into the pickup. "Is this general knowledge?"

The secretary knew him by sight. "It could hardly be suppressed."

Svyatog turned heavily toward Huruva. "I believe, Commissioner, that a general meeting must be called."

✧　　✧　　✧

At times like these, Huruva's traditionalism was appropriate. Virtual reality was out of the question for a conclave of mutually distrustful parties. So all the Enclave residents who counted packed their physical bodies into the seldom-used auditorium.

Behind a raised table at one end of the hall sat the four resident commissioners of the gevahon represented here. All were equal by diplomatic fiction, though everyone recognized that Huruva'Strigak of Gev-Harath was *primus inter pares*. They were dressed formally, with open-fronted sleeveless robes over the double-breasted, open-necked tunics that were ordinary business dress.

Facing them was a crowd of merchants belonging to various hovahon. Sitting in the front row as befitted Hov-Korth's stature, Svyatog could feel as well as hear the unease behind him. The merchants were behaving pretty much as per stereotype—voluble Lokarathon, stolid Rogovon, boisterous Tizathon, and (Svyatog told himself) steady, imperturbable Harathon. But all were worried and angry. Many had been availing themselves of the nearby wet bar.

Huruva called the meeting to order and set forth the facts, thus defusing the wilder rumors. "And now," he concluded, "we must decide on our course of action in response to this outrage. All views will be heard; but inasmuch as this involves diplomatic relations with the local rulers, it is ultimately a governmental decision. I therefore ask that the hovah representatives restrain their understandable indignation until after the resident commissioners have spoken."

Against a low grumbling sound from the floor, Valtu'Trovon motioned to be recognized, rubbing the cilia that grew along his cranial crest much as a human might have cleared his throat. Huruva spoke formally. "We will hear the resident commissioner for Gev-Rogov."

Valtu, descended from ancestors who'd been genetically modified for a higher-gravity planet than the original Lokaron world, was short, thick and squatty. (*Not unlike the humans, come to think of it,* Svyatog reflected. But the humans were *supposed* to look that way.) His green skin was an unintended concomitant of the Rogovon genotype, as was the basso voice that now filled the auditorium.

"Am I correct in gathering," he addressed Huruva, "that the attack was a professionally mounted assassination?"

"That is believed to be the case. Local law enforcement could doubtless have dealt with an angry mob of unarmed civilians."

"In that event," Valtu rumbled, "our course is clear. We should retaliate immediately, targeting their capital city with kinetic strikes from orbit. Afterwards, we should present them with a deadline, by which they must turn over the perpetrators to us, along with an indemnity, or else face further punishment."

Despite Huruva's injunction, a hubbub of talk arose, some of it aghast but much of it approving, in certain cases vociferously so. The Tizathon resident commissioner gestured to Huruva and was recognized.

Jornath'Gorog at least *looked* right. Gev-Tizath was a secondary colony, sprung from Gev-Harath, and the colonists had required little modification. Relations between parent and child had had their ups and downs, but they were currently allies. Belonging to essentially the same subspecies doubtless helped. Jornath's blue skin was now dark with anger. "This is outrageous! We don't know for certain that the local government was implicated in the attack. It could have been some very well-equipped and well-led renegade group, or some other human government, or—"

Valtu interrupted him rudely. "Whether the local rulers were behind the attack or not is unimportant. Even if they weren't, they're in the best position to find out who was."

"But we can't use mass violence against them before even presenting our demands!"

"Violence is the only thing natives are capable of understanding!" Valtu turned dismissively away from Jornath and faced Huruva. "I recognize that this is primarily a matter for Gev-Harath, inasmuch as the victim was Harathon. Nevertheless, such terrorism constitutes a threat to *all* Lokaron on this planet. Gev-Rogov will be honored to lend whatever assistance we can in any military response you decide to undertake."

The implication couldn't have been much clearer. Gev-Harath normally maintained the preponderant military force in orbit overhead. The Tizathon and Lokarathon contingents were mere tokens—as the Rogovon one had been until recently, when one of their deadly *Rogusharath*-class strike cruisers had arrived. It was enough to place their military presence in a class of its own, for it outclassed the largest single Harathon ship on hand. It had, however, avoided the provocative gesture of taking up low Earth orbit. Instead, it orbited in the leading-Trojan position of Earth's moon, ostensibly to conduct certain training exercises in private.

There were a few more exclamations of approval from the floor, from the duller or more drunken individuals present. Svyatog ignored them, as he watched Huruva glare at Valtu. The commissioner had clearly decided his earlier suspicions had been correct: the Rogovon *wanted* the standing arrangement on this planet to break down, and be replaced by an outright annexation in which they had a share. *And*, Svyatog reluctantly found himself concluding, *Huruva is right*.

There were things besides their appearance that he found unpleasant about the Rogovon. Long in a state of arrested sociological development as they'd struggled to tame a harsh environment, they still had a centralized government that seemed to most Lokaron an archaic survival—as did the nakedly militaristic quality of their expansionism. They'd been pariahs until they'd adopted civilized commercial practices. *But it's only skin-deep*, Svyatog thought. *Their hovahon are little more than disguised government agencies. They exist at the government's sufferance, rather than the other way around. Unnatural!*

But however anomalous and even distasteful its system might be, Gev-Rogov was too big to ignore. Gev-Harath was even bigger, and far richer, but to stay in first place militarily it found itself forced into expenditures that elicited howls of anguish from the hovahon that footed the bills.

Huruva was still glaring in silence when a rather supercilious voice broke the tension. "Before we rush to a decision," said Branath'Fereg, the resident commissioner for Gev-Lokarath, "I, for one, would like more information on the Americahon—excuse me, *American*—power structure. I suggest we solicit the input of those with the best sources of information on local conditions." He inclined his head toward Svyatog.

Svyatog returned the gesture. Branath's suggestion was a reasonable one. The military was the province of the gevah governments—indeed, it was perhaps the primary function for which the hovahon had set them up. But the megacorporations insisted on keeping for themselves the business of intelligence gathering. They were too jealous of their many secrets to be willing to entrust anyone else with that particular capability. Hov-Korth, as the biggest operation here, was careful to be the best informed. And, in addition to his hovah's intelligence apparatus, Svyatog had a carefully guarded private source.

Still, Svyatog couldn't help wishing Huruva had solicited his help in this matter, rather than letting Branath take the lead. He didn't altogether trust the Lokarathon commissioner . . . or any of the Lokarathon, come to that. Their gevah was unique in not being descended from a colony, for it comprised the original Lokaron home system and its immediate interstellar environs. They had never entirely gotten over the colonial subspecies' effrontery in going their own ways. *They've paid a price for their affectations,* Svyatog told himself. *They've been insisting so long that the home system is the only place where it's possible to lead a truly civilized life that by now they believe it themselves. It's hampered them in interstellar competition almost as much as their location, as far from the frontiers as you can get.* These thoughts ran through his mind as he looked at Branath's rather satiny bluish-white skin and narrow features—the *true* Lokaron genotype, the Lokarathon smugly asserted, to the others' intense irritation. Indeed, the other gevahon denied Gev-Lokarath's pretensions almost as assiduously as they copied its fads and fashions.

Not that Svyatog was prejudiced. He prided himself on his fearlessly enlightened views. He didn't even mind the fact that Branath was a *primary male,* in accordance with Gev-Lokarath's abandonment of traditional gender roles. Even Gev-Harath was tending in that direction.

"I'll do my best to help, Commissioner," Svyatog said, then paused to gather his thoughts. "The local power structure is difficult to make sense of. By our standards, it's arcane: a centralized, self-perpetuating caste of career functionaries, responsible to no one, insensately hostile to any social institutions that interpose themselves between the individual and the government. In fact, they lay contributions directly on individuals—*taxation*, they call it." A mutter of incredulous distaste ran around the room. "It's these functionaries we've always dealt with—layers and layers of them. They all claim to be working for the *President*."

"The what?" Recollection awoke in Branath's face. "Oh, yes, I remember now: the high priest."

"Not precisely, Commissioner. But it's true that he's merely a figurehead. The real ruler is an entity called the *Central Committee*—a group, not an individual. The functionaries are coy about it, insisting when pressed that it isn't part of the government. This seems to be accurate; it just tells the government what to do."

"Incredible," Valtu muttered. Never noted for his sense of humor, he'd completely missed the dig hidden in Svyatog's remarks about centralization. And, to be fair, not even Gev-Rogov really approached the humans' oppressive, cumbersome, labyrinthine farrago of a government

"If this Central Committee is so shadowy," Branath inquired with his Lokarathon air of faint superiority, "are you certain it exists?"

"Quite certain, Commissioner." Svyatog forebore to reveal the special source of information that enabled him to be so certain. Instead, he gave an explanation that was, as far as it went, factual. "You see, we've learned that nine local years ago the reigning President was opposed to signing the trade treaties with us. *Publicly* opposed, in defiance of custom. But the Central Committee went ahead anyway."

"Why?" inquired Jornath.

"At first, it was simple realism: they'd learned they couldn't resist us militarily, and generations of science fiction had filled their heads with images of rapacious, all-destructive monsters from space, avid for their females—"

"Whatever for?" Jornath was genuinely puzzled.

"Er . . . never mind. At any rate, they signed. And since then, we've become one of the pillars of their power. As the sole organ through which we deal with Earth, they control the flow of modern technology, not only for their own people but for the whole planet. And they use for their own purposes some of the items they've outlawed for everyone else." The rapid-fire clicking sound of Lokaron laughter ran around the room. "The point is, the real rulers here have no interest in antagonizing us. It is my considered judgment that neither they nor anyone allied with them were behind this terroristic act."

"Then who was?" growled Valtu.

"Presumably some group of socially marginal xenophobic fanatics, outside the government and therefore lacking the capability to threaten us here in the Enclave."

Valtu continued to glare, but he said nothing, and a sound of relief rose from the majority. Jornath, however, looked worried. "But what about the human semiskilled workers you Harathon have employed? What if some of them are sympathetic to this terrorist group you're postulating? Couldn't they constitute a . . . a . . . ?"

Fifth column, Svyatog recalled from his studies of the idiom-rich local language. But Huruva spoke up, apparently deciding it was time to reassert his control of the meeting. "The beings to whom you refer are carefully screened, and kept under equally careful surveillance—in both cases, by means beyond their civilization's understanding."

Svyatog frowned at that last. He wasn't so sure about the humans' inability to visualize the capabilities of the technologies involved. In fact, for reasons he couldn't reveal, he *knew* Huruva was indulging in wishful thinking. *We're so used to equating "non-Lokaron" with "primitive" that we haven't yet adjusted to what we're dealing with here. The humans are just advanced enough to be able to accept the notion of a still more advanced civilization. They know our technology isn't magic, even if they can't duplicate it.* But Huruva spoke on, in tones intended to bring the meeting to a close.

"For the present, our security will be tightened. In particular, the resident human employees will be subjected to added restrictions. In the meantime— tomorrow, in fact—I will communicate with our human contacts in their *State Department* and demand a meeting with high-level officials. Rest assured, there will be reparations. And now, if there is nothing further, the meeting is adjourned."

CHAPTER FOUR

"Well, that tears it!" Dan Pirelli leaned back in his chair and flung his napkin down disgustedly. "The whole operation is screwed, blued and tattooed!"

"What are you farting at the wrong end about?" Ben Roark inquired. He'd just entered the canteen, after an exercise in which he'd been able to demonstrate in satisfactory fashion to that young puke Carl Travis that forty-two was not old enough to merit the nickname "Pops."

"Hadn't you heard, Pops?" Roark gritted his teeth but let Pirelli continue. "A Lokaron trade delegation in New York was attacked. A couple of local cops got killed. But the important thing is, so did one of the Lokaron. Now they're shitting in their pants, or whatever it is they do. They've buttoned up the Enclave tighter than old lady Kinsella's ass. We'll *never* get in there!"

Travis had come in out of the Nevada sun just behind Roark, in time to catch Pirelli's words. "Did any of the attackers get caught?"

"No. Nobody knows who they were . . . or if they

do they're not saying. But it's a pretty easy guess, isn't it?"

"Yeah." Travis seemed to want to spit. "Who else? The goddamned grandstanding Eaglemen!" He turned to a machine and punched up a coffee with unnecessary violence.

An uncomfortable flurry of frowns and hastily averted glances ran through the few men in the canteen. Travis' vehemence clearly wasn't popular. These were all picked members of various specialized military units, temporarily assigned to the Company for the operation that now looked like it might have to be abandoned. Among them and others like them, admiration of the Eaglemen ran deep and—of necessity—silently. Even the ones who disapproved of the secret organization didn't like to listen to *other* people doing so. Some of them, Roark imagined, knew Eaglemen—or at least people they strongly suspected were Eaglemen—personally.

But none of them spoke up to take issue with Travis. They wouldn't have done so even if this had been an ordinary military base—you never knew who might be listening. The same went double for a place as spooky as Area 51.

Could that be why you're sounding off? Roark wondered in Travis' direction. *Performing for the microphones?*

He walked to a window and looked out toward Wheelbarrow Peak and the dusty Nevada desert beyond. It was a sunny day, as usual. A silvery glint in the sky caught his eye: a plane circling around to land on the airstrip on the dry lake bed. It wasn't one of the potbellied transports that ferried supplies and occasional personnel out here to the ass end of nowhere. It was a lightweight, modern executive jet— the sort he'd been expecting Havelock to arrive in.

"I think," he remarked to the room in general, without turning around, "that we're about to find out where the operation stands."

Havelock was a civilian, so they all remained seated as he entered the briefing room, accompanied by a young Hispanic-looking woman in camo fatigues with Army captain's bars and parachute wings sewn on. A couple of Air Force enlisted men followed, carrying an unfamiliar device which they set up on one of the two folding metal tables at the head of the room while Havelock and his companion stood behind the other one. (The accommodations at Area 51 were most generously described as "functional.") They then departed, leaving Havelock to face the half-dozen men.

"Good afternoon, gentlemen. This is Captain Rivera, Army Special Forces. She'll be your on-scene control in the Enclave."

Nobody said anything, but Roark was conscious of an undercurrent of discomfort in the room. Havelock felt it too. His neatly trimmed gray mustache quirked upward. "Set your minds at rest. Lieutenant Rivera has certain specialized knowledge necessary to the mission's success—indeed, it makes the entire business possible. It's perhaps unfortunate that she hasn't had the opportunity to train here with you. But she's at least as familiar as you are with our intelligence concerning the Lokaron in general and the Enclave in particular. And you need be in no doubt as to her qualifications."

Roark didn't doubt it a bit. Rivera was only about five feet two and economically built, but she was obviously one solid muscle. Her dark eyes were as hard as the rest of her. His companions, appraising her, wore a variety of expressions. Pirelli looked like he was in love.

"Now, then," Havelock continued briskly, moving on from the *fait accompli* of Rivera's inclusion in the operation. "Knowing as I do the workings of Rumor Central, I'm sure you've all heard about the incident in New York. And there's no point in denying that it's queered the pitch for us." He paused significantly. "Nevertheless, I believe we can get you people into the Enclave despite their heightened security precautions. So does the Director. Therefore, the operation's timetable is unchanged."

All at once the atmosphere in the room somehow tightened. Havelock picked up a remote, and the obscure device on the other table projected a simulacrum of the Enclave.

Lokaron stuff, Roark knew. They'd all studied maps and diagrams covering the same ground, and gone through dry runs in mockups of certain portions of it. But now they gazed at a holographic image so real that a solid, though translucent, model seemed to have magically popped into existence out of thin air. Staring at this product of technologies from beyond the sky, Roark felt the hairs at the nape of his neck bristle.

Near the center of the irregularly shaped area, the towers of the main buildings soared skyward. None of the architectural conventions represented—and there seemed to be several—were any more Islamic than they were anything else from Earth's repertoire; but it was hard not to think of a cluster of minarets from the *Arabian Nights.* The Lokaron preferred buildings which were, to most human eyes, disproportionately tall and slender, giving them a fragile look which Roark knew to be completely spurious. It had nothing to do with a shortage of square footage on the ground—spacious plazas and lawns stretched between the towers—or any other utilitarian consideration. Nor could the relatively low gravity which Earth's scientists had postulated for their homeworld account for it. No, it was an aesthetic impulse, doubtless unconscious—an aspiration for the infinite.

Jerry Chen's face reflected a struggle of emotions. His curiosity won, as it so often did. "Excuse me, sir," he addressed Havelock, "but there's something I've wondered ever since I've been here, and now I'm wondering even more. How did we get such detailed information about the inside of the Enclave?"

Roark grunted agreement. "It's not as if we had spy satellites like we used to."

"Strictly speaking, you gentlemen do not need to know that. However, at this stage of the game it can't do any harm to tell you the broad outlines. The fact of the matter is, some time ago the Eaglemen managed to get an agent in there. In the course of an operation against their organization, we came into possession of the data with which their agent had supplied them."

"But, sir," Chen spoke above the flabbergasted hubbub, "is this agent still in place?"

Havelock spoke in measured tones. "Even at the time of the operation to which I've just alluded, their agent had apparently ceased reporting. So"—he gave a wintery smile—"you'll have to get along without whatever help or hindrance an Eagleman agent might provide."

"But," Chen persisted, "how did they—?"

"The same way we're going to insert you people, Lieutenant Chen: under the guise of hired local workers. Of course, they did it back in the days when the Lokaron were, by our standards, remarkably uninterested in security. Now, for reasons to which I alluded earlier, it will be much more difficult."

"Then, sir . . . " Chen began.

"I said 'difficult,' Lieutenant, not 'impossible.'" Havelock permitted himself a look of self-satisfaction. "We've already sent your well-prepared doubles through the screening process for employment in the Enclave. Those doubles were supplied with your documented genetic records. You will, of course, appear in their place for the actual arrival at the Enclave. Thus you'll be able to pass muster when you're scanned on arrival, as you will be."

Now Chen's face was a mask of incredulity. "I can't believe the Lokaron simply take the genetic documentation we give them at face value."

"They used to, Lieutenant. I theorize that's how the Eagleman agent was able to get past their security, if it can be so dignified. But now they verify the data with their own scanners at the time the workers are hired."

Chen struggled to cope with the unaccustomed sensation of just not getting it. "But if they did their own scan of these doubles of ours, it must have been immediately apparent to them that the documentation was faked."

"As you're all aware, the Company is allowed a certain latitude in making use of illegal Lokaron technologies. Some time ago, we learned that they have a device which can deceive their own ranged genetic scanners. They never offered it to us for sale, of course. But they freely discussed the principles involved, secure in their belief that we could never duplicate it. But by intensive study, and at enormous expense, we *have* duplicated it, using components from other devices which are part of their trade inventory. Using this cobbled-together equipment, we were able to get your doubles past the scanning, without any discrepancy between its results and their official records—which, of course, are *your* records."

Roark broke an uncomfortable silence. "You're saying they *sold* us the stuff from which this gizmo could be put together? But . . . but . . . "

Chen put it into words for him—an irritating habit of his for which, just this once, Roark was grateful. "Damn it, sir, a race of interstellar spacefarers can't be *stupid*!"

"No, unforunately they're not stupid. Far from it. But they're unused to taking aliens like ourselves seriously as security threats. We've gathered that ours is the most advanced civilization they've ever happened on . . . the only one, in fact, to have discovered the scientific method."

"You mean," Pirelli asked, "they were expecting us to take these components and try to work a magic spell with them?" Uneasy chuckles chased each other briefly around the room.

"Something like that," Havelock allowed, in a tone of subject-closing dryness. "And now, let's go into the details of how you're going to establish yourselves in the Enclave."

Chen spoke up. "May we also know some of the details of what we're going to be called on to do once we're there?"

"No," Havelock replied with an axe blade's finality. "That falls into the realm of things you don't need to know just yet. And, inasmuch as you're all grown-ups, I shouldn't need to recite the platitude that you can't be made to tell that which you don't know— not by *any* technology. Suffice it to say that you've been given the knowledge and training you'll need. Now, let's get down to cases. . . . "

❖   ❖   ❖

They had transferred to ordinary civilian transport at Denver, and proceeded onward to the various eastern cities from which they would arrive at the Enclave, for it would have been poor technique for them all to arrive as a group. Roark and Chen were the only ones aboard the commuter jet to Washington Dulles. So they were the only ones to get a glimpse of the Enclave itself from aloft.

Roark had a port window seat, and he gazed out at the rolling landscape east of the Blue Ridge Mountains. Here the copper and bronze of autumn still glinted amid the dead gray-brown of winter which now reigned unchallenged in the upper reaches of the mountains. The jet was sweeping around from the southwest, over Warrenton, where Mosby's raiders had once galloped. . . .

"There!" Chen exclaimed, looking over his shoulder and pointing.

Yes! In the haze of distance, rising out of a countryside where only a few farmers had needed to be bought out to make room for something that didn't belong there, soared the gleaming alien towers.

After a while, Roark became aware of Chen's voice. "Ever think about how differently it turned out from the way people used to expect?"

"Huh?" Roark turned to his right and considered his traveling companion. He hadn't gotten to know any of the other men at Area 51 closely—you didn't, under these circumstances. But Chen had stood out, and not just by being the only Asian-American in the group. He had an irreverent, inquiring intelligence which couldn't have been further removed from the traditional stereotype of a Marine, which he was. Not that any of these men were dummies; Havelock hadn't picked that sort. But Chen stood out as the unit intellectual . . . or the unit smart-ass, depending on one's perspective. Roark hadn't always found him comfortable to be around—actually, in his first week or so away from booze he hadn't found *anybody* comfortable to be around, and the feeling had been entirely mutual. "What're you talking about?" he demanded. "What's *it*?"

"Alien contact. Back before it actually happened, people were always imagining what it would be like if extraterrestrials appeared in the sky. Hell, a lot of people thought they already *had*, and were waiting to reveal themselves to us after we'd 'proven ourselves worthy' by eliminating war and pollution and prejudice and so forth, so they could welcome us into the Galactic Federation of do-gooders." Chen grinned as Roark made a rude noise with his mouth, then resumed. "The *other* version was a bunch of slobbering, slavering uglies out to exterminate humanity, either so they could colonize the Earth or just out of sheer meanness."

"Yeah," Roark said, recalling some of the movies he'd watched as a boy. "Always angels or devils. Why didn't it ever occur to anybody that they might be just simply *people*? Odd-looking, sure, and probably with some funny ideas, but subject to the same basic needs and driven by the same basic motivations as ourselves. I guess that way they wouldn't have been much use as a substitute for religion."

Chen gave him a sharp look. Like the others, he'd never known quite what to make of Roark. The ex-Company man (they knew that much about him, at least) was the only one among them who wasn't active-duty military; and he was old enough to be, if not their father, certainly an uncle. But rumors about his reputation in covert ops abounded, and he'd proved able to keep up with them physically. And whenever you got past his habitual surliness, he was capable of startlingly out-of-character insights.

"Right," Chen agreed. "And the idea of 'incomprehensible alien worldviews' was always a crock. If they weren't rationalists, they wouldn't be able to get here in the first place. It's like George Orwell once said. In religion or philosophy, two plus two may equal five; but when you're designing a rifle or an airplane, they'd damned well better equal four."

"And the same probably goes double for designing a starship." Roark nodded. He stared moodily out at the glistening intruders in the autumn-clothed northern Virginia countryside. He spoke as much to himself as to Chen. "So why should we be surprised that they're treating us exactly like we've always treated other cultures on a lower technological level? Whether those cultures lived or died wasn't important, except as it affected the balance sheet."

Chen, suddenly worried, gave his companion another narrow look. Area 51 had buzzed with stories about "Pops" Roark's past, concerning which he was so reticent. One of them had dealt with an incident which had left him with a score to settle with the Lokaron as well as souring him on the Company. If he was on some kind of personal vendetta . . .

"You just got through saying they're people," Chen ventured cautiously. "Nonhuman people, but people."

"So they are," Roark agreed quietly. "So were the Europeans in Asia and Africa, century before last. At that, I suppose we ought to be grateful. The Nazis and the Khmer Rouge were *people* too, and we don't seem to be dealing with anything like that. No, the Lokaron are here just to make a buck."

He fell silent, and as the distant Enclave dropped out of sight astern he ceased to see the view. Instead, he was seeing his familiarity-dulled waking nightmare.

It was a nightmare in two colors: the black of night, and red—the redness of the flames, of the highlight those flames brought out in the dying woman's hair, and of her blood. . . .

They spent the descent into Dulles in a silence Chen wasn't about to break, for Roark had clearly reverted to his surly norm. After getting through baggage claim, they proceeded not to Ground Transportation—for their destination was too far off the main roads to make conventional vehicular transport practical—but to a special, fenced-off area just off the runway where a wingless vertol awaited them. Its driver, a human, wore a nondescript uniform. He took them aloft, heading into the westering sun.

CHAPTER FIVE

The formalities of arrival were less formal than Roark and Chen had expected. Landing on a small expanse of what seemed to be perfectly ordinary concrete, they passed through a small building where their luggage went onto a conveyor belt that whisked it past devices whose function was easy to guess. The scanning must have been as perfunctory as it looked, for no questions were asked about certain small components, meaningless in isolation, which each of them had brought. Next they walked past a console where a Lokar operated what Roark recognized as the instrumentation of a ranged genetic scanner. It was the first time he had ever seen a Lokar close up in person, and his reaction was that intimate blend of fascination and flesh-crawling revulsion which many humans had owned to ever since the aliens' arrival. *Why?* he wondered, seeking to analyze his own feelings. *Nobody thinks a horse or a dog looks wrong because he doesn't look like a human.*

But horses and dogs don't talk, or wear clothes, or make tools. The Lokaron do these things, and all the other things that only humans are supposed to do. In fact, they do the tool-making part a hell of a lot better. He studied the scanner operator's hands, so different in skeletal and muscular structure from his own but at least as apt to manipulation, with their two opposable "thumbs" on opposite sides of four long spidery "fingers." *I suppose we'll just have to get used to it.*

There was still more to get used to as they proceeded into the structure to which they were directed, passing through (Roark was sure) additional layers of invisible, impalpable security. It was a subsidiary building adjacent to one of the towers. In addition to the occasional Lokaron, other nonhumans walked the corridors. Most were bipeds like humans and Lokaron; but their varyingly proportioned forms were clothed in a many-colored diversity of flesh, scales, fur and less familiar coverings, and one slender being's overall body-plan suggested the centaur of Classical mythology. (Roark was old enough to remember those tales, for the EFP hadn't suppressed them as "irrelevant" and "politically inappropriate" until after his childhood.) But whatever their differences, the non-Lokaron all wore the unmistakable look of menials. It was something that earlier human employees here had mentioned, and it had given rise to much perplexed theorizing. Even Earth's rudimentary technology had long since rendered domestic servants unnecessary . . . which was just as well, inasmuch as its leveling effect on the economy had simultaneously made them unobtainable. And yet the immensely more advanced Lokaron complicated their logistics by supplying the dietary necessities of a gaggle of life-forms, so that living beings might perform tasks that could surely have been automated at a fraction of the expense.

The mystery deepened when Roark and Chen arrived at their quarters. Bachelor human workers were billeted two to a room, and the total square footage was none too generous even on those standards. Some wondered what attracted highly trained people to employment under such conditions. The salary, paid in trade vouchers, was usually—and plausibly—cited as the reason. But Roark could immediately see that the quality of the accommodations could not be measured by their size. This became even more apparent as he listened to an English-language explanation, complete with holographically projected illustrations, of the apartment's amenities. He sat down on a chair whose self-cleaning covering was made from the same kind of smart fabrics as the uniforms they'd been provided, whose sizes adjusted to fit all wearers. As he watched Chen examine a tube of general-purpose nanotechnic detergent gel, he reflected that while most of this stuff was now available outside the Enclave as trade goods, its cost made it a status symbol for the rich. Not like the cheaper Lokaron items that everybody but the invincibly old-fashioned and the incurably xenophobic now used. . . . He blinked unconsciously. He hadn't thought of his quasi-living contact lenses for months. No need to, as they never needed changing or cleaning. And having twenty-twenty eyesight again was surprisingly easy to get used to.

Chen put down the tube of miracle gunk and turned an unreadable face to him. "I guess they figure they're just providing us with the basic civilized necessities."

"I dunno. Maybe we semiskilled workers have it better than the *real* primitives."

"Right. Maybe the shoeshine boys, or whatever, merely get the kind of stuff that the human upper-middle class in First World countries can afford." Chen sat down on his bed—not very wide, but made of something that reconfigured itself to the sleeper's contours so instantaneously that it was almost like floating in midair—and scowled.

"The real question," Roark mused, "is why the Lokaron hire humans for what they apparently consider low-level technical jobs. Even if these jobs can't be automated, surely it would be cheaper to bring in their own personnel, who wouldn't have to be trained in the basic fundamentals—even language."

"Oh, so now you're an authority on interstellar logistics?" Chen's irritability, Roark reflected, might have something to do with the prospect of commencing that training in the morning. It apparently involved certain techniques which all humans found novel and some found disturbing.

"Well, I guess I shouldn't complain," Roark said with careful casualness. "Whatever the reason is, it's why we got hired." His eyes met Chen's and he silently completed the thought: *And why this operation is possible.* The perfectly legitimate Lokaron-retained employment agency through which the Company had secured their positions had ventured no opinion as to whether or not their living quarters would be bugged. Roark didn't consider the question worth asking. There was, after all, absolutely no way to prevent the Lokaron from doing it, if they thought it worth the trouble. Even had his debugging skills not been useless in the face of a wholly unfamiliar order of technology, he couldn't have used those skills without tipping his hand. So he simply took for granted that he was under surveillance and behaved accordingly. Ordinary grousing and speculating—the term *bulkheading* came to mind, from the hitch he'd spent in the Navy a couple of decades before—were all right. Indeed, their absence might have aroused suspicion among the Lokaron, who'd had years to observe human behavior. But there could be no open talk of their mission.

Chen's almond eyes met his for a moment that wasn't allowed to last too long. Then the younger man nodded. He didn't have Roark's years of experience, but he'd been briefed. The moment ended, and he spoke perhaps just a little too casually. "Yeah. Well, let's see what's on. We can probably get D.C. from here."

They could. But it was a little eerie, watching a TV screen that floated immaterially in midair.

The first training session, like so many ventures into the threatening unknown, didn't live down to expectations. It was mostly an orientation, presided over by a professorial late-middle-aged human.

As they filed into the small auditorium and took seats that configured themselves into human proportions, Roark surreptitiously noted his fellows from Area 51, who had arrived the previous day from their various staging areas. Last to enter was Ada Rivera, who scanned the group as though scoping out a battlefield. Then the elderly gent, evidently a long-term Lokaron employee, stepped to the podium.

"Good morning, and welcome to the Enclave," he began. "I'm Training Supervisor Edward Koebel. Now, all of you are trained in the fields for which you were hired—the agency wouldn't have sent you otherwise. Nevertheless, you'll understand that the equipment you'll be working with is on a higher level of sophistication than what you're used to, in addition to being just simply unfamiliar. Besides which, it will be necessary for you to learn the Lokaron common language—the written language, that is."

"Not the spoken one?" The speaker, a scholarly-looking young woman, sounded disappointed. "Why? Can the human voicebox simply not form the sounds?"

"Not properly, although we can produce a more-or-less-understandable approximation. But it's unnecessary. All the Lokaron you'll be dealing with directly will be equipped with translator devices." Koebel gave a wintery smile. "Never fear, you'll have plenty to learn without that. Indeed, under ordinary circumstances it would be necessary to send you back to school for at least a year. However," he continued into the appalled silence, essaying a pleasantry, "in case it's escaped your notice, circumstances here are *not* ordinary by human standards.

"Now, you've undoubtedly heard stories—mostly exaggerated and sensationalized—about the Lokaron technology of computer interfacing by direct neural induction. I must now tell you that these stories have a basis of truth. No great surprise, really. Our own civilization has long recognized this kind of capability as a theoretical possibility . . . although we were, it turns out, a good deal further away from actual realization of it than various popularizers and science-fiction writers had supposed. Indeed, the Lokaron themselves consider it to be on the cutting edge. As such, it has not been marketed for humans. Nevertheless, it has been adapted for human compatibility—and you will be using it to expedite your training."

A rustle of awed unease ran through the room. A young man raised his hand for attention. "Uh, is this going to involve some kind of . . . surgical implant?"

"Set your mind at rest. The technology is entirely noninvasive." Koebel held up what looked like a plastic headband supporting an openwork skullcap of metallic wires. "You merely don this, and insert the proper storage medium in the slot here." He indicated the left side of the headband, where it bulged outward a bit. "The necessary skills are then directly imparted to your mind."

The young man looked no less ill at ease, and a lot more incredulous. "So you're saying that I slip the right software into the headband, boot the system, and presto! I'm a sixth-degree black belt in Tae Kwon Do."

Koebel laughed. "Of course not! But I remember the subgenre of fiction such notions came from. It was all part of the mysticism of computer geeks, as they were called in my youth. They also imagined the datanet taking on a tangible physical form. It was their version of what other mystics—the ones who *admitted* they were mystics—called the 'astral plane.'" He chuckled reminiscently. "No, if that kind of thing were possible there would have been no need to hire trained people. But in fact there has to be a foundation to build on. Additional information will be put at your disposal in fields for which you already have the appropriate mental orientation, the necessary habits of thought and action. Put simplistically, it gives you more of what you've already got. And it reduces training time by a factor of four or five, depending on the individual."

No one spoke, as they all contemplated the possible implications. Koebel didn't let the silence last long. "Each of you will receive a headset like this one after lunch, along with a set of instructions for linking it with the computer terminals in your rooms, and a set of exercises to be performed using it. You will have the afternoon to study this material and complete the exercises. In addition to the obvious benefits of familiarization, this will allow a more precise evaluation of your aptitudes, using the data from the terminals." He raised a hand as though hastily warding off an anticipated question. "Have no fears for your mental privacy. This isn't 'mechanical telepathy' or any such fantasy. There are, indeed, such things as shared virtual realities; our own civilization has that capability, albeit on a level the Lokaron consider laughably crude. But that requires its own special equipment. What you're going to be using is specialized in an altogether different direction. And now," he concluded in a brisk tone that did not invite further questions, "I believe the lunch break is upon us."

They stood up and filed out. Mealtimes here, with their locally purchased food, were clearly going to be a source of comforting familiarity as much as nourishment. They passed through corridors that seemed to have been grown as much as built, and as they proceeded the crowd gradually thinned out. Roark and Chen were alone when they came abreast of a kind of alcove, of obscure function. They were just past it when a loud whisper came from within.

"In here!"

They stopped, looked at each other, and turned toward the shadowed alcove. A hand gripped Roark's arm and hurried him in. He tensed for a breakaway move, then relaxed as he saw it was Rivera.

Chen followed him into the shadows. "What the hell?" he hissed. "They could be watching!"

"We don't think so—not here. We've got to assume we're being watched in our rooms, but they can't possibly have every inch of the Enclave under surveillance at all times. And we have to talk somewhere." Rivera drew a deep breath. "We can't stay here too long, so listen carefully. Roark, tonight after dinner you're to announce that you're going for a stroll to settle your food. There's nothing prohibited about that. In fact, there are few restrictions on our movements as long as we stick to this building, the tower we're adjacent to and the common areas."

"We know," Roark put in. It was part of the basic instructions that had been waiting for them in their room. In particular, the other towers were off limits. No reason was given.

"Shut up and listen! You're to go to G-14." They had all memorized the arbitrary grid that the Company had placed over the map of the Enclave, and Roark visualized the location, in the common areas near an ornamental something that couldn't really be called a sculpture. "Travis will be waiting for you there. You'll appear to strike up a casual conversation with him."

Roark frowned. "Why Travis? He's not my partner." Nor did he like or trust him, on the basis of their acquaintance at Area 51. "Have I got to—?"

"Yes, you do," Rivera snapped. "He has your instructions. Things are going to start happening faster than we'd anticipated. That's all I can tell you at this point. But you're going to have to be prepared for anything, at any time. And you're going to have to follow orders unhesitatingly—and unquestioningly. Got it?"

Roark forced down a rebellious impulse. Havelock, after all, had made it clear that Rivera was their control. "What about me?" Chen asked.

"For now, nothing. Just sit tight in your room tonight, and act no more than normally puzzled when Roark is late returning. Now let's get moving, before we're missed."

❖   ❖   ❖

The afternoon passed quickly, as they explored the use of the headsets that were waiting for them in their room.

All their vague anticipations of awesome and unpleasant mental sensations, complete with appropriate special effects, vanished when they donned and activated those headsets. There was no stunning invasion of their minds by terrifying mental energies, no subtle insinuation of coldly alien thought-tendrils. There was, in fact, nothing perceptible at all. But then they set to work on the exercises that accompanied the headsets—theoretical problems in the fields for which they'd been hired, requiring them to adapt their knowledge to Lokaron technology. Roark's initial reaction was to reject the whole business out of hand as preposterously difficult without more background instruction. But then, without any dramatic transition, he found the problems becoming less hard, as he drew on knowledge that seemed to have been in his mind all along.

He looked up and stared at Chen, sitting across the table from him. The other man was already staring at him. He started to say something, then thought better of it.

Thus the afternoon went. The dinner hour arose, and they ate in the midst of an unwontedly subdued group. Roark was careful not to pay any special attention to Rivera or Travis, across the room at other tables. Afterwards, on returning to their room, he waited a reasonable length of time before offhandedly announcing his intention of taking a stroll.

Hands jammed into jacket pockets against the late-September evening, he walked through the dusk between the bases of the towers. It was rather like walking in a downtown area whose buildings reared too high for their tops to be seen without conspicuous neck-craning, but on a smaller scale, for the towers lacked the brutal mass of Earth's typical urban skyscrapers, soaring skyward from much smaller ground areas. Also, there were no streets, only landscaped common areas; the Enclave's total area was too small to require vehicular traffic, especially inasmuch as each Lokar seemed to live and move and have his being pretty much within the confines of a single tower and its appurtenant lesser buildings. It was a facet of the aliens' behavior that had been noted before, and pyramids of theory had been erected on that slender foundation.

He turned a corner and saw Travis up ahead in the twilight, sitting on a bench that was a little too high for human legs. He walked casually past, halting within earshot as though to look at something in the middle distance.

"About time you got here, Pops," Travis muttered. "Listen up. We're going to infiltrate the Hov-Korth tower tonight." He jerked his chin in the direction of the tower—the largest of the lot—to which the humans' building was appurtenant.

"What? Tonight?" To Roark's inexpressible annoyance, this little rodent had caught him flat-footed. Things were moving a lot faster than he'd expected. And . . . "Uh, what kind of tower, did you say?"

"It's the name of the Lokaron outfit that employs us humans."

"This is the first I've heard of that."

"What makes you think you know everything that Havelock does? Remember his need-to-know-basis-only mentality. He always keeps information as compartmentalized as possible, so no single leak can compromise too much. We know more about the Lokaron than you've ever been told."

Roark controlled his annoyance. "In everything I

have heard about Lokaron organization, the units have had a different prefix. It's always *Gev*-something or other."

For an instant, Travis' smug superiority faltered a bit. "We're still not sure about the details. The . . . gevs, whatever they are, seem to be composed of . . . things beginning with *Hov*. And Hov-Korth seems to be the dominant component of Gev-Harath, which is the top-dog outfit." Travis scowled, evidently suspecting that he'd somehow lost ground. "We're wasting time! You and I are to enter the tower—"

"You mean just walk in?"

"Sure. Their human employees go in and out of there all the time in the course of their work. What we've been in so far is just sort of a dormitory. We won't even be noticed. Hell, they probably think all humans look alike!"

"What are we going to be doing once we're inside?"

"You'll be told when necessary." Travis was back in his usual engaging form. "Now let's go!"

Their entry into the tower seemed to confirm Travis' confidence. They passed through sliding doors of a crystalline transparency that was not glass, and proceeded across the darkly gleaming floor of a spacious foyer. Only a few Lokaron were in sight, moving across the expansive space in the oddly stately way they had of walking, like tall ships navigating a mirror-calm sea, and none of them evinced the slightest notice. Roark followed Travis to a bank of elevators which, he knew, did not depend on cables and pulleys. Once inside, he followed the younger man's cue by maintaining a poker face—it was an obvious locale for surveillance. They descended, and once they emerged Travis' entire body-aspect changed

to one of taut, purposeful haste. He led the way
unhesitatingly down deserted corridors that lacked the
polished ornateness of the ground floor.

*He evidently has reason to think there aren't any
spy-eyes down here,* Roark thought. *And he sure
seems to be certain of where he's going. I suppose
the little prick* does *have information I don't.*

"Are you ready to let me in on the big secret
now?" he asked aloud.

Travis looked irritable, but he answered in a low
murmur as he strode along. "I'm carrying a spool
of some very special string: a kind of reconfigurable
fiber-optic cable, so thin it's effectively invisible. I've
also got a very small socket that allows it to connect
with any piece of electronic gear. We're heading for
a completely automated data processing center. If we
can get in—and I think we can, given how lax their
security becomes this deep inside the installation—
then I'm going to set up the connection."

"Connection to what?"

"Nothing, yet. We can't get the necessary communicator in here . . . yet. But when we can, it'll be
ready."

"I've never heard of this stuff you're talking
about."

"Neither has anybody else. It's a completely illegal
Lokaron import. And I mean illegal under *Lokaron*
law."

"Then how—?"

"Quiet! Somebody's coming."

The figure had turned a corner far up ahead. As
it came closer Roark could see it was a human
female, despite the ungenerous lighting and the
gender-deemphasizing costume the aliens issued their
hirelings. He and Travis donned expressionlessness
and walked on, neither too slowly nor too rapidly,

prepared to exchange nods as they passed the woman who was approaching . . . moving in a way that was . . .

Funny, Roark thought, as an odd chill seemed to slide along his flesh, *it's almost as though. . . .*

Now in the middle distance, she passed under an overhead light. It brought out a reddish undertone in her dark brown hair.

No! I mustn't expose myself to the pain. I mustn't make myself vulnerable to the dreams.

But then she was almost level with them, and he could no longer pretend it wasn't true, no longer keep up the barrier of dull hurt he had interposed for so long between himself and a universe which held far greater hurt.

"Katy," he croaked.

She jarred to a halt, her hazel-green eyes meeting his and widening with a recognition that was the final proof.

"Ben." Yes, it was her voice.

But then, as she seemed about to say something else, a new sound invaded Roark's shock-dulled consciousness: a kind of snarl from Travis' direction.

As though in slow motion, Travis launched himself forward. His right hand swept up from a hip pocket of his Lokaron-issued uniform, holding a handle from which a knife-blade suddenly sprang.

How did he get that *in here?* Roark wondered, in some storm-center where his mind could still function, locked away from the reality that had suddenly become too strange and inexplicable to be dealt with.

Katy blinked quickly, and fell into fighting stance, backing up and fending off Travis' knife thrust with a hand and forearm raised into a textbook blocking-move. But trained reflexes couldn't altogether compensate for total surprise. She lost her balance, and as she staggered Travis slipped under her guard, moving behind her, sliding his left arm under her left armpit and around her throat, bringing his right hand up for a blow with the switchblade which she couldn't possibly parry.

"Ben!" This time her voice was a choked gargle.

All at once, the state of protracted time in which he'd been existing snapped back into synchronicity with the universe. All the impossibilities could wait. So could thought.

His right foot shot out in a side-kick that connected with Travis' right hand, and the switchblade went flying. He completed the turning movement and found himself face-to-face with Travis, for Katy had taken advantage of her attacker's startlement to slide out of his grasp.

The two men met in a blinding series of blows, delivered by opponents equally well-trained, the experience of the one counterbalanced by the other's youthful reflexes.

But only for a moment. For Katy had scooped up the dropped switchblade, and now she brought it around in a very precise and scientific slash.

There was an obscene amount of blood, and the fight was over.

Roark stood panting for a moment, as his mind sought to catch up with reality. The final collapse of Travis' swaying, lifeless body to the floor seemed to complete the realigning of his time-scale with the world's, for it was at that instant that he began trying to blurt out all his questions.

But there were so many of them that they got in each other's way. "Katy, how did you . . . ? I mean, why did he . . . ? That is . . . ?"

She made a quick sideways hand motion that cut

off his attempts to speak. "No time! We're in luck. This level isn't subject to surveillance, and nobody ever comes down here at this time of night. Better still, there's a garbage disposal chute just beyond the corner. Take him there and drop him in. It reduces stuff to the molecular level."

"But . . . " Roark looked at the spreading pool of red-black blood on the floor.

"I'll take care of it!" And she was off, sprinting in the direction from which she'd come.

Moving more by inertia than anything else, Roark grasped Travis' body under the arms and dragged it toward the corner. Seeing the only thing that could be a garbage disposal, he hoisted the corpse up to the opening and slid it downward into oblivion.

Turning around, he saw Katy returning with a tube of the detergent gel and a bunch of paper towels. She set to work, spreading the stuff over the blood-stains. The nanomachines of which it was composed proceeded to reduce the blood and all other organic remains to a dry powder, which she wiped up as Roark watched with a numb sense of unreality. It was all he could do. Too much had happened too fast.

Finally, she stood up and took a deep breath. "So much for the forensic evidence. But questions will be asked when he's missed. And, knowing them, he's not the only Eagleman here."

"*Eagleman?* Travis? No, you're wrong. This is a Company operation. And I need to report this to Rivera, our control."

"*Rivera?* That tears it, Ben. You've got to lie low—we both do. And my room is the only place. Come on." She turned in the direction from which she'd originally come.

"Wait a minute! Aren't you going the wrong way,

to get to the dormitory or whatever they call it? And aren't the rooms there under surveillance?"

She shook her reddish-brown head. "No. I live here, and—"

"Here? In the tower?"

"Yes. And I know for a fact there are no spy-eyes in my quarters. Now come on!" Underneath her urgency, there was something awakening in her eyes which belied her peremptory tone. "There isn't time, Ben! I'll explain everything. But now we have to get you out of sight."

As they hurried through the passageways, his thoughts began to untangle themselves. And among all the chaos of unanswered questions—notably, how Katy had known Travis was an Eagleman, and why he had attacked her with instant, homicidal fury— a single memory arose: Henry Havelock's voice, back at Area 51.

"Some time ago the Eaglemen managed to get an agent in there . . . apparently ceased reporting some time ago."

He glanced at the woman striding along beside him and started to open his mouth, but then snapped it shut. Like everything else, the new question would have to wait.

For now, he was chiefly conscious of how much he needed a drink.

At last, although I knew it, he amended. It was one of the many things he had a chance to reflect on if he awaited her return.

CHAPTER SIX

Katy's apartment (it wasn't just one room) was in the middle levels of the Hov-Korth tower. She'd obviously been living there for some time—it had that undefinable but unmistakable air of long-term female occupancy.

Katy left immediately after they arrived, with a hurried explanation that she had to complete the original errand that had taken her down that subterranean corridor, and a needless admonition to Roark to lie low. It gave him time to explore the place, and to get over his initial skepticism about Katy's assurance that it was surveillance-free. After all, she seemed quite certain of it, and he knew her well enough to know she wouldn't feel that way without good reason.

At least I thought *I knew her,* he amended. It was one of the many things he had a chance to reflect on as he awaited her return.

That downtime didn't help as much as it should have. Without the press of action and urgency that had held it at bay, he was left face-to-face with the wreckage of his reality structure, an unsatisfactory but familiar object that now lay shattered on the floor. All he could do was sit and stare at it, occasionally picking up and examining a shard with numb bewilderment.

But, rising out of that debris, a single realization grew and grew: *Katy is alive.* He had to cling to that.

He was clinging to it when she returned, hastily closing the door behind her and leaning on it as she turned to face him.

"All right," she said, catching her breath. "I shouldn't be missed by anybody. I won't be expected anywhere until tomorrow." Her words dropped tracelessly into a bottomless well of awkward silence. She drew another deep breath. "It's hard to know where to begin, isn't it?"

"Yes, it is." Oddly, it never for an instant occurred to Roark to use what some might have thought the obvious conversation opener: *Are you really Katy Doyle?* There was no room for doubt in his mind, so full was it of well-remembered gestures, motions, facial expressions, husky soprano voice, coppery-red glint of overhead lights off deep brown hair. . . . No, there could be no possible question. It was as undeniable as it was impossible.

He wanted to take her in his arms. But it wasn't right—not yet.

Almost desperately, she broke the silence again. "Ah, would you like a drink? I've got rum."

Roark forced back down that which leaped in him—possibly the most difficult thing he'd ever done. "No, Katy, I'd better not. I don't always know just exactly when to stop. And we've got to talk. I've got to know . . . " But there were too many questions. How could she be alive? How was it that she was living here, in the heart of this Lokaron tower? How had she known Travis was an Eagleman (if, indeed, she was right about it)? How . . . ? *"How?"* he finally blurted out, concentrating all his bewilderment into the one word. "You *died*!"

She winced, and averted her eyes as she began to speak. "No, I *almost* died. I was dying when you last saw me. Then the security guards arrived. They thought I was too far gone to be worth trying to save. But . . . there was a Lokar with them."

"Yes, I remember." Roark nodded, recalling the tall nonhuman figure silhouetted against the lights and the flames, towering above the human guards. "That was why I held my fire."

"Damned good thing you did. His name is Svyatog'Korth, and he's what you might call a VIL—a very important Lokar. A very, *very* important Lokar. I'll tell you more about him later. Anyway, he saw that I was still alive—barely. He told them to take me to his personal shuttle. There I was put into some kind of cryogenic suspension until they could get me here, to the Enclave." Her eyes seemed to gaze with incredulous awe at something unattainably far away. "You simply can't *believe* what Lokaron medical science can do, Ben! The stuff they've sold us is nothing. They can revive a corpse that hasn't been dead too long—which was, I'm told, precisely what I was. They can stimulate cellular regeneration of destroyed tissue. Things they can't regrow in place—major organs, or an entire arm or leg—they can selectively clone, and force-grow in no time as replacement parts. They can . . . Well, suffice it to say that they put Humpty-Dumpty back together again."

"But why did this . . . Svyatog'Korth go to so much trouble to save you? A human, and one who'd been engaged in an operation counter to Lokaron interests, at that."

"I asked him that, using their translators, as soon as I was in shape to say anything. His motives were complex. Part of it was guilt—and *don't* give me that look! I didn't believe it either, at first. But I eventually came to realize there was a genuine feeling there. Not really guilt, though. I think it was more a case of being *appalled*. Svyatog's not a soldier or anything. He'd never actually seen what automatic weapons do to bodies."

"I'm surprised he didn't simply order the guards to put you out of your misery."

"Svyatog's not like that!" Surprised by her vehemence, Roark didn't contest the point. After a moment, she resumed. "Anyway, he had another motive as well, although he didn't think it through until later. You see, in his position he needs accurate intelligence on humans. And he'd come to realize that mere data wasn't enough. He needed a human advisor, someone he could trust, to interpret the data in terms of human culture, human psychology."

"What is this 'position' of his? You mentioned before that he's some kind of high muckety-muck."

"I'll have to explain about their system." The generous mouth quirked upward in a smile that would have banished any remaining doubts that this was really Katy, had he still been harboring such doubts. "You've heard the expression, 'everything you know is wrong.' It's always been a favorite graffito of college twerps. Well, in the case of what humanity at large thinks it knows about the Lokaron it happens to be absolutely true." She paused as though organizing her thoughts. "In the first place, while the Lokaron are all one species they're not politically unified. They want us to think they are, but they're not. We're dealing with divided sovereignties."

"Huh? You mean like our nations?"

"You could say that. But don't lean too heavily on the analogy. The Lokaron 'nations'—gevahon in their language, like Gev-Harath, to which Svyatog belongs—are rooted in differences that mean a lot more than the differences between a Frenchman and a German . . . or, for that matter, a Frenchman and a Melanesian. As you know, ever since they arrived we've noticed that there are physical differences between them."

"Oh, yeah: the blue ones that are typical, and the greenish ones who aren't quite as attenuated, and the bluish-white ones who're even more so. You're telling me that each of these types equates to the members of a certain, uh, gevah? Everybody's always assumed that we were looking at racial groups like our whites and blacks and Asians and so forth."

"I'm sure the Lokaron had such groupings in their early history. But by the time they'd left their native star system their geographical gene pools had pretty much blended, just as ours have been blending ever since the day Columbus' sailors first started making whoopee with the Arawaks. No, the different-colored Lokaron belong to different *subspecies*—artificially created subspecies at that, designed to colonize various planets. Listening to Svyatog, I've gotten the impression that they're a lot less queasy about genetically engineering their own species than we would be.

"It's a state of affairs we find hard to imagine, because humans have all belonged to the same subspecies for tens of thousands of years. 'Ain't nobody here but us *Homo sapiens sapiens.*' Try to picture us carrying on diplomatic relations with a nation of *Homo sapiens neanderthalensis.*" She smiled again. "You might say the members of different gevahon really *are* as biologically different from each other as human nationalists have always *believed* their own nationalities to be!

"But the comparison to our nations is valid in that the gevahon are just as sovereign. More so, since no one of them is enforcing a hegemony like the U.S. is on Earth—not even Gev-Harath, the most powerful of the lot. They're all expanding in a rough-and-tumble way, complete with occasional inter-gevah wars, although there seem to be unwritten rules that restrict the actual fighting to the frontiers."

Roark struggled to assimilate the new data. "So all along we've been dealing with a gaggle of rival power-groupings, and never known it." His voice trailed off as he pondered the implications.

"Makes you realize why they've kept it a secret." Katy smiled.

"I'd say so! But to get back to your buddy Svyatog, I suppose you're leading up to telling me he's a government official of this Gev-Harath outfit."

"There you go again, thinking in terms of human assumptions. You'll never understand the Lokaron unless you grasp the fact that a gevah is *not* organized like a human government. They're like . . . Have you ever heard of the Hanseatic League?"

Roark blinked. "I seem to recall the term from somewhere."

"Probably some required history course a long time ago. I was never a history buff myself, but I've read up on it lately, trying to find human parallels to the Lokaron setup. There are no exact ones, but the League comes about as close as any. It was an alliance of North German city-states in the late Middle Ages, run by the great merchant houses, who'd set it up for mutual defense and other bare-bones governmental functions. Likewise, the gevahon aren't 'states' as we understand the term, ruling directly over individuals. They're set up and financed by the *hovahon*, or corporations—at least I think of them as corporations, even though they're still family-run to a large extent. What we'd call 'government officials' have the status of . . . well, not exactly 'hired hands.' The gevah functionaries get the respect they need in order to function. For example, each of the gevahon that are operating on Earth has a government representative—a 'resident commissioner' as the machine translates it. But they serve, not some deified abstraction of the nation, but the currently dominant coalition of hovahon. And everybody recognizes this."

Roark gave a skeptical head shake. "For a civilization way beyond our technological horizons, it seems . . . primitive."

"That's your indoctrination talking! I know damned well you don't *like* the centralized bureaucratic state. But you still think of it as the most 'advanced' form of human association, the end-result of 'progress,' and all that crap, because that's what you've been told to think."

"*Nobody* tells me what to think! But . . . damn it, you can't deny that history has in fact taken that route."

"*Our* history. But it doesn't have to be that way. Listen: the Lokaron had states like ours a long time ago, and think of them as something 'primitive' that they've struggled up from! They look back on things like conscript armies and direct taxation of individuals the way we look back on slavery and human sacrifice! And they see us much like we'd see a civilization that had gotten as far as the scientific revolution but still had god-kings like the pharaohs." Her tone softened, and for the first time she reached out and tentatively touched Roark's arm. "I know Ben—it's a hell of an adjustment. But I've made that adjustment. I've come to see that the course of modern human history hasn't been inevitable at all—it's just been a series of mistakes."

Roark wanted to reciprocate her touch—wanted it even more than he'd wanted to take her up on her offer of a drink. But he held her eyes with his and spoke in a very controlled voice. "Is that why you decided to stop working for the Eaglemen?"

For several heartbeats the silence reverberated around the room. Then Katy slumped down onto a couch. *Funny,* Roark thought. *We've been standing all this time. I hadn't even noticed that we'd never sat down.*

"How did you know?" she finally breathed.

"It was the only logical answer to a lot of questions. You were certain—not just suspicious, but *certain*—that Travis was an Eagleman. But what bothered me even more than that was the way he tried to kill you, with no apparent motive. Then I recalled what Havelock told us: his knowledge of the Enclave had been captured from the Eaglemen, who'd gotten it from an agent who'd ceased reporting. The only explanation that made sense was that you were the agent, and that Travis was an Eagleman who they'd managed to plant in this operation. He recognized you and immediately decided that, not being dead, you must have been turned. So you had to be eliminated." He paused and allowed the train of thought to proceed to its logical destination. "The mention of Ada Rivera really spooked you. I suppose she must be an Eagleman too." *My God!* he thought to himself even as he spoke. *How deep does the infiltration of the Company go?*

Katy nodded. "Yes. We followed the cell system, each member of the higher-level cells controlling a cell on the level below. Rivera was my cell's control—a member of the command cell, as you might call it, with nothing above it but the ultimate leader, whose identity we never knew."

Roark released the breath he became aware he'd been holding. "So you were a member of the Eaglemen all that time you were working for the Company. All that time you and I were. . . . " A montage of memories flashed before his mind's eye, too rapidly to separate the different times, rooms, beds, precise intertwinings of bodies. . . . He became aware that he was standing over her where she sat slumped on the couch. He forced his fists to unclench and his vocal chords to function. "Why didn't you tell me, Katy? God damn it, you could have told me! You could have trusted me! I would have—"

"You would have what?" she flared. "You're telling me you would have *understood*? Cut the crap, Ben! I knew what you thought of the Eaglemen. You've never exactly been bashful about voicing your opinions. And the subject came up often enough, what with all the people we knew who were sympathizers or, you suspected, actual members. Even if you hadn't betrayed me—and no, I don't really think you would have—you would have been eaten away by guilt. I wasn't about to inflict that on you . . . on both of us, really, because your frustration would have eventually come out in the form of resentment of me for putting you in such a dilemma." She subsided again and spoke in a voice that was normal save for its dullness. "Anyway, after I'd started working for Svyatog I managed to get word out to Rivera that I was alive and inside, through a human employee here who was sympathetic enough to the Eaglemen to be willing to do a message drop. And yes, it was through me that the Eaglemen got the detailed plans of this place."

Roark found that he'd joined her on the couch
and was facing her from a couple of feet. "Couldn't
you have used the same methods to get word to
Havelock? After all, you'd been working for both him
and the Eaglemen before."

"But no more! Even with Lokaron medical treat-
ments, wounds like mine took a lot of convalescing.
So I had time to do some thinking. And I narrowed
down the possibilities of who could have set us up,
until there was only one left." She shot a challenging
gaze at Roark, who didn't meet it. Then she nodded
grimly. "I see you've reached the same conclusion.
So you understand how I felt. I'd always suspected
that Havelock was a consummate son of a bitch, but
finally I *knew* it. So I was perfectly content to let
him go on thinking I was dead." She gave Roark a
look that made him wince. "I can't believe you went
on working for him."

"I didn't! I quit the Company and . . . sort of went
to pieces for a while. I signed back on for this job
because I wanted revenge."

"Revenge? You mean against the Lokaron? For . . . ?"
For a while there was silence, because no words
were needed. Finally she spoke with the briskness
of embarrassment. "Well, anyway, I went to work for
Svyatog. Partly it was simple gratitude for saving my
life. Partly it was . . . Well, I felt I was in a unique
position to help humanity by helping him understand
our species. You see, he's the top representative here
on Earth—the 'factor,' I suppose you'd have to call
him—of Hov-Korth, the biggest hovah in Gev-
Harath, which as I mentioned is the most powerful
gevah. In short, the fate of the human race is pretty
much in his hands. And no, I don't like that any
more than you do. But my likes and dislikes don't
change the facts. All I can do is give thanks that he's

a fundamentally decent individual, and do my best to make sure his decisions are based on an accurate assessment of human behavior. Any misunderstandings could be fatal—for us! And it's not easy to convey an understanding of us to a Lokaron; underneath the superficialities, they're more alien than you imagine. To take just one example, they have no conception of the male-female duality that's so basic to human psychology."

"What? But I always assumed . . . well, I never really knew . . . "

"Of course not. The sex lives of the Lokaron are nobody else's business. But the fact is, they have three genders. The 'primary males' function pretty much like our males, except that they impregnate what I think of as the 'transmitter,' which produces the eggs. But the transmitter doesn't give birth. It just carries the fertilized egg for a while, after which the egg dies unless it's implanted in the third gender—the 'female,' as I think of it because it *does* give birth, although that's really a fallacy. The transmitter does the implanting using something similar to the male sex organ." She looked uncomfortable.

Roark goggled. "I'm trying to visualize this. Let's see: the transmitter is Lucky Pierre . . . "

Katy's glare stopped him. She resumed with emphatic seriousness. "Svyatog is, of course, a transmitter—"

"Huh? Why 'of course'? And you've been referring to Svyatog as 'he.' "

"I suppose it isn't really 'of course' in this day and age—I was just falling into Lokaron gender stereotypes. And my use of 'he' for the transmitters as well as the primary males is part of my *own* leftover stereotypes. Also, it's the convention the translator software uses. You see, the transmitters are the large, strong, aggressive ones. In primitive Lokaron societies, the traditional pattern was a transmitter sultan with *two* harems. And a solid wall between them! The primary males can . . . well, *perform* with the females directly. Lokaron religions have always inveighed against this as perversion, because it can't possibly lead to conception. But . . . " Katy's discomfort deepened. "But the primary males and the females both *enjoy* it. And no," she added hastily, "I don't know the details of just why they do. But I have some inkling of the tangle of guilt, hypocrisy and confusion this has led to."

"I think I'm beginning to," Roark said slowly. "Holy shit! And I thought *our* lives were complicated!"

"It's different now. Urbanization dissolved traditional social patterns for them much as it did for us. Nowadays, all Lokaron societies have legally abolished gender discrimination. But in practice, they haven't even gone as far in the direction of equality as *we* have." (A flash of bitterness, quickly suppressed.) "Transmitters like Svyatog still dominate the power elite. And he's no saint—he's completely committed to the interests of Gev-Harath in general and Hov-Korth in particular. But I think I've been able to make him understand us better, and . . . put a sympathetic face on humanity for him. Make him see that his interests and ours dovetail."

"I suppose that's why you were able to rationalize working for him while continuing to work for the Eaglemen. I imagine they'd consider you a traitor to the human race." Roark expected an explosive reaction to this calculated bit of provocation. He got a flicker of fire in her eyes that was too brief to be called a glare. Then she averted her gaze and spoke with quiet earnestness.

"I'd had doubts about the movement even before being brought here. But I still fully agreed with them that we Americans have to get rid of the damned EFP. On the strength of that, I was willing to send them the information they wanted—for a while. But then, the longer I stayed here, I came to understand certain things. First of all, it's a pipedream to think we can simply throw the Lokaron off Earth and go back to the way things were before they came. We've got to face the fact that we've joined a Lokaron universe."

"Been made to join it, you mean."

"How does that change anything? The point is, we can't turn our backs on that universe. We've got to make a place for ourselves in it."

"Will the Lokaron *let* anybody not of their species do that?"

"Who said anything about asking their permission? We've got to beat them at their own game. And we can! Living among the Lokaron, I've come to two conclusions about them. First of all, I've never seen an iota of evidence that they're inherently any more intelligent than we are. And secondly, their civilization has become . . . self-satisfied." She laughed shortly. "Not exactly a big surprise. It would be amazing if they *didn't* feel that way, considering what they've accomplished. But they've fallen into what military people call 'victory disease.' Once we acquire their knowledge, we can bring a fresh viewpoint to bear on it. We'll try things their scientific establishment says are impossible . . . and make them work, because we won't *know* what's impossible!"

"Well, then, you ought to approve of the mission

I'm on. The whole idea, as Havelock explained it to me, is to steal Lokaron technology."

"Havelock! If he said it was nighttime I'd swear the sun was shining. But even if, for once in his life, he's telling the truth . . . Don't you *see*? Their advanced technology isn't their secret. They wouldn't have *become* advanced in the first place if they didn't have a society that frees creative individuals to create and productive individuals to produce. The Eaglemen are right about that, at least: the EFP has got to go. It's that kind of state—the kind that keeps itself in power by locking as much of the population as possible into a culture of dependency—that's left humanity eating the Lokarons' dust. But the purpose of getting rid of it isn't to return to some womb of an idealized Lokaron-free past. We've got to adopt Lokaron technology and become a respected member of an interstellar society which is—let's face it—going to be predominantly Lokaron for the foreseeable future."

"Havelock might be more in agreement with that than you think," Roark suggested, recalling words spoken in the light of a burning airplane one night on Grand Cayman.

"Maybe. But his little operation seems to have been well and truly infiltrated by the Eaglemen, doesn't it?" Katy seemed about to say more, but then her face froze into an inward-looking mask of intense thought. Roark restrained his questions, and waited. When she finally turned back to him, her eyes were haunted.

"Ben, I don't know why it took me so long to think of this. But now I remember. When I was a member of the Eaglemen, we used to sit around a lot and hash out plans for attacking the Enclave. It was our favorite wet-dream . . . but that was all it ever was. All our brainstorming always led us to the same conclusion: it was hopeless without inside help. But now . . . "

"You're saying that's why they insinuated their people into Havelock's operation?"

"It's got to be! And now that they've gotten their people in here . . . Ben, they must actually plan to try it!"

"But they wouldn't dare! Hell, even if they succeeded, Earth would face retaliation from the Lokaron forces in space, which they can't touch."

"Ben, trust me. I know these people, and you don't. They've convinced themselves that if the Enclave were swept away the Lokaron would just give up on Earth as a bad job. And then the Central Committee, which agreed to the trade treaties, would be so discredited that the EFP would fall. They have the true idealist's capacity for self-deception. In reality, the only winner would be Gev-Rogov."

"Who?"

"Remember, we're dealing with several . . . nations. One of them, Gev-Rogov, is a partial exception to a lot of what I've told you about the Lokaron. The Rogovon—they're the green ones—are the closest thing among the Lokaron to genuine statists and militarists. They'd like to see an outright conquest and partition of Earth. Gev-Harath and the others don't agree. But if we provoke them too far, they may decide that the Rogovon have been right all along. Even Svyatog may be unable to argue them out of it. And if they decide to go with the military option, don't even *think* about Earth resisting them."

"Maybe you've been among them so long you underestimate your own race," some rebellious part of Roark argued.

Katy took a deep breath. "Ben, forget all those old bullshit science fiction movies. H. G. Wells, who invented the 'alien invasion' genre, knew damned well that his 'war of the worlds' wouldn't have been a war at all, but an annexation. In order to provide a happy ending, he had to cheat. His Martians, after blowing away Earth's military, were killed off by Earthly microorganisms to which they had no resistance—as if a super-scientific civilization wouldn't have foreseen that problem! No, until we modernize ourselves up to Lokaron standards, the only thing keeping us alive is that our fate is in the hands of Svyatog and others like him." She leaned forward and grasped his hands. This time he returned the pressure. "Ben, we've *got* to stop the Eaglemen."

"Well, is there any way you can get word out to Havelock, and let him know his organization is crawling with Eaglemen?"

"That bastard? And even if we could trust him, would he be able to stop them? Especially considering how totally they seem to have penetrated his security."

"Yeah," Roark acknowledged the point. It was, on reflection, strange. Havelock might be slime, but nobody had ever called him *incompetent* slime. How had the Eaglemen outfoxed him so completely?

"There's only one way," Katy said, interrupting his uncomfortable thoughts. "We'll have to deal with this ourselves, right here. Which means we'll have to go to Svyatog with it."

"Huh? To Svyatog? *We?*"

"Yes. I'll get you in to see him. You'll be able to tell him the details—in particular, which human employees he needs to watch closely." She eyed him narrowly, recognizing the conflict playing itself out behind those familiar features. "Yes, Ben, I know: asking you to break security is like asking a doctor to poison a patient. But is Havelock really worth your loyalty?"

"It's not Havelock. It's my own . . . honor, I suppose," he finished in an embarrassed mumble.

"I understand, Ben. But this is bigger than your personal code of behavior . . . however much I may admire that code." Their eyes met for a significant instant before she hurried on. "We're talking about the fate not just of America but of the entire human race. And the hell of it is, there are no bad guys here. As you've probably gathered, I don't hate the Lokaron; and I certainly don't hate the Eaglemen. But they're playing with forces they don't understand, and we've got to stop them before they cause a tragedy beyond their comprehension. Will you help me?"

Roark nodded slowly. "All right. I'm with you. Let's go see Svyatog."

"Not now. It's too late. But I'll have access to him tomorrow morning. You'll just have to spend the night here."

Their eyes met in silence. Roark noticed that their hands had never unclasped.

"I've . . . I've missed you," he finally said, fully aware of the inadequacy.

She nodded jerkily. "Yes. I know what you mean. I'd resigned myself to the idea that I'd never see you again. So tonight . . . I didn't know how to react."

He tentatively leaned forward. She didn't shrink from his kiss.

After a time, she took a breath. "Are you sure you won't take me up on that drink?"

"Yes, maybe I will at that . . . in a little while."

they walked up to the large desk where they simply stopped. She'd explained that no formal courtesies were required of an coming into the presence of

CHAPTER SEVEN

Roark was grateful for the view through the lofty transparencies of Svyatog'Korth's private office, in the highest reaches of the Hov-Korth Tower. That glimpse of autumn-clothed Virginia countryside was a homelike anchor for his sense of reality as he and Katy passed through silently sliding doors and faintly tingling invisible curtains of stationary security nano-bots, and crossed a darkly gleaming marblelike floor between walls paneled in what looked like priceless jade but glowed faintly from within. The matter-of-fact, human-crowded functionality he'd seen so far had not prepared him for this realm of hushed alienness.

He reminded himself that it was all old hat to Katy, and stayed shoulder to shoulder with her as they walked up to the large desk, where they simply stopped. She'd explained that no formal courtesies were required when coming into the presence of Earth's arbiter.

Svyatog'Korth was a Lokar of the blue-skinned, average-proportioned sort Roark had always thought of as simply the majority type but now knew to be characteristic of Gev-Harath and its offshoots. He'd also learned of certain age indicators to look for, and from the smooth texture of Svyatog's hairless skin he knew the Lokar to be a fairly young one, without the coarsening that came with middle age, accompanied by a thickening of the body that was scarcely noticeable to human eyes. (Katy had mentioned that Svyatog was young for his position in Hov-Korth. She'd waxed indignant when Roark had suggested that he might owe that position to his surname, even while admitting that the hovahon were still largely run by their founding families.)

He also knew how to recognize the Lokaron equivalent of a smile, a stretching of the mouth which concealed the hard ridges which served as teeth. (The Lokaron, like humans, were omnivores, but with a strong predisposition toward a meat diet, which lent them some of the characteristics of carnivores.) Svyatog's face now wore that expression. He gave the rather high-pitched sounds of Lokaron speech. The minute but sophisticated single-purpose computer in the pendant he wore translated those sounds into an American English flawed only by its flawlessness, which it transmitted to the hearing aid-like earpieces the two humans had been issued. "Ah, Katy! This must be the man you spoke of earlier this morning when you asked to see me." The unhuman head turned and the yellow slit-pupiled eyes focused in their disturbing way. "Mr. Roark, I believe."

"Yes, Factor," Roark murmured. Svyatog didn't need one of the earpieces; he had a surgical implant which performed the same function, among others. "Thank you for taking time out of your busy schedule to see us on short notice."

"Don't mention it. Katy indicated that the matter is one of extreme urgency. Won't the two of you sit down?" Svyatog's gesture indicated a spot behind them. Roark turned and saw two odd-looking but human-proportioned chairs that hadn't been there a moment before.

Toto, I don't think we're in Kansas anymore. Roark ordered the prickling at the nape of his neck to subside as he sat down with a mumble of thanks.

"Factor," Katy began, "as you know, from the circumstances under which you originally found me and also from my subsequent account, I formerly worked for the chief American intelligence-gathering organization."

"Yes. A government instrumentality, as I recall." The near-microscopic translating computer could convey tone, and it clearly hadn't been instructed to edit any out, however unflattering to the listener. Katy had explained that the hovahon adamantly refused to entrust spookery to the gevah functionaries.

"Just so," Katy resumed. "At any rate, Mr. Roark is an old . . . colleague of mine."

Svyatog looked at Roark with new interest. Roark met his gaze and suddenly decided he'd identified what was so unsettling about those eyes: they were the most *animal*-like thing about the Lokaron. He also decided he should follow Katy's advice and be completely forthright. "Actually, Factor, I was a member of the group that included Katy, that night when you saved her life . . . for which, by the way, I owe you a debt of gratitude."

Svyatog's facial muscles did a quick, indescribable expansion and contraction which, Roark suspected, answered to a sudden lifting of a human's eyebrows over widened eyes. "Are you, by any chance, still in this same . . . line of work?"

"I wasn't, but recently I've resumed it. And yes, I became an employee of yours in order to spy on you."

Katy flashed him a sharp glance, even though she herself had counseled him not to try to conceal anything from this being, who knew humans far better than Roark knew Lokaron. But he kept his eyes on Svyatog's face, expecting an exaggerated version of the look he'd just seen. Instead, the alien face was a mask of control. "I'll say this for you, Mr. Roark: you've succeeded in getting my undivided attention. May I inquire as to your reason for coming to see me now? Would it perhaps be . . . ?" Svyatog's eyes flicked back and forth between the two humans, members of their species' two sexes, and gazed at them across a chasm as wide as the abyss between the stars.

"No," Roark answered the unspoken question. "Well, it has something to do with it. I can't deny that. But"—a sudden flash of resentment—"we humans aren't mindless slaves of our sexual patterns, any more than you are of yours! Oh, all right, some of us are," he backpedaled, recalling certain people he'd known, and also the President under whom the U.S. had ended the previous century, whose demeaning of the office had helped create the institutional vacuum the EFP had eagerly filled. "But not those of us who've outgrown adolescence."

"What, then, is the basis for what seems a rather dramatic change of sides on your part?"

"*Not* a change of sides! I want that clearly understood. My loyalty is still to the United States of America, and to the human race in general. But I have to make my own ethical decisions as to where my loyalties must take me. It's called being an adult."

Svyatog regarded him in silence for a couple of (human) heartbeats before speaking gravely. "Yes. I agree. Although . . . I gather that the notion of individual responsibility for the consequences of one's actions has fallen out of favor in your culture over the last two or three generations."

Roark felt his ears heating up, but he couldn't argue the point. "What others think is their business. I can only answer for myself. And Katy has convinced me that the interests of my nation and my world are bound up with yours. I wouldn't be coming to you if it were a matter of betraying my government— the government that sent me in here, along with five others."

Svyatog's face took on the goggle-eyed-equivalent look once again, but the translator conveyed only dryness. "Evidently our security needs work."

"So does ours. You see, I've learned that at least two of those five were, in fact, members of a secret organization called the Eaglemen."

"Ah, yes. Katy has told me about them: fanatical xenophobes with respect to us, and romantic reactionaries with respect to their own country's current regime. And they've attached themselves to an espionage operation of the very government they oppose, in order to infiltrate the Enclave. How can you be sure of this?"

Katy answered for him. "Because I recognized one of them, who is dead now, and knew the other one by name. I myself am a former member of the organization."

The English-speaking voice in Roark's ear grew even more expressionless. "This is new data."

"Yes, I concealed it from you. And for a while after entering your service, I continued to work for them. Later, as I've learned from Ben, the government captured some of the information I'd supplied to them. This made possible the operation which has resulted in Ben's presence here."

Few humans could have equaled Svyatog's absolute motionlessness. Outside the transparency a flock of migrating birds fared heedlessly southward toward Florida without breaking the silence.

"Why are you telling me this now?" the alien finally asked, with a lack of intonation that represented the translator software's abject surrender in the face of unmanageably complex emotions.

"To convince you that I'm in earnest. Yes, I withheld this from you for a long time, despite my gratitude and my . . . high regard for you." Human and Lokaron eyes met, and Roark, observing from the outside, strove to define his own emotions. Jealousy was, of course, unthinkable. Biologically, Katy had less in common with this being than with an armadillo, or an oak tree. Still, those locked pairs of eyes held a tale of shared thoughts and now-disappointed trust that were forever outside his own world of memories.

After a moment, the eyes slid apart and Katy resumed. "I withheld it even after I stopped considering myself a member of the Eaglemen. I broke with them even though I continued to share their opposition to my country's current government—"

"Understandable, from what I know of it." Svyatog's smooth urbanity was back.

"—and still share it. In fact, I shared it so strongly that I was willing to go along with the other half of their agenda—expelling you Lokaron—even though I suspected it was an impossible dream, and not even a very beautiful one at that. But finally that suspicion became certainty. Our future lies in today's universe— *your* universe. So I stopped communicating with them. After a while, I pretty much forgot about them. I also forgot about their pet idea of attacking the Enclave."

"*What?*" Svyatog leaned forward in an altogether human way. "Why haven't you told me this, if you've abandoned your loyalty to them?"

"It didn't seem important. The notion was never anything but an impossible daydream. The only plans that rose above the level of fantasy required people on the inside, which we never had. But now . . ." Katy's voice trailed off, for it didn't take an expert on Lokaron body language to know that Svyatog had ceased to listen as he worked out the implications for himself.

"You say there are two of these infiltrators?" the alien finally asked.

"There *were* at least two. Now there's at least one; we killed the other, Travis, last night." Katy spoke tersely of the moment of shared recognition in the corridor, and Travis' murderous attack. "But there could be other Eaglemen. And the one we *know* is left is a fairly high-level one—she was my cell leader. And if our government inserts additional agents, some of *those* may well be Eaglemen. They've shown it's not beyond their capabilities."

"Also," Roark put in, "the Eaglemen can make unwitting tools of the agents who don't even belong to their organization. That cell leader—Ada Rivera is her name—is our on-scene control. If she tells the others to act in support of an outside attack, they'll assume she's transmitting orders from higher up."

Svyatog flopped back in his chair and stared at them. "But this is terrible! If such an attack takes place . . ." He seemed to catch himself, and his mouth snapped shut as he darted a slit-pupiled look at Roark.

"I've told him about Gev-Rogov," Katy said quietly. "And given him all the background he needed to understand what I was telling him."

"That was not information you were authorized to release." The artificial voice was very level.

"No, it wasn't. But he had to be let in on it. And I trust him—completely."

Svyatog gazed at the two humans. They sat unflinching under his regard. "Very well," he finally said, addressing Katy. "I've learned to rely on your judgment. And, at any rate, you seem to have presented me with a *fait accompli.*" He turned to Roark. "You understand, then, the possible consequences if these idiots make their attack. Of course," he added as a complacent afterthought, "they'd have no hope of success. But they wouldn't *have* to succeed. The mere attempt would be enough."

"But you can stop them!" argued Roark. "You can apprehend Rivera and all the others, and use whatever means necessary to get confirmation of what we've said." *My God,* he thought, suddenly hearing himself, *these are humans I'm talking about, and Americans at that.* "And then . . . uh, deport them, or whatever."

"Unfortunately, it's not quite so simple. That kind of overt act would cause such an uproar among our human employees that everyone would hear of it. The truth would come out: the Enclave has been infiltrated, not just by American government operatives but also by the kind of xenophobic terrorists I've constantly assured everyone we need not fear. It would create precisely the climate of paranoia the Rogovon are counting on."

Roark stared at the Lokar. "But there must be *something* you can do!"

"Of course. I can have them kept under subtle surveillance. But more important at the moment is what *you* can do."

"Huh?" Roark was uncomfortably aware of how stupid he must look as he sat, blinking. "Me?"

"Yes. You." Svyatog's face had never looked more alien. "You claim to understand what is at stake here. Prove it. Resume your place among your fellow infiltrators, where you'll be in an ideal position to know when Rivera is preparing the groundwork for an outside attack. And when that moment comes . . . stop her. Abort the attack quietly."

Katy regained the power of speech before Roark did. "Do you have any idea what you're asking of him?"

"I do. I'm asking him to act in his own people's interests, as viewed in the larger perspective you've made him see."

Sheer irritation at listening to himself being discussed in the third person brought Roark out of shock. "Wait a minute! Aren't you overlooking a few little problems? Right now, Rivera and the others must be wondering what happened to me and Travis. When I show up without him, there are going to be some awkward questions."

"I can provide you with a cover story. You'll be returned to your fellows with a stern warning about straying into unauthorized areas—where, it seems, Travis was killed by automated defenses. We'll let it be known that you were questioned but that your answers satisfied us."

"Rivera won't buy it. She'll never trust me again."

"It will be up to you to allay her suspicions. It shouldn't be too hard. With only four subordinates left, she'll be open to justifications for not rendering herself even more shorthanded."

Had Svyatog been a human, Roark would have been certain he was getting dangerously pleased with his own cleverness. As it was, he was even more certain of it. *Katy said that cockiness is their abiding vice,* he reflected. *It may do them in, eventually. But right at the moment, I'm on the leading edge of what gets done in!*

"What about me?" Katy asked.

"You must remain out of sight. If this Travis individual recognized you and assumed that you had been turned, Rivera will surely do the same, as will any other Eaglemen still surviving in the group. We can set up prearranged rendezvous times when Roark can communicate with you—and, through you, with me."

The man and the woman exchanged a quick eye contact, eloquent of their knowledge that what had been miraculously restored was about to be undone again. Roark unwillingly ended that shared moment and turned to face the alien across the desk. "So you want me to deal with this situation in a low-profile way—meaning, as a practical matter, unsupported. What if I make a good-faith effort but something goes wrong? Can you guarantee to keep me and Katy alive?"

"Yes, I can. If all else fails, I will—" Svyatog stopped abruptly, then resumed in a carefully expressionless way. "There's no need to go into the details at present. Suffice it to say that I can put the two of you beyond any possibility of reprisal by the Eaglemen, and that I will do so if it comes to that."

Roark locked eyes with Katy once again. She gave a small nod, into which she seemed to be trying to concentrate everything she'd already told him about what this being's word meant. Roark nodded in return. It had to be enough.

He turned back to Svyatog. "All right. Let's get down to cases."

❖   ❖   ❖

The next few days went by in a mist of unreality for Roark. He'd been a lot of things in his time, but never a double agent.

But then, he told himself, *that's not really what I am, strictly speaking. So what* am *I? I'm not sure human experience provides a word for it.*

His return to the human dormitory, as he'd decided he might as well call it, went pretty much as expected. Chen showed every evidence of relief to see him back, tempered by shock at the official version of Travis' fate. The others, who weren't supposed to know him, concealed whatever reactions they may have had as they listened, along with all the other human employees, to the lecture about restricted areas. All but Rivera, who shot him a surreptitious look compounded of puzzlement, suspicion, and emotions less easily defined.

Afterwards, he reported to her personally at the same secluded alcove where she'd given him and Chen their instructions two days earlier. "They had a laser sensor system," he concluded his fictionalized account. "Only it doesn't operate in the visible light frequencies, or even close to them. So the aerosol spray Travis was using didn't reveal the beam. And it has one other difference from our systems: when it's tripped, it instantaneously steps up its energy output to weapon-level intensity. Travis never knew what hit him."

Rivera muttered a bilingual string of obscenities. "We never learned about this system from our—" Her mouth snapped shut as she seemed to recall Roark's presence. "Anyway, they took you alive. What did you tell them?"

"Nothing! Oh, I don't doubt that they could have gotten the truth out of me with drugs or . . . whatever the hell they use. But they didn't think it was worth the trouble. They accepted my story that we were just idle sensation seekers, and sent me back here with a scolding."

"How can you be so sure of that? For all anybody knows, they could have put you under without you knowing anything was going on, sucked you dry of knowledge, and left you without any memory of it."

Roark found exasperation easy to counterfeit. "Sure. And for that matter, they could have zapped us all with this magic mind-ray you're postulating as we were arriving. Hey, as long as you're spinning paranoid fantasies, why fuck around? How about this: they're telepathically eavesdropping on all our innermost thoughts, all the time, and—"

"All right, all right. Cut the sarcasm." Rivera chewed her lower lip and scowled with concentration. "I suppose we'd all be dead or in custody by now if you'd spilled your guts. So I'm going to proceed on the assumption that we haven't been compromised, and advise Havelock accordingly. You're to hold yourself in readiness for a major shift in this operation's entire orientation."

"Huh? What's that supposed to mean?"

"You'll be informed at such time as you have a need to know."

"You know something, Captain? I'm getting awfully goddamned sick and tired of that canned phrase you picked up while brown-nosing some OCS instructor. I may have resumed my affiliation with the Company, but I'm *not* in the military."

"You insubordinate son of a bitch! You heard Havelock: I'm in charge inside the Enclave. My orders are his orders. And, last I heard, you work for him."

"Yeah . . . without any great enthusiasm. But I'm not some twerp fresh out of boot camp who's going to wet his pants when you bark at him. If you want to get the maximum performance out of me, you'd better start talking to me like a grown-up. Which means, among other things, sharing information."

The discipline Rivera visibly imposed on herself extended even to her lips, which barely moved as she spoke in a tightly controlled voice. "Very well, *Mr.* Roark. You'll have to know anyway. The decision has been made to adopt a policy of overt action against the Enclave."

Even though this was what Roark had been awaiting, he found he wasn't prepared for the shock of actually hearing it. Rivera's euphemism somehow made it even worse. "You must be crazy!" he blurted. He retained enough presence of mind not to specify just *who* must be crazy. "An attack can accomplish nothing except to bring down a reprisal that will—"

"It's been determined at higher levels that the risk of retaliation is within acceptable parameters. Instead, we believe the loss of the Enclave will make them lose heart and pull off Earth. We'll be free of them for good!" Rivera could no longer keep exultation out of her dark eyes. They blazed with an unaffected enthusiasm that, for the first time in Roark's experience, made her actually sympathetic.

Even if I didn't know she's an Eagleman, I'd be pretty sure of it now. "You really do believe this, don't you?" he asked quietly.

"Come on, Roark! They're nothing but a bunch of interstellar hucksters! If we convince them they can't operate here at a profit, they'll give up on Earth as a bad job, and cut their losses. It's the way minds like theirs work."

How would you know? Roark wanted to ask. But he wasn't here to engage in a debate.

"All right. When is it going down?"

"Night after next." Rivera saw Roark's expression and nodded grimly. "Yes, I know, it's all happening fast. But those are my instructions."

"What are mine?"

"You and Chen are to meet me at oh-one-hundred that night, at Charlie-eight-five." She used the coordinate system they'd superimposed on the map of the Enclave and memorized. "We're going to disable the perimeter warning system."

"With what?"

"Remember all those odds and ends you brought in here in your luggage? Chen has been filling in for you while you've been in custody, so now I've got it all." They'd established a schedule of drops by which all the agents delivered their various smuggled items to Rivera, who knew how to assemble them. It hadn't been difficult; the Lokaron were serenely confident that nothing they needed to worry about could possibly have gotten through the entry scanning-net.

"Have you put together weapons for us?"

"No, but you'll be surprised what I *have* put together. And the important thing is that we take out the warning system—especially in light of what you've told me about this lethal beam sensor of theirs. The attacking force will be inside before the Lokaron know what's going on."

"Still—"

"Yes, I know, they'll take a lot of casualties. But it can be done, given the element of surprise. It *has* to be done, for America and for the whole human race! Oh, and don't worry: they'll have extra weapons for us. We'll be able to get in on the party." Once again, Rivera seemed to glow from an inner flame of honest idealism, a blaze she could barely contain, and Roark was struck by how attractive she could be when she forgot to be a martinet.

I wonder, came the unbidden thought, *if she'll be looking like this when I kill her.*

"Over here!"

Roark and Chen moved furtively through the night in the direction of Rivera's low voice. They wore their darkest clothing—there was no formal curfew for humans, but neither was there any legitimate reason for them to be out at one in the morning among the thin scattering of trees in this part of the Enclave's western edge—and, under it, multiple layers of underwear against the late-autumn chill. Aside from the few lights still showing from the towers behind them, there was only a quarter-moon and a scattering of stars to see by, and with no high-tech aids like starlight scopes they proceeded cautiously. But their eyes had adapted, and presently they saw Rivera's equally dark-clad form up ahead beside a tree, motioning to them. Beyond her was a relatively clear slope, and beyond it was the deeper blackness of a densely wooded area. Still further west, the mountains occluded the stars.

Fallen leaves crackled as they settled down beside her. She wore a backpack to which a fiber-optic cable connected a paperback-book-sized object in her hands. The top face of that object gave off a faint varicolored glow. Roark looked at it more closely, and sucked in a breath of the chill air.

"A Lokaron tactical sensor," he breathed.

Rivera's teeth gleamed in a grin. "Not exactly, but cobbled together using mostly Lokaron components. I *told* you you'd be surprised at what all the junk you brought in could be assembled into!"

"What do you need it for?"

"To let me know the attack force is in place. I couldn't communicate with them, even if I had a communicator to do it with; the Lokaron would detect that. But this thing is a cluster of strictly passive sensors—thermal, sonic and so forth. Watch." She laid the unit on the ground, pointed west. "See, it displays the landscape out there . . . and *these* are the troops concealed in the woods. They've been brought in quietly over the past week."

So this isn't such a sudden change of strategy after all, is it? The unsurprised thought occupied only a small fraction of Roark's mind; with the rest he was gazing, stunned, at the sheer number of ruddy little blotches marking the human bodies concealed in the woods. *My God! I never knew there* were *so many Eaglemen! They must have brought in their entire organization for this. But how could so many military people absent themselves from wherever they're stationed, at exactly the same time?*

"Where are Pirelli and Stoner?" Chen asked.

"Over on the far side of the Enclave. They were here half an hour ago, to pick up these." Rivera reached inside her apparently general-purpose backpack and produced several small objects, which she distributed to the two men. In the darkness, Roark felt rather flimsy metal frameworks enclosing some kind of lightweight electronic hardware.

"These aren't bombs," Chen stated positively.

"Of course not. We couldn't have brought explosives in with us; the Lokaron chemical scanners would have detected those in our luggage. No, these are very crude, one-shot applications of Lokaron technology. They produce an EM pulse that disrupts electronic systems. You four are to affix them to the generators of the security sensors, all around the perimeter, by means of these adhesive patches on the sides. From our standpoint, they're *better* than bombs. Explosions out here just might wake the Lokaron up! But since the whole security system is automated, they probably won't even know it's ceased to function until our people are on top of them."

"I suppose these devices are set to all go off at a predetermined time," Roark ventured cautiously as he stuffed the little objects into his pockets.

"No. We had to keep things as simple as possible, given the conditions under which we're working. This is a command-detonation system. As soon as you've finished, report back here to me. When I know all the devices are in place, I'll activate them simultaneously, with this." Rivera displayed a simple remote. "Our people outside can detect the sensor field around the perimeter, so they'll know when it goes down. That'll be their signal to move."

And if it doesn't *go down, they'll know something's gone wrong, and abort the mission,* Roark thought, knowing what he must do.

"All right, here are your orders." Rivera assigned each of them certain generators, the locations of which they'd long since memorized along with everything else Katy had ever told the Eaglemen about the Enclave. "All right, any questions? No? Then move!"

They moved, Chen to the south and Roark to the north. The latter proceeded a short distance, until he was well out of Rivera's sight and was sure Chen was also. Then he turned and doubled back under the fitful moonlight.

He paused behind a tree and peered at Rivera. She was still in position. She'd taken off her backpack and laid it beside the sensor display, in which she seemed absorbed. Very carefully, lest his steps on the carpet of dried leaves give him away, he began to circle around behind her. He worked his way to the tree closest to Rivera's back and paused, readying himself. This would have to be done quickly and quietly. . . .

There was a sound of hastily approaching steps. Cursing under his breath, Roark flattened himself against the tree as two figures emerged from the darkness and joined Rivera.

"All done," said Pirelli. *Yeah*, Roark recalled, *he and Stoner started earlier.*

"Good," Rivera said. "As soon as Roark and Chen report back, it's a go. Now get to your assigned coordinates and stand by."

"Right." The two headed off, in different directions. Rivera turned back to her display. Roark drew a long slow breath and relaxed from motionlessness. *Now, where were we?* He drew a length of cord out from inside his jacket's lining through a tiny slit. He'd turned down Svyatog's offer of a real weapon, which he would never have been able to keep concealed from Chen in their quarters. But it hadn't been hard to improvise a garotte.

Again the sound of approaching footsteps sent him flat against the tree, exasperated. A figure emerged from the darkness and joined Rivera.

"What's the status?" asked a voice Roark recognized as Stoner's.

"On schedule," Rivera replied. "Roark and Chen should be done shortly. They're competent men. And, like Pirelli, they think they're acting in support of a government military operation . . . which they *are*, after all."

Stoner too, Roark thought. *So fully half of the six of us were Eaglemen! Jesus Christ! How could they have penetrated the Company so completely?*

And . . . what did that last remark of Rivera's mean?

Stoner was staring at the sensor display. "Are all our people in place?" he asked nervously.

"How should I know?" Rivera's voice was brittle with tension. "All I know is what Havelock told me the last time I was able to exchange messages with him. He assured me that Kinsella, having let him talk her into this attack, had given him a free hand in selecting the personnel. So he should have been able to put plenty of us in key positions."

What the hell is she talking about? Roark wondered irritably. *She's not making sense. . . .*

Then, with a jolt, reality rearranged itself into a pattern in which Rivera's words made perfect sense.

As though from a vast distance, he heard Rivera resume. "You'd better get moving. It won't be long now."

"Right." Stoner slipped away into the night.

After a time, Roark shook himself and stepped cautiously out from the tree. He looked at Rivera's back, where she crouched over the display. And he dropped the cord onto the ground.

Don't be stupid, he told himself. *Rivera is Special Forces. She knows all the tricks you do, and is a lot younger. The surest way to disable is to kill.*

Oh, shut up, himself replied. *The only thing I'm certain of just now is that I'm not certain of anything any more . . . and I'm damned if I'll kill anybody without a definite reason.*

He took a couple of very careful steps, which brought him close enough to spring the rest of the distance.

Pushing off for that leap, he disturbed the dead leaves. Rivera twisted around at the sound. Her eyes widened with recognition.

Then he was on her, just as the turning movement put her off balance. He grappled her from behind, forcing the kind of fight where sheer weight and strength counted. She started to snarl his name, but it turned to a choking gurgle as his left arm went around her throat. She strained and writhed, seeking to escape his grasp. It was like trying to hold onto a spring-steel wildcat. Her left elbow jabbed backward into his ribs, with a pain that almost made him lose control of her. He had just barely enough time to turn her head sideways, exposing a certain spot, and deliver a short right jab. She went limp.

He made sure her unconsciousness wasn't feigned, then checked his ribs. Nothing broken. He turned to her backpack and found the remote. Simply stomping on it might have inadvertently activated it. He opened the plastic panel on its back and removed the batteries, then pocketed it.

Someone—it had to be Chen—was approaching from the south. Roark scooped up the backpack and its attached display pad and scuttled away into the trees. He watched as Chen rushed over to Rivera, tried the usual revival techniques, then looked around with bewildered frustration. Finally Chen swung the unconscious form over his shoulder and went back into the Enclave.

Roark waited a while, staring at the display. Finally the little blotches of color—some of which, but not all or even most, represented Eaglemen—began to move with military orderliness, withdrawing from the woods as their instrumentation told them that the Enclave's security system had not gone down as promised.

Only then did Roark head back . . . but not toward the dormitory. *It seems,* he thought, oddly calm, *that I'll have to take Svyatog up on his offer of sanctuary, or whatever, after all.*

CHAPTER EIGHT

Entering the plush, dimly lit conference room, Henry Havelock could tell this was going to be bad.

Colleen Kinsella had arrived earlier, and she sat across the oval table from the room's four other occupants. There was only one empty chair, immediately to Kinsella's left. As Havelock settled into it, Kinsella gave him a sidelong look whose poison was brewed from humiliation at the grilling she'd been undergoing and anger at him for the position he'd placed her in.

Soon her opinions will cease to matter. The thought left no visible or audible spoor on Havelock's face or voice. He inclined his head graciously. "Gentlemen. Ms. Ziegler."

The man directly opposite him wasted no time on pleasantries, but cut in quickly before Central Committeeperson Vera Ziegler could launch into a time-wasting denunciation of Havelock's old-fashioned (and therefore ideologically unacceptable) way of addressing the three Central Committee members and the chairman of the Joint Chiefs of Staff.

"Director Kinsella has indicated that you can explain to us the intolerable position her agency's machinations have placed us in."

Havelock gave an eyebrow lift of bogus astonishment as he studied the speaker. Murray Morris was fat, bald, and totally unremarkable in appearance. For once, appearance was not deceiving. He possessed no talents whatsoever except the one that mattered: political survival. That single ability was also his single conviction. Under a regime of fascists or monarchists or plutocrats, he would have risen to prominence just as he had under the present one, by sheer longevity. He was a power on the Central Committee, and one of those who'd approved Kinsella's (meaning Havelock's) proposals to infiltrate, and later to attack, the Enclave.

"If memory serves, Mr. Morris," Havelock murmured, "the Central Committee authorized these 'machinations,' which otherwise would never have been set in motion."

"Yes, yes." Morris gave a pout of overweight petulance. "We believed the potential benefits of the original plan outweighed the dangers. Then, after the terrorist killing of a Lokar, we allowed ourselves to be persuaded that direct action against the Enclave was the only way out of the impasse in which we found ourselves."

"If you'll recall, sir, I offered you an alternative at the time. Shortly after the New York incident, I obtained definitive evidence that the Eaglemen were responsible." *No great feat, inasmuch as I'd directed them to do it.* "I suggested that you offer this evidence to the Lokaron as proof of the government's innocence. I renew the suggestion now."

"But that won't satisfy them!" Morris' voice rose to a plaintive bleat. "It didn't even satisfy them before

this new fiasco. They were demanding reparations—
a demand to which we couldn't possibly accede—"

"How typical!" Ziegler cut in shrilly. "What else
can one expect of the Lokaron? They're bloodsucking
capitalist exploiters of the masses, who naturally think
exclusively in terms of money! If it hadn't been for
their interloping, America—under our guidance—
would by now have attained a higher state of consciousness, rising far above the profit motive and all
the other obsolete, individualistic social patterns in
which these grotesque, unhuman monsters are
hopelessly mired. And without the temptation of their
technological gimmickry, we would have achieved a
sustainable society, living in harmony with the
environment!"

The other two Central Committee members
rolled their eyes resignedly heavenward. Among the
cynical *nomenklatura* that ran the EFP, Ziegler was
that rarest of birds, an old-line true believer.
Permanently ensconced on the Central Committee
as a sop to those of like mind among the Party's
rank and file, she could always be relied on to
support any action against the Lokaron, whose very
existence was ideological anathema to her. Unfortunately, the price of her support was staying awake
through her speeches.

"Of course, Vera, of course," Morris soothed her.
"You are, as ever, the conscience of the Party. We
can always count on you to remind us of the great
ideals that gave birth to our movement."

"Especially," Earl Drummond added, deadpan,
"when we're in danger of straying into mere practicalities."

He'll go too far, one of these days, Havelock
thought as he eyed Drummond, the solitary Central
Committee member for whom he had any respect.

But Ziegler, too stupid to recognize sarcasm, just blinked twice and looked vaguely puzzled.

Drummond was black, by the logic-defying North American definition—his face was the color of butterscotch and his features suggested about as much genetic material from West Europe as from West Africa. But his hair and neatly sculpted beard were wooly, and their snowiness contrasted beautifully with his skin. He was the only nonwhite on the Central Committee of a Party that had always taken care to exempt itself from the racial quotas it imposed on everyone else. His status was unique in another way as well, of which he proceeded to remind them without unnecessary subtlety. "And I certainly agree on the desirability of expelling the Lokaron and tearing up the trade treaties—to which my cousin, President Morrison, was opposed from the beginning."

Morris flushed. "*All* of us agree on the unfortunate nature of the treaties which we were *unavoidably* constrained to sign, as *everyone* is aware . . . at least everyone *here*," he intoned.

Havelock grinned inwardly as he recognized the defensiveness. It was curious: members of the EFP hierarchy were no more immune than anyone else to the mystique of the Presidency, an office which they themselves had politically emasculated. As John Morrison's cousin, Drummond partook of that *mana*. He was a voice on the Central Committee for the President's well-known and politically awkward opposition to the treaties. It was one reason he'd supported Kinsella's proposal, the other being that they were old friends and allies. Now he nodded pleasantly in acknowledgment of Morris' unsubtle point.

"Precisely, Murray. So perhaps we can return to

the practicalities I mentioned before . . . such as the failure of the Company's attack on the Enclave." He swung his dark eyes toward Havelock.

"Strictly speaking, Mr. Drummond, the attack didn't fail. Rather, it never occurred. The on-scene commander quite properly called it off when his instrumentation indicated that our agents in the Enclave had not succeeded in deactivating the Lokaron security system."

"Pettifoggery!" snapped Morris. "The fact is, the Lokaron are quite aware the attack was planned. They aren't saying so openly, for obscure reasons of their own. But the point has been made abundantly clear to me by, uh, Huruva'Strigak, who seems to be in ultimate authority among them—he presented the original demand for reparations. Can you shed any light on this?"

"I believe I can, sir. Since the night of the abortive attack, I've been in communication through our message-drop system with Captain Rivera, our top person inside the Enclave." This got the attention of everyone—especially Kinsella, to whom it was news. "According to her, one of the agents under her control, Ben Roark, sabotaged the operation. She concludes that he has evidently been turned."

General Hardin stirred into attentiveness and consulted his electronic notepad, "Roark? Roark? Oh, yes! A former agent of yours—not a military man like the rest of them. Just goes to show." He puffed himself up and looked around, gleefully meeting Ziegler's glare of concentrated and distilled hate. "What can you expect of goddamned pansy civilians?"

Havelock, who knew the total fictitiousness of the citations behind all the fruit salad on Hardin's chest, restrained a laugh as he always did in the presence of the JCS chairman's affectations. (Rumor held that, had he dared, Hardin would have worn a brace of pearl-handled revolvers with his seven-star general's uniform.) The EFP, committed to generations of antimilitary rhetoric but just as dependent on the military for its survival as any other regime, had packed the upper echelons with creatures whose sole qualification was political reliability. Not too surprisingly, those bureaucrats in uniform had a tendency to overcompensate. It was a tendency Hardin took to extremes, although behind his posturing lay all the actual combativeness of the well-fed lap dog he resembled.

I shouldn't complain, Havelock reminded himself. *If the* real *military people; the warriors, hadn't found themselves in a dead end in today's U.S. armed forces, I wouldn't have found it so easy to mold the Eaglemen into the instrument I needed. Their frustration was my tool, and the EFP created it. For that, it's even worth listening to Hardin's bluster with a straight face.*

"Actually, General," he cut in, forestalling a diatribe by Ziegler, "I recruited Roark personally, believing his expertise in operations of this sort outweighed any doubts as to his reliability."

"A serious error in judgment," Ziegler said with venomous satisfaction.

"Undeniably. I take full responsibility for its consequences. And I offer to make amends by having him eliminated."

"What?" The outburst came from Kinsella, though all of them looked gratifyingly astonished. "But . . . but how can you get at him? He knows all your people in there, and—"

"Not any more, Director. Even now, we're in the process of infiltrating three more agents into the Enclave—understudies of the original six. They were trained separately, for security reasons based on this very type of contingency."

"Still," Drummond observed, "now that he's gone public with his betrayal, surely the Lokaron have taken him under their wing. Which means he's untouchable."

Havelock spoke in carefully measured tones. "I believe that our agents can get to him even though, as you surmise, he's under direct Lokaron protection. I have reasons for this belief. For the present, I must ask you to not trouble yourselves about the nature of those reasons . . . and to give me a free hand in carrying out this operation."

Drummond gave him a narrow look. "I find myself intrigued by this Roark, Mr. Havelock. What could possibly have led him to betray not just his country but his very species? What could the Lokaron offer him?"

"Ha!" Hardin snorted. "What else? Money, of course. Damned civilians . . . !"

"Oh, come, General." Drummond smiled. "How would he spend it? He must know he'll never be able to show his face outside the Enclave again." He turned a shrewd look on Havelock. "Can you shed any light on his motives? I seem to recall that his earlier parting from the Company was less than entirely amicable."

"True enough, sir. He blamed me for the death of a female agent with whom he was romantically involved. But the actual killing was done by the Lokaron, or at least by their human hirelings. So he was at least equally embittered against them, which was what enabled me to recruit him. What could have led him to transfer his allegiance to them, as he seems to have done, is beyond my understanding."

Actually, Havelock understood it only too well.

Anger stabbed painfully at his gut as he contemplated his blunder. *It's Doyle, of course. It had been a long time since I'd even thought of her. So it never occurred to me to consider that she might still be alive inside the Enclave . . . and that if she was, then the cessation of her reports to the Eaglemen could only mean she'd somehow been turned. And it also never occurred to me that if she was alive and working for the Lokaron, Roark might meet her, and be influenced by her.*

And that, it appears, is exactly what's happened. Murphy's Law stands confirmed! Only decades of practice at controlling his facial muscles kept his teeth from grinding together.

"So now you want us to let you assassinate him," Morris said, bringing him back to the present. "Even if, as you claim, the thing is possible, why should we assume you won't fail again?"

"And," Drummond added, "aside from revenge, why should we want him dead now? The damage is done."

"I must beg to differ, Mr. Drummond. This isn't just a matter of vengeance. Roark must be eliminated as a necessary precondition to getting our original plan back on track."

Kinsella stared at him. "Do you mean to say . . . are you actually suggesting that we try *again*?"

"Why not, Director? The arguments in favor of an attack are still as valid as they ever were. And our plan is still fundamentally sound."

"But we're hopelessly compromised! Roark has surely revealed the identities of all the other agents. The Lokaron must be watching them like hawks."

"Ah, but he doesn't know the *new* ones to whom I alluded a few minutes ago. Using them, we can try again. But *not* with Roark still alive inside the Enclave, working for the Lokaron. He's an uncontrollable factor which makes any planning impossible."

"Hmm . . . " Morris pondered for a moment. "Very well. If you think you can reach Roark, I'm inclined to let you try. Is this the sense of the meeting?"

"I suppose so," Drummond allowed. Hardin emitted a vaguely affirmative-sounding growl.

"Yes!" Ziegler's eyes held a feverish glitter of eagerness. "Kill the traitorous motherfucker! Vermin like him deserve to be exterminated! I wish they could be forced to watch their children being anally gang-raped to death first!" She raved on for a while in the same vein, while Havelock reflected that she was a typical advocate of "compassionate government": her love of ethnic and class abstractions was exceeded only by her loathing of actual people. "But," she finally concluded, getting her breathing under control and addressing Havelock, "you'd better not screw up this time."

"All right, then," Morris said with heavy finality. "We will so report to the full Central Committee. And we won't detain you any longer from putting the operation into effect."

As he departed from the Company building, Havelock decided it could have been a lot worse, all things considered. The thought was less than comforting as he proceeded through the Washington night toward his Massachusetts Avenue hotel and the meeting he *really* had to worry about.

Once in his suite, he went for the bottle he kept for such occasions. It was colored water, but he was a virtuoso at simulating the drunkenness that Kinsella's observers would think an appropriate reaction to his time on the hot seat. Once he'd reached a suitable state of simulated inebriation—not an extreme one, which would have been out of character—he stumbled to bed and turned off the lights, leaving the room in that darkness which was the object of the entire charade. He lay awake for a time, until he was sure any surveillance monitor would have concluded that no further vigilance was called for. Then he slipped from the bed and felt his way to the walk-in closet. It was the one place he'd checked out in old-fashioned (and therefore undetectable) ways, satisfying himself that it was bug-free.

He sat down on the shoe ledge in the darkness and fumbled in a hidden compartment under the ledge. He found what he was searching for: a small, flat console attached by a fiber-optic cable to a latticework headpiece. He touched a button on the console, activating a signal undetectable by any human instrumentality, and waited. Presently an orange light blinked in acknowledgment. He put on the headset, touched another button, and was, to all the evidence of his senses, seated in an office in one of the Enclave's towers.

It was a technology so illegal that the Party hadn't even allowed it to be procured for limited use by government agents. Havelock gazed across a table at the being who'd provided it. The green Lokaron face showed that heightening of its bluish undertone that Havelock had learned to recognize as denoting intense emotion—notably anger.

Valtu'Trovon wasted as little time as Murray Morris had earlier. His mouth formed Lokaron words, but the virtual-reality software provided translation. "You're late," Havelock heard.

"I'm sorry, lord." By trial and error, he had arrived at this form of address, which the translator rendered as something acceptable to the Rogovon resident commissioner. "But I had to take security precautions. And before that, I had been detained in a meeting where I was called upon to explain the attack's failure."

"Well, now you can explain it to *me*."

"Of course, lord," Havelock murmured. The software faithfully conveyed his obsequiousness. It was how he always dealt with his superiors. (*Who aren't as clever as I am*, ran the automatic mental addendum—but barely above the level of consciousness, for it went without saying.) It seemed to work regardless of species.

He gave a succinct and accurate account of what had happened. Valtu heard him out, then spoke in portentous tones. "This is not good. You assured us that in your dual role as a high-ranking government intelligence operative and clandestine leader of the Eaglemen, you were in a unique position to create the kind of political climate we require. We accepted your assurances, and agreed to your price. This could have resulted in serious embarrassment for Gev-Rogov. Fortunately, I was careful to take no irrevocable steps in advance, knowing the inadvisability of relying on natives."

Havelock sustained his expression of polite attentiveness despite Valtu's insult and his own inward gloom. The plan really *had* been perfect, from his standpoint as well as Valtu's. The Rogovon, forewarned, had been standing to arms in their tower that night. The attack, having swept everything else before it, would have smashed itself against that obstacle. All the Eaglemen would have died, and with them the knowledge of his duplicity. All the other surviving Lokaron would have come around to the Rogovon viewpoint on how Earth should be dealt with. And Henry Havelock would have ruled Gev-Rogov's share of occupied Earth as the native governor he'd persuaded them they would need to squeeze the maximum return out of their human subjects. *Damn Roark to hell! Him and that bitch, Doyle! Yes, she dies too.*

"Fortunately, lord, I've already laid the groundwork for persuading my superiors to authorize another attack. The organization for it is still in place. And as I've explained to you, it's easy to exploit the personal and familial ambitions of the director of the agency I work for. But a necessary precondition is the removal of the two rogue agents involved. I've already obtained permission to mount such an operation against the man, Roark. Naturally it will also target the woman, Doyle, of whom my government superiors know nothing."

Valtu cogitated for a moment. "I've known for some time that Svyatog'Korth, the factor for Hov-Korth, has a confidential advisor on human affairs. Evidently it is this Doyle female. Why didn't you ever tell me about her?"

"If you'll recall, lord, I did mention the Eagleman agent who'd ceased reporting. I had no way of knowing she had become a confidant of Svyatog'Korth and, through him, a source of information for Gev-Harath in general. I probably never mentioned her name, considering it unimportant."

"All human names sound alike anyway," Valtu acknowledged offhandedly, dismissing the point. "At any rate, she's not part of Gev-Harath's general human labor population. She must live in the middle residential levels of the Hov-Korth tower. Among the Harathon," he added parenthetically, "each hovah has its own tower." The translation pitilessly reproduced a tone Havelock had heard often enough among humans: envy of affluence masquerading as contempt for extravagance. "And now, after his little escapade, Roark has doubtless joined her there. What makes you think your assassins can reach them?"

"That very point was raised by the more intelligent of my human superiors. I assured them that I had reason for optimism. Of course I couldn't tell them what that reason was: your help."

Havelock permitted himself a moment of satisfaction at having taken Valtu aback. The Rogovon commissioner spoke slowly. "This presents difficulties. Remember, Gev-Harath is almost as powerful as Gev-Rogov." Havelock had learned to recognize this as the closest the Rogovon could bring themselves to admitting Gev-Harath's primacy. "Naturally, we have nothing to fear from them," Valtu went on, a little too emphatically. "Still, the kind of involvement you request could result in . . . diplomatic awkwardness. So it's quite out of the question."

Havelock looked up from his humble posture, met Valtu's slit-pupiled eyes, and held them. "I can only remind you, lord, that the plan is unworkable as long as Roark and Doyle are active within the Enclave. And, as you yourself so rightly pointed out, they are invulnerable to my merely human efforts as long as they are under Harathon protection. The corollary is obvious: if you want me to undertake a second, successful attack on the Enclave, you *must* give me the support I need to eliminate them."

"You *dare* to tell me what I *must* do, you . . . you . . . you *native*?" The volume rose to an ear-hurting level as the software sought to reproduce Valtu's rage.

"Not at all, lord. I merely suggest that Gev-Rogov's clandestine operations resources—naturally far superior to Gev-Harath's security apparatus—should enable you to give my agents access to Roark and

Doyle without involving your gevah in the kind of public embarrassment you naturally wish to avoid."

Havelock waited patiently while Valtu got himself under control and considered the practicalities in light of the prestige-preserving formula he'd just been offered. *The Rogovon really are impossible,* he reflected. From what he'd been able to infer about Gev-Harath and the others, editing all the bias out of what the Rogovon said, he often wished he'd been able to go to work for them instead. But, he admitted to himself, it was no accident he'd gravitated to Gev-Rogov. None of the other gevahon had the kind of limitless ambition to which he could attach his own.

And, he told himself, there were compensations. Since going on Gev-Rogov's payroll he'd learned more about the Lokaron than any other human. . . .

Except, of course, Doyle. And now Roark.

Yes, they must definitely die.

"So be it," Valtu interrupted his thoughts. "The necessary arrangements will be made. You will be contacted in the usual way." Abruptly, the connection was severed and Havelock was back in the darkness, alone with his certainty that he'd be able to manipulate this alien just as he'd always manipulated his own kind.

Valtu'Trovon sat brooding for a few moments after removing his headset. His assistant, Wersov'Vrahn, who hadn't been included in the shared virtual reality but who'd been observing Havelock's half of the byplay in noninteractive format on a two-dimensional screen, waited patiently while his boss brooded.

"I shouldn't lose my self-control like that," Valtu finally said.

"Who could blame you?" exclaimed Wersov. "What a creature!"

"Yes. Utterly beneath contempt, like all of them. But useful." Valtu laughed. In the Rogovon sub-species, the rapid-fire clicking held a vaguely metallic resonance. "You know, don't you, that he thinks *he's* using *us*?"

"So you've explained to me. He's convinced himself that we're going to make him our puppet ruler among his own species." Wersov made his own sounds of amusement. "Odd. He seems shrewd . . . for a native."

"He is. But he's also a human. Their thought processes are incomprehensible." Privately, Valtu wasn't so sure. He'd known many a Lokar who, after successfully manipulating his fellows for too long, had fallen into a solipsistic conviction of invulnerability, feeling himself safely removed from the universe his victims inhabited. Could it be that it worked the same way among humans? Valtu instinctively shied away from the vaguely subversive thought. He stood up and strolled over to the nearest transparency, and gazed at the landscape which never failed to interest him.

Soon, of course, it would become less interesting . . . but only temporarily.

Havelock couldn't really be blamed, he thought indulgently. After all, the Harathon and all the rest of Gev-Rogov's enemies among the Loakron hadn't guessed it, either. The reason for *their* failure was easy to understand. They could manage tours of duty on this planet, but its gravity—over a third again that of the species' birthworld and its Harathon and Tizathon offshoots—dragged at them. They would never think of it as a potential *home*. It never dawned on them that the Rogovon actually *liked* it. It was similar to the environment the Rogovon genotype had been engineered for, only better in all respects.

Except, of course, for its indigenous race, Valtu amended. *But that will be corrected, after war is provoked and Gev-Rogov is found to be the only gevah still in a position to wage it. In such an atmosphere of outrage against the humans, no one will complain when we deal with the situation in our own way. . . .*

Afterwards, it will be simple enough to reseed a world that nobody else wants. And such a colony, once it matures, will put our power base in a class by itself. Gev-Rogov will be a giant step closer to assuming its rightful place as the preeminent gevah.

Havelock will be dead with all the rest, of course. But he'll have served his purpose.

CHAPTER NINE

Svyatog'Korth studied the ruined remote that Roark had appropriated from Ada Rivera. Then he set it down on his desk, and leaned back in his chair and gazed over steepled fingers in a way that was eerily human.

"Let me make sure I understand," the translator said in the English that Roark no longer had to keep separate from the Lokaron actually emerging from the factor's mouth—he automatically edited the latter out as background noise. "This Havelock, a high officer of American intelligence and your superior, is also the leader of the Eaglemen—who, in addition to opposing us, seek the overthrow of the very American regime he serves. How can you be certain of this?"

"I can't. But it's the only explanation that makes sense of what I overheard Rivera tell Stoner, her Eagleman subordinate. And it makes sense of a lot of other things I've been wondering about. For example, how did the Eaglemen penetrate the Company's security so completely as to get three of their people placed among the six agents sent here, including the controller? Simple: Havelock was in charge of personnel selection—he could pack the operation with Eaglemen. Same goes for the attack force that was waiting out there. I had thought the attack was an Eagleman stunt that Rivera was manipulating us into supporting. But it really was a Company operation—organized by Havelock, who was able to put Eaglemen in crucial positions."

"It also explains how the Company got its in-depth information about the Enclave," Katy put in. "Back when I was reporting to the Eaglemen, I was unwittingly reporting to Havelock. I wasn't high up enough in the organization to know the identity of our real leader; only the command cell knew that."

"So," Svyatog mused, "for an unknown length of time the Eaglemen have been making a tool of the American intelligence apparatus."

"Unless it's the other way around," Roark cautioned. "We don't know where Havelock's real loyalties lie."

"Ha!" Katy's voice was rich with scorn. "'Real loyalties'? Havelock? You've *got* to be kidding! *Nothing* is real where you're dealing with that lying cocksucker." (Roark couldn't help wondering how Svyatog's translator rendered *that*. Something appropriate, no doubt.) "The only thing you can be certain of is that he's got his own private agenda, which has nothing to do with the Company, the Eaglemen, or America. They're just means to whatever end he's pursuing, and he wouldn't hesitate a second to sell out any or all of them!"

"Katy's right," Roark said quietly. "The man's a compulsive intriguer. And we have no way of knowing what his 'private agenda' is."

Svyatog seemed to think out loud. "We could bring in Rivera and Stoner for questioning on the subject. . . . " The Lokar gave his shoulders the odd backwards-and-forwards shake Roark had come to recognize as reflecting a negative decision. "No. It would defeat our efforts to keep the whole business quiet and thus avoid creating an awkward situation within the Enclave for the Rogovon to exploit."

"It wouldn't do any good anyway. They know him in his Eagleman persona, which is probably no less phony than his Company one."

Svyatog again looked thoughtful. "Huruva has direct diplomatic contact with the American government. Through him, I could enable the two of you to bypass Havelock and inform his superiors of his involvement with the Eaglemen."

"They wouldn't believe us. Remember, in their eyes we're traitors. They'd think we were just spreading disinformation on your behalf." Roark looked glum. "Same goes for the idea I had—for about two seconds—of contacting Chen and Pirelli, the two non-Eaglemen left among the agents here, and telling them they're being played for suckers."

"And," Katy added, "it would do even less good to try to make contact with the Eaglemen. We can't tell them anything they don't already know about his double-dealing. In fact, Rivera and the rest of the command cell must spend a lot of time congratulating themselves on having their fearless leader highly placed in the Company—they don't know him like we do. And anyway, they'd be even less likely than the Company to listen to us . . . especially to me."

"They're not exactly a fan club of mine either," Roark said grimly. "Not now. Speaking of which, I fully expect them to try for me—and for Katy, since Havelock's probably deduced that she's still alive in here. And when I say 'them' I include Chen and Pirelli. They'll obey Rivera's orders. Chen, at least, won't like it . . . but he's a Marine."

"Have no fears on that score. I told you I would guarantee your safety, and I fully intend to honor that promise. You've certainly earned our gratitude. Not," he added with a complacency Roark found less than entirely comforting, "that there should be any real danger, now that you're both living in the middle levels of this tower. Especially considering that we know exactly which humans to watch for suspicious moves."

"I suppose not," Katy conceded. But she sounded like Roark felt.

They kept their own counsel all the way back to Katy's apartment. (Svyatog kept promising them something bigger, but Roark was in no particular hurry—the place was more spacious than the room he'd shared with Chen, and the company was a lot more inspiring.) Once there, Roark dropped onto the couch. Katy lowered herself into a chair with its back to the door. They looked at each other for a moment in silent seriousness.

"I don't like it," Katy finally stated.

"Neither do I," Roark agreed. "Svyatog's getting cocky again. Granted, it's hard to see how Rivera and the others could get at us here. But—"

"No, I wasn't even thinking of that. I was thinking of Havelock. Ben, what can he be up to?"

"How the hell should I know? Sorry, I know I'm irritable. But who can follow the ins and outs of a mind that devious?"

"I sometimes wonder. . . . Does he have a goal at all, or is he just driven by a compulsion to duplicity?"

"To be exact, I think he unconsciously picks the goals that let him follow that compulsion." Roark grinned crookedly. "On our flight here, Jerry Chen and I were talking about the way space aliens finally landed after all, though not the way people in the

last century expected. Now, we seem to find ourselves in the middle of another old wet-dream: the
shadowy, high-level conspiracy."

Katy sought for recollection, then grinned in turn.
"Oh, yeah. I remember. After the Watergate business,
it was fashionable to believe that some vast, sinister
secret government was running everything from
behind the scenes."

"Right . . . although it really started before that,
with the various assassinations in the decade before
Watergate. No conspiracy theory was too far-fetched
for people back then to swallow." Roark's grin turned
nasty. "There was only one theory they *weren't*
willing to believe, because it was the most night-
marish of all: that there *wasn't* any omnipotent
conspiracy, and that the U.S. government was *exactly
as it appeared to be*. In other words, that they really
were ruled by the clueless nebbishes they saw on
the TV news every night . . . and that they had
nobody to blame but themselves."

"I think," Katy said, turning serious, "that you've
just put your finger on the reason those old conspiracy theories were so popular."

Roark laughed harshly. "Yep. They told the Americans of that era precisely what they wanted to hear:
'It isn't your fault! You're just victims! It's the
Illuminati, or the multinational corporations, or the
military-industrial complex, or whoever. *They're* the
reason the government's the way it is—not the fact
that you're a flock of silly sheep who vote for
whoever the opinion makers tell you to vote for.'"
His bitter humor abruptly fled—or at least the humor
did, leaving only the bitterness. "No wonder the EFP
took over a generation later. It pandered to the
fashionable paranoia of the age . . . which meant,
underneath all the bullshit, that it was promising to

shield people from what they *really* feared: having to take responsibility for their own choices."

Katy's serious look shaded over into grimness. "I was more right than I knew. It really will take more than technology for us to make a place for ourselves in the modern galaxy. Our people are going to have to be reeducated from the ground up in things they once picked up from the culture without having to be taught."

"Yeah, that's the long-range problem. But for now, our immediate concern is that we really *are* looking at the kind of clandestine high-level double-dealing in the intelligence community that people used to get their jollies fantasizing about. Good God, Katy, how many ends can Havelock really be playing against the middle?"

"I don't know. All I'm sure of is that we haven't learned the full extent of it yet."

"No, we haven't. And we can't do a damned thing about it." Roark stood up slowly, as though very tired. "Katy, I need a drink."

She looked at him sharply. It was the first time he'd used that exact combination of words since they'd set up housekeeping together, and he'd partaken only in self-consciously metered moderation. She started to open her mouth to caution him . . . but what came out was, "So do I."

"Coming up." Roark started to turn toward the kitchenette.

With a roar, and a stench of burning plastic, a ring of flame as blinding as burning magnesium erupted around the door's security lock. Before the human nervous system could react, a six-inch circle of plastic enclosing the lock, its edges blackened and ragged, fell away and two figures—human, male, unknown to Roark—smashed the door in, taking a tiny instant to get their bearings in the room as they brought up small hand-weapons Roark recognized as spring needlers.

Even as Roark's brain was absorbing all this, his body was acting for him, dropping to the floor and roaring something inarticulate that included the two syllables, "Katy!" It wasn't necessary, for at the same instant she was tumbling forward, taking her chair with her so that it covered her as she landed on her hands and knees. One of the intruders opened up on her as she went over. Several needlelike flechettes stitched through the back of the chair. She screamed as one of them lacerated her scalp.

The other attacker was bringing his needler into line with Roark's head.

Roark swept up a small end table by one of its legs and flung it clumsily from his crouched position. It missed, and wouldn't have done any damage even if it had connected. But it threw the man's aim off, and the needle missed by inches. It gave Roark time to gather his leg muscles and spring before the semiautomatic needler could get off another shot.

He was in mid-spring when the second needle lanced through fleshy part of his upper left arm. It was only a dimly sensed stinging impact at the edges of his time-accelerated consciousness. Drilled-in techniques for keeping it there clicked automatically into place, allowing him to function. He crashed into his attacker, grappling with him, grabbing the wrist of his gun hand with his own weakened left hand.

Off to the side, some detached and time-accelerated part of him observed, Katy had flung herself backwards, carrying the chair with her, ramming it into the man who'd fired at her and pushing him back against the door frame. He was still there, struggling to free himself from the confining chair legs, as Roark wrestled his own opponent back against the wall beside the door. The man tried to bring the needler around and press it against the side of Roark's head. Pain shrieked in Roark as he made his left arm force that hand back, and in the very act of overcoming that pain he summoned up a surge of strength that slammed the gun hand to the wall just as its trigger finger convulsed. The needle entered the other assassin's head just under the left ear, at an upward angle; his right eyeball exploded outward with the force of its exit. Otherwise, his face merely wore a look of surprise as he slid down to the floor.

Katy struggled out from under the chair and rose unsteadily to her feet, blood from her scalp wound matting her hair and streaming down her face. She managed to grip the right wrist of Roark's opponent, lending her strength to his efforts to hold the gun hand pinned to the wall. Roark brought a knee sharply up, eliciting a strangled cry of pain and breaking the deadlock. The needler dropped to the floor. An elementary judo move sufficed to bring the man's right arm behind his back and painfully up, forcing him to go to his knees to avoid dislocating his shoulder. Roark forced him the rest of the way down, flat onto his stomach, and planted a knee in the small of his back to assure that he'd stay there.

Katy scooped up one of the fallen needlers and held it on Roark's captive. Roark spoke to her raggedly, for waves of pain were lapping over the barrier of his ability to hold them at bay. "Katy, call Svyatog. Tell him to send his security types." The act of speaking seemed to release a fresh onset of pain. Reality wavered as he glanced down at his blood. He commanded himself to steadiness. "Tell him we've got a prisoner for interrogation."

The man on the floor managed to turn his head around far enough to bring one eye to bear on Roark. It was blue, Roark noticed, now that he had time to notice individual details of the men who'd sought his life and Katy's. Her assailant was dark in a Mediterranean or Semitic sort of way. But this guy was pure redneck, and so was his speech. "Maybe that's what *you* think, you pig-fucker! See you in hell!" And his pain-twisted smile took on a look of triumph just before he bit down, hard, in a way Roark recognized but hadn't been prepared for.

Frantically, he rolled the Eagleman over onto his back and pried his jaws open—not too difficult, as his muscles were already going slack. He thrust a finger down the man's throat, to force him to disgorge whatever the hollow tooth had contained. But it was no use. He was dead by the time Svyatog's security personnel arrived.

Just as he had gazed at the remote-control unit the day before, Svyatog'Korth examined the spring needler. Then he turned to the two humans across his desk. "I gather this weapon is not unfamiliar to you."

Roark nodded dully and spoke mechanically. Lokaron first aid had gotten their wounds under control, and their artificially stimulated healing was proceeding at a rate unheard-of on this planet. But nothing could prevent them from being shaken. And they were both short of sleep. "It uses a gas-operated spring. No propellants, no electronics—so all the components can be disguised as something innocuous, even to your scanners. That, and the fact that it's silent, has always made it popular for black ops."

"But I gather it wasn't issued to you."

"No. I guess only the Eaglemen got them. Same goes for that hollow tooth." Roark forced his numb brain to try to function. "Couldn't you have revived him? He hadn't been dead long."

"We tried, of course, and got some response from the body. But the poison was evidently designed with that possibility in mind—it was a nerve agent that worked directly on the higher neural functions. His memory was already gone."

"Who the hell *were* they?"

"Newly inducted employees. Evidently your Mr. Havelock had additional strings to his bow." Even in his current state, Roark admired the translator's facility with English idioms. Equally impressive was the way it conveyed Svyatog's gloom. "Naturally, we cannot be sure they are the only Eaglemen who've arrived since you did. Nor am I prepared to assume that they are, having learned my lesson about underestimating these people." Roark suspected that the word *people* represented a bit of diplomacy on the translator's part. "At any rate, there is really no warrant for the assumption we've been making that these assassins *were* Eaglemen. They could have been legitimate agents of the American government, dispatched by Havelock in his official capacity."

Katy shook herself out of her torpor. "How did they know where we were? And how did they get to us there? Damn it, you promised—"

"I'm aware of what I promised," Svyatog cut her off bleakly. "And I abase myself for my failure to protect you. All I can say in my own defense is that a new factor has come into play." The alien gathered his thoughts—Roark had come to recognize that look. "The assassins took care to use only items of local manufacture, smuggled in by themselves, in the actual attack." He indicated the needler. "Even the compound they used to burn away your lock was a binary propellant whose two components, when separate, did not activate our chemical scanners. But, as you surmise, nothing of local origin would have enabled them to penetrate our security and reach your quarters. For that, they needed inside help."

Katy spoke while Roark was still trying to make sense of Svyatog's words. "Inside help? You mean . . . *Lokaron* help?"

"There is no other possible explanation. We have deduced how they did it. The details are unimportant. Suffice it to say that it is beyond any present human technology."

"But . . . who . . . ?"

"Who else? Gev-Rogov, of course."

"But why?"

"Unknown. They're not necessarily helping either the American government or the Eaglemen, as such. We're agreed that Havelock's agenda and theirs may not be the same."

Roark made himself think through the implications of what he'd heard. He looked nightmare in the face.

Katy's voice seemed to come from a great distance. "Svyatog, you can go before your fellow Lokaron with this. You can expose the Rogovon for—"

"No. The Rogovon have covered their tracks too well. Their involvement is as unprovable as it is obvious. They would simply deny it."

"But surely you can do *something*!"

"Oh, I'll inform Huruva. But he will be unable to make any use of the information—except, of course, to tighten up what has proven to be our laughably inadequate security."

"Isn't that a little like locking the barn door after the horse has run off? And is your tightened security going to suffice to assure our survival? Maybe in some area of the Enclave that's better defended—"

"No. I will be completely candid. With Havelock using the resources of both the American government and the Eaglemen to seek your lives, and Gev-Rogov aiding him, I cannot guarantee your safety anywhere on this planet."

Well, Roark thought with an odd calmness, *I should have left well enough alone. I'm not staring at nightmare anymore. I'm inside it, living it, and there's no waking up.*

As she often did, Katy regained the power of speech before he did. "All right, Svyatog, what's the punch line? Surely you're offering us some alternative to a death sentence."

"Death sentence?" The translator conveyed puzzlement.

"Well, if *you* can't keep us alive, what hope have we?"

"But I haven't said this."

"In a pig's eye you haven't!" snapped Roark, irritated at the Lokar for being so uncharacteristically dense. "Your exact words were that you couldn't guarantee our safety anywhere . . . on . . . " His voice ran slowly down as he realized what he was saying.

"On this planet," Katy finished for him in a voice that said she, too, had figured it out.

Svyatog spoke briskly. "My private shuttle can be ready to depart in a few hours, to rendezvous in orbit with an interstellar vessel." He looked down on them from his great height, with his luminous amber eyes. "I promised to safeguard your lives. And I make a point of keeping my promises. But I can no longer do so if you remain here. Therefore, if you wish to remain under my protection, you must accept the offer I am now making: to transport you offworld, where you will be beyond—*far* beyond—your enemies' reach."

Roark stared at the being across the desk, and a chill ran through him. He had fancied that he was getting used to Svyatog, adjusting to his alienness, settling into a kind of spurious familiarity. Now he saw the Lokar with soul-shaking clarity, not as an individual who could be dealt with once one got past his physical oddities, but as the embodiment of forces beyond human aspiration.

"Uh, where exactly do you propose to take us?" Katy managed to keep her voice steady to the end of the question, then yielded to a nervous laugh that almost rose to a giggle. "Not that we'd know the difference!"

"I had in mind Harath-Asor, the homeworld of my gevah. I think you'll find it . . . interesting. And while it is several hundred light-years away as you measure interstellar distances, the actual travel time is quite reasonable. The fact that we are able to conduct interstellar commerce on a profitable basis should tell you that much."

"Will you be taking us there yourself?"

"No. I have to remain here a while longer. But you'll be in good hands. And I'll be joining you there presently."

Roark shook free of the oppressive sense of tininess that had crept over him and rejoined the conversation. "Wait a minute. Wait a minute! This is getting altogether too matter-of-fact. Are you saying that if we want to survive we have to give up our homeworld forever?" His eyes strayed to the waning Virginia autumn outside the office's transparencies.

"By no means. I have reason to believe that your . . . exile, if you insist, will be only temporary."

"But still," Roark persisted, "you're asking us to—"

"To be the first two human beings to venture beyond the moon!" What he heard in Katy's voice brought Roark's head around. Her face was transfigured. "To see what others have only dreamed! Ben, this is a chance no one has ever been offered!"

"In addition to being the only way to save our buns." But Roark's cynicism was sheer habit. His grin matched hers. Their hands found each other and clasped.

Svyatog looked from one of them to the other. They were in no mood to notice that his face wore the arch-looking (to humans) expression that was a Lokaron smile.

Their hands were tightly clasped once again as they sat in the Lokaron shuttle, watching the interstellar transport grow from toy to intricate artificial mountain in the view forward.

The shuttle's drive converted the angular momentum of spinning atomic particles into linear thrust in a manner beyond the compass of Earth's science, but it wasn't magic—the way takeoff had pressed Roark and Katy down into their acceleration couches had left no room for doubt on that score. It hadn't been as bad as it might have been, though, for the craft was designed for beings whose native gravity was 0.72 G, and its freedom from any need for reaction mass allowed it to take its time accelerating up to orbit. There, things got worse, with the alternating acceleration and weightlessness that accompanied the rendezvous maneuvering. But then they got better and stayed that way, for the Lokaron could generate artificial gravity fields. Such a field clamped comfortingly down on them as the shuttle slid through some kind of nonmaterial barrier into the great ship's cavernous docking bay and settled onto the deck. They emerged, inarticulate with wonder, and gazed at the cloud-marbled blue curve of Earth outside that wide opening that seemed so impossibly open to vacuum.

After a moment, an approaching figure drew their attention from that spectacle. It was a Lokaron of the medium-blue Harathon subspecies, wearing the "business suit" of loose sleeveless robe over double-breasted tunic, all in subdued reddish shades. When he spoke, the translator produced the same perfect English in which it rendered Svyatog's speech . . . but not in the same voice, which came as no surprise given what they already knew of the software's sophistication.

"I am Thrannis'Woseg, an employee of Hov-Korth. Svyatog'Korth has assigned me to attend to your needs during the journey, which I trust you will find comfortable."

Katy, the more experienced of the two in dealing with the Lokaron, spoke for them. "Yes, thank you. The artificial gravity is a great help—at least until the ship departs."

"It has, in fact, already done so." Thrannis indicated the entry port. The blue planet below was no longer motionless, but seemed to be drifting at an accelerating rate. "The ship's departure was delayed until your arrival, and the captain is eager to make up the lost time."

The evidence of Svyatog's pull held no surprise. But . . . "Thrannis, shouldn't we be feeling the acceleration?"

"No. The ship is designed in such a way that 'down' equals 'aft.' The artificial gravity is under the control of the central computer, which reduces it to correspond with the drive's current acceleration. So apparent weight is constant."

And hadn't fluctuated in the slightest. . . . But, Roark told himself, such things were to be expected. Before entering the shuttle and the Lokaron world it represented, he'd steeled himself against mental vertigo. That, like so much good advice, was evidently going to be easier to give than to follow.

"And now," Thrannis continued, "let me show you to your quarters."

"Uh, wait a minute, Thrannis," said Roark, a little desperately. "First, can't we go someplace where we can watch as . . . as . . . " He gestured vaguely toward the portal, where Earth was no longer visible. The realization hit him: by departing Earth orbit he and Katy had already gone further than any humans had in their lifetimes. Aside from robot probes, the United States government had unofficially turned its back on deep space after the last Apollo missions, a generation before the EFP had made it official.

"Ah!" The translator conveyed Thrannis' dawning understanding. "You wish to watch as your world recedes. Don't worry, you'll have ample time. At this modest acceleration, our velocity is building only gradually. And your cabin viewscreen can give you a view aft. You'll find that all your cabin functions will respond to voice commands in your language." He paused, giving the two humans a chance to contemplate the kind of reprogramming he'd implied so offhandedly, performed in the brief time since Svyatog had known they'd be taking passage aboard this ship. "However, when we arrive at the transition gate, you may wish to make use of the ship's more elaborate observation facilities. I believe you'll find transition . . . impressive. Or, at least, completely foreign to your experience."

"Yes, I think we just might," Roark acknowledged as Thrannis led them away.

The advent of the Lokaron had demonstrated the existence of extraterrestrial life to the satisfaction of even the most skeptical. It had also laid to rest the conventional wisdom that interstellar flight, while perhaps not impossible in an absolute sense, was inherently impractical. Unfortunately, a decade later, no one on Earth was entirely clear on how they did it. They themselves hadn't been altogether helpful. They'd hastened to assure anxious human physicists that, yes, Einstein had been quite right, as far as he went, and that their ships didn't violate the lightspeed limit but merely *evaded* it. But they'd been unable— or, some suspected, unwilling—to explain in any intelligible way just how this was done. The information they'd doled out had provided more questions than answers.

The unambiguous facts were these: there was a higher space, congruent in some mysterious way with our own, in which points in our space—or, rather, the points *corresponding* to those points—were far closer together. The Lokaron translators called it "overspace," a label which might or might not be deliberately misleading. Entering or departing from it—"transition"—required the creation of a multi-dimensional "tunnel" in spacetime. A ship could carry an engine that wrapped such a tunnel around itself— an engine so massive, and such an energy hog, as to render the ship that carried it unable to earn its keep as a carrier of cargo or passengers. Military ships, and the exploration ships that pushed the frontiers of Lokaron space ever outward, mounted such engines. But for commercial uses, there was another way: the "transition gate," which produced the same effect *externally to* itself, creating a tunnel for other objects to pass through. This was even more technology- and energy-intensive than the shipboard transition engines. But it made interstellar traffic an economically viable proposition, for once in place it could be used by any and all ships that could reach it . . . like the ship that Roark and Katy now rode.

Reaching it took time, for transition was impossible in a significant gravity field and so Gev-Harath, like the other gevahon, had built its transition gate in an orbit skirting the inner fringes of the asteroid belt. It was currently almost seventy degrees ahead of Earth as they both circled the sun. But at a constant acceleration and deceleration of almost one Lokaron G, little more than two ship's days (the thirty-nine-plus-hour days of their destination world, to which they adjusted with difficulty) passed before Thrannis told them it was time.

He led them to a circular chamber whose domed overhead was a viewscreen, as though it was open to the stars. The few Lokaron present stared at them with frank curiosity as they settled uncomfortably into loungers which, unlike their own cabin's furnishings, had not been designed for humans. Nearby was a small auxiliary pickup showing the view aft, including the little light-blue dot that was Earth. Above their heads was the view forward. The ship had flipped over and decelerated for the second half of the journey, to arrive here at a velocity at which it could maneuver. But now it was forging ahead again, toward the tunnel the transition gate had bored through the structure of reality.

So far there was nothing to see. The gate's physical plant was small, and there was little sunlight out here for it to reflect anyway. And the nonmaterial tunnel would not become visible until they began to enter it. They waited in edgy silence.

Then a chime sounded. The two humans, who'd been warned what to expect, emulated their Lokaron fellow spectators and settled into the loungers in preparation for acceleration. Roark stole a glance at the small viewscreen to the side. Earth was still there: blue, lovely. . . .

Without further warning, the ship surged—not pushed by its drive, but *pulled* by forces that accompanied transition—and they were pressed down into the recliners. At the same time, the stars directly above them—and therefore directly ahead of the ship—faded out, or rather were pulled down to merge with those around the sides and flow sternward, forming a tunnel of light that ran through the visible spectrum before vanishing. Then their weight was normal again and there was only blackness in the dome above them. The ship was in the enigmatic realm of overspace, where it could navigate only by the high-tech lanterns of the Lokaron beacon network, and from which it could emerge only through another transition gate.

But a split second before that, Roark's eyes had gone back to the auxiliary screen, in which the waterspout of scintillating colors was streaming backward toward the little blue spark. Then that screen, too, was black, and the spark was extinguished.

He saw that Katy was also staring at the infinitely deep well into which their world had fallen and vanished. Then their eyes met, and there were no words, for none had been invented—at least not in English or any other Earthly tongue.

CHAPTER TEN

To Roark, the world of Harath-Asor seemed to exist simultaneously in the distant past and the remote future, with nothing of the present about it at all.

The sense of ancientness belonged to the planet itself, rising like a mist from the worn-down hills—you couldn't call them mountains—and slow-flowing rivers of its mature landscape, for this was an old planet of an old sun. That sun hung larger and yellower than Sol in a deeper-blue sky than Earth's. It moved slowly across that sky, for its tidal drag had slowed the planet's rotation over the ages. At some point in its past, Harath-Asor had given birth to a race of beings capable of erecting the awesome but unintelligible edifices whose ruins dotted the planet's waste places. But something had wiped them out—some mutant microorganism, probably, for there was no indication that they'd possessed the technology to do the job themselves. When the Lokaron pioneers had arrived, they'd found a fecund but untenanted world into whose biochemistry a Lokaron-friendly ecology could be insinuated with minimal genetic modification of most species, including the colonists themselves. For these latter, it was effectively their homeworld, the natural habitat of their subspecies—or, to be precise, the habitat for which their subspecies had been designed. They were part of it, and it of them, as though they had spent millennia of history and eons of prehistory among its ripe landscapes.

But it was only later that this aspect of Harath-Asor made itself manifest to the two humans. To reach it, they first passed through realms of technology beyond Earth's engineering horizons.

The transport, after emerging from a transition gate, threaded its way insystem through the crowded spacelanes. They sat under the observation dome and watched in openmouthed wonder. Ponderously turning space habitats surrounded by firefly-swarms of small craft . . . vast spidery communications arrays . . . inconceivable powersats . . . all drifted silently by. Finally the planet waxed in the display, its nightside a constellation of city lights, its dayside less blue and more sandy-white than Earth's. A barely visible silvery thread extended three diameters straight out from a point on its equator.

"Is that an . . . an orbital tower?" Katy asked Thrannis, pointing unsteadily at the impossibly rigid thread.

"Yes. I gather your civilization is familiar with the concept."

"In theory, yes. But as a practical matter it's well beyond our materials technology." Bitterness entered Katy's voice. "It probably would be even if the EFP hadn't halted our development a generation ago."

"Ah." Roark could practically hear the wheels turning as Thrannis contemplated a potential market. "Actually," the Lokar resumed, "this one has become largely a tourist attraction since the advent of reactionless drives." If there was any condescension in his voice, the translator edited it out.

A shuttle took them down to the surface, crossing the terminator from day to night before descending over a cityscape like a glowing forest of lofty, brightly lit towers, and settling onto a landing platform with scarcely a bump. They emerged under a sky from which the city lights and the orbital powersats banished the stars, leaving two crescent moons as the only vestiges of the natural night. The platform on which they stood extended out from one of the towers near its base, only a few stories above the vehicle-teeming streets. Staring at that base's massiveness, they saw at once that the needlelike slenderness they'd marveled at from aloft was an illusion. The tower was slender only in relation to its inconceivable height. Only by looking at the more distant towers could they form any real impression of these edifices' dimensions.

"They must need pressurization on the top floors," Katy said in a small voice. It was chilly, but her breath didn't steam in this somewhat thin, dry air to which their sinuses had had to adjust aboard the ship.

Roark looked at her, saw that familiar profile silhouetted against the light-blazing cityscape, and all at once he *knew*, with a certainty beyond mere intellectual understanding, just how far beyond ordinary human ken they'd wandered. Deep within him, something he'd forgotten was there wanted to run until it found a certain sunlit street of small neat houses, and keep running until it was through the screen door of one of those houses and in the arms of she who, like the street and the house, would surely never change.

A trio of tall Lokaron figures stepped from the shadows that hemmed in the harshly lit landing platform. Though armed with no visible weapons, they bore the unmistakable look of security guards. Their leader spoke briefly with Thrannis, who then turned to his human charges. "All is in readiness. Let's go inside. I'll show you to your quarters."

"Uh, Thrannis," Roark said hesitantly, "aren't there any . . . well, formalities?" He hadn't expected quarantine procedures; it was widely known that human and Lokaron biochemistries had enough subtle differences to prevent either species from playing host to the other's microorganisms. But . . . "Surely there must be some kind of customs or immigration check."

Thrannis looked vaguely puzzled, and Roark sensed that the translator had conveyed something subtly different from his intended meaning. "No, no, don't worry. There's nothing irregular about your arrival here. And there's no need for the gevah functionaries to concern themselves. This is purely a Hov-Korth matter. I've brought you directly to the hovah's headquarters"—he indicated the architectural mountain from whose side the landing platform was cantilevered out—"for convenience, and to avoid premature public exposure. The sight of you might occasion more comment than we want at this stage."

"Are you saying we're going to be confined to this place?"

"Oh, no. Your excursions will, of necessity, be subject to a certain degree of supervision. But I have every intention of showing you as much of this planet as possible in the time we'll have available. This is Svyatog's express wish. But for now, let's proceed."

They followed him inside, where they found themselves on a gallery surrounding a central well whose floor was several stories below, at ground level,

and whose ceiling was lost in the dimness far above.
For all the structure's titanic mass, there was an air
of ethereal grace, born of advanced materials and
transcendent architecture. The vastness and the
unfamiliar artistic idioms rendered the scene a swirl
of strangeness, impossible for their minds to grasp
before Thrannis hurried them on. They took an
elevator which used a powered-down version of what
made the Lokaron space vehicles move. In an
amazingly short time they were in a small suite of
rooms whose windows overlooked the illimitable
cityscape from an aircraftlike altitude.

"And now," Thrannis said as they settled in, "I'll
let you get some rest. I know you must be tired."
(This was tact; the ship's day/night cycle had been
slaved to Harath-Asor's, thus avoiding the interstellar
equivalent of jet lag.) "There are some people who'll
want to see you tomorrow."

Roark groaned inwardly as he visualized Lokaron
graduate students in anthropology asking about the
quaint native mating customs. Katy dragged her eyes
away from the panorama outside the windows and
spoke up. "What about showing us the planet, as you
said a while back?"

"Have no fear. You'll be able to get out and play
tourist soon enough, subject to the restrictions I
mentioned. I think I can safely predict you'll find
it rather different from your usual tourist experience!
And now, I'll bid you good evening."

The "people who'll want to see you" turned out
to be Hov-Korth security types, with sensible questions about how the Company and its uninvited
Eaglemen guests had gone about infiltrating the
Enclave on Earth. Roark suppressed the closed-
mouthed habits of decades and answered them

truthfully. It took most of the long day, leaving them drained and out of sorts.

But afterwards Thrannis proved as good as his word, taking them over, through and beyond the city, which was of vast extent. They viewed from close range the orbital tower, just as impossible-seeming as it had been from a distance. They walked slowly through wonders in the Lokaron equivalent of museums. They saw what had to be called factories, where the manufacturing was done on the molecular level.

It was at one such place that Katy asked a question that had perplexed them, and many other humans. "Thrannis, why do you Lokaron bother to engage in trade at all? I mean, if you can just make goods to order on the spot—?"

"Ah, yes. Svyatog told me to expect this question. I gather that your civilization has reached the stage of being able to conceptualize nanotechnology, but that the concept is still at the . . . the . . . "

"The 'gee whiz' level," Roark suggested.

There was a pause as Thrannis tried to make sense of the translator's rendition of that. "I believe I catch your drift. Yes. The dazzling possibilities have distracted you from certain practical limiting factors involving both energy and precise control. And as for the self-replicating nanomachines that certain of your popularizers have visualized . . . well, atomic energy is a harmless toy by comparison. It is self-evident that no sane society would tolerate them."

Roark wasn't certain it really was all that self-evident, but he held his peace as Thrannis continued. "No, nanotechnology isn't magic. It is, however, a revolutionary industrial process. Indeed, it increases manufacturing capacity by such orders of magnitude that it promptly creates a shortage of the rarer elements. Transmutation on a large scale is not feasible, for any number of excellent reasons. So we have to look elsewhere to fill the demand."

"But," Katy persisted, "why trade with less-developed races on inhabited planets for what you need? Why not just strip-mine lifeless planets and moons and asteroids?"

Thrannis started to speak, then stopped and began again, as though what he was trying to say was so obvious to him as to be difficult to put into words. "First of all, the elements of which I speak are more likely to be present on large planets than on space rocks. But aside from that, consider the economics of interstellar commerce. The kind of operation you're visualizing would require us to transport everything necessary to set up a hostile-environment colony, at staggering cost. Worlds where we can live without elaborate life-support are a more attractive proposition. Likewise, when we can offer the inhabitants of those worlds technology so far beyond their ability to duplicate that we can set our own prices, trade is far cheaper than . . . " The translator subsided as Thrannis left "conquest and enslavement" unsaid. Before the pause could grow awkward, the Lokar proceeded briskly. "And as long as we're trading in bulk anyway, we've built up a very profitable sideline trade in luxury goods for the Lokaron market, which has an insatiable appetite for novelty as long as it's *authentic* novelty."

"Like authentic personal servants?" asked Roark. Since arriving on Harath-Asor he'd seen members of some of the same non-Lokaron species he'd noted in the Enclave. *No humans*, he thought. *Yet.*

"Yes. It's economically indefensible, of course— as are most luxuries. It's a matter of . . . prestige. Of status."

"You're very forthright with us," Katy observed.

"I've been instructed to be. But now, let's proceed. There is much else for you to see."

That was an understatement. They lost track of time as one strangely long day followed another in this world of disorienting alienness and awesome power. In their moments of privacy—or at least what they chose to assume was privacy—they sought each other with even more than their usual eagerness, for at such times they could, together, create a private universe of the humanly familiar. Roark suspected he would have gone mad if he'd been alone in a world which held not a single accustomed reference point.

Then there came a day when Thrannis' air-car, returning to the Hov-Korth tower, slanted upward rather than descending toward its accustomed landing platform. "What's happening, Thrannis?" asked Roark as he watched the mists of low-lying clouds in the cabin's wraparound viewscreen. "Where are we going?"

"There." The Lokar pointed ahead and upward, toward a small landing flange that jutted from the cliff-wall of the tower. "Someone wants to see you."

"More Lokaron spooks," Roark muttered to Katy.

"Must be a better class of them, though." She indicated the flange. It was near the prestigious top of the tower.

Roark turned back to Thrannis. "Uh, is it going to be cold at this altitude?" It was summer in this hemisphere of Harath-Asor, and they were dressed accordingly.

"Don't worry about it."

They soon saw what Thrannis meant. The air-car touched down on the flange against the ruddy backdrop of Harath-Asor's setting sun, then moved slowly through a version of the Lokaron spaceships' atmosphere curtains, and came to rest in a kind of hangar-*cum*-reception area alongside another craft, essentially similar but bearing what they now recognized as the hallmarks of VIP-level luxury. Thrannis led them past unobtrusive security devices into hushed, softly lit corridors where only a few Lokaron moved. He motioned them through a door that slid aside for them.

They were at one end of what was unmistakably a conference room, with a long oval table surrounded by Lokaron-proportioned chairs. But it held only one occupant, silhouetted against the sunset outside the window at the far end of the room.

Katy, with more practice at recognizing individual Lokaron, spoke before Roark. "Svyatog! We thought you were still on Earth."

"So I was, until very recently. I've only just arrived, but I wanted to see you without delay." Svyatog sat down at the head of the table, and motioned them to do the same. They perched uncomfortably, despite the chairs' efforts to reconfigure themselves.

"How are things on Earth?" Roark ventured.

"Well enough. After much diplomatic procrastination, the American government representatives have finally agreed to pay the reparations we demanded for the New York incident. They also claim to be making every effort to apprehend the Eaglemen responsible, and we claim to believe them. This has defused the crisis, and all has been quiet at the Enclave. We have continued to keep the infiltrators there under unobtrusive surveillance, and while they are obviously engaged in communication with their contacts they attempted no overt acts." The Lokar gave a dismissive gesture. "But what of you? Are you finding your time here interesting?"

"Interesting?" Roark echoed. He sought for words. "Yes, you might put it that way. It's been . . . "

"There's no describing it," Katy blurted. "Beyond what we owe you for sending us to safety, we owe you even more for letting us see all this."

"I am glad you feel that way, inasmuch as I am about to ask a favor of you."

"What?" The last of the sunset brought out reddish highlights as Katy gave her head a puzzled shake. "Svyatog, what can a couple of exiles like us possibly do for you?"

"Yeah," Roark agreed, "here on this planet where we're aliens, and the only members of our race at that."

"You misapprehend. What I want you to do isn't here on Harath-Asor, but on Earth. And it's only partially for me. The chief beneficiaries will be your own people, because what I intend—with your help—is to open up the future for them."

Roark and Katy exchanged a puzzled glance. Before they could respond, Svyatog resumed.

"From the beginning, we Harathon have recognized, on the intellectual level, that your world is more than merely a source of raw materials and folk art. But we've never really thought out the implications of that fact. Deep down, we've continued to think of you as primitives. This was, I suppose, understandable. We've had no other model for dealing with aliens, as the only non-Lokaron societies we've encountered have been prescientific and preindustrial." Svyatog must have noted their expressions, for he continued hastily. "No, don't be offended. I have come to the conclusion that this was a mistake. There is a qualitative difference between your civilization and those others, to which we were blinded by common alienness. You have the capacity to develop, in a relatively short time, into something more: a *real* trading partner for Hov-Korth and the other hovahon of Gev-Harath.

"Furthermore . . . " Svyatog paused as though preparing to voice distasteful conclusions. "Gev-Harath and the other mainstream gevahon are, in the long run, at a disadvantage in resisting the expansionism of Gev-Rogov. You might say we lack antibodies against that virus. We need allies. And, given Earth's weakness, you have even more reason than we to fear their . . . imperialism." This time the translator's pause suggested that Svyatog was awkwardly verbalizing an alien concept. "So you and I have a common interest: a strong Earth."

Roark found himself recalling what Katy had said to him the night of their reunion, explaining her willingness to work with the being who had now paralleled her thoughts so closely. He repeated an objection he'd voiced to her that night. "But *can* Earth become strong? I mean, with the universe already preempted by your race—"

"Not so." Svyatog touched the controls on the tabletop in front of his chair, and a holographic display appeared above the center of the table. It contained a myriad of tiny lights, filling a space which, Roark decided after a moment's thought, must represent a segment of a disc. Around the edges, the lights were white; but the circular region at the center was filled with all the shades of the spectrum, grouped very roughly by color although there were no sharply delineated boundaries between those groups.

"Shouldn't the density be thicker in bands, to represent the spiral arms?" Katy asked.

"That's a misconception. The density of stars is fairly constant throughout the galactic disc—the spiral arms hold only about five percent more stars per cubic parsec than the regions between them. What's denser in the spiral arms is the cosmic dust from which stars are formed. That's why they show up so clearly when viewing a galaxy from the outside: they're full of young supergiant stars that don't live long enough to wander away from their nurseries. But that's all beside the point. As you've gathered, this is a representation of the part of the galaxy in which our race is active. The colored lights are the stars within the control of the various gevahon." Svyatog manipulated another control, and a white light at one side of the varicolored swarm began to flash stroboscopically. "That is your sun. It lies on the very wave-front of our expansion, in the direction of the galactic core. So coreward of you there is an open frontier, into which you can spread along with Gev-Harath and the other three gevahon active on that frontier.

"Nor is the other direction, toward the galaxy's rim, as closed to you as it may appear. No gevah claims whole volumes of interstellar space—the very idea of such boundaries is too absurd for discussion. Only star systems are claimed, and those only by actual occupation or at least garrisoning. Interspersed among those systems are many others which no one has thought worth claiming, but which hold planets that could readily be terraformed—something we've never been inclined to do. If you were prepared to make the initial investment, you could reap a rich harvest of potential colony-worlds, your title to which no one would question."

Katy turned her eyes from the display and addressed the Lokar. "Why are you telling the two of us all this?"

The English echo of Svyatog's voice grew stern, and his words again echoed Katy's. "Before any of this can happen, you humans must set your own house in order. The regime that currently rules America has to go—your Eaglemen are right in this, if in nothing else. It has locked your country—and, through your country's dominance, the entire planet—into a state of arrested development. It is a parasitic entity, draining away your race's future in order to perpetuate its own meaningless power in an unending present."

Given his total agreement with every word the alien had said, Roark wondered why his ears were growing hot with resentment at those words. *Precisely because it was an alien who said them,* he admitted to himself. "Damn it," he said aloud, "you Lokaron haven't exactly helped! By doing business exclusively through the EFP, you've cemented its power. Everybody on Earth has to come to it hat in hand for access to your technology."

"True," Svyatog acknowledged. "We have followed our ingrained practice in dealing with primitives, using the most powerful local chieftain as our go-between. Thus we have enabled the regime to achieve its long-standing goal of keeping the rest of the planet stagnant so America could stagnate in competition-free safety. This must be rectified. To fulfill its potential, Earth must be unified, not under the hegemony of America—or of any other one power, which would be just as bad—but as a genuinely representative federation. America will continue to be the leader, at first. So America must be under the rule of people committed to bringing Earth into the modern galaxy, for unless pushed the majority will always choose safety over risk and serfdom over individual responsibility."

"You still haven't answered my question," Katy said stubbornly. "What's this grand design of yours got to do with *us* in particular?"

"The answer is simple: I want your help in bringing it about."

"*How?*"

"We have to start somewhere. We can't impose change on your country—we have to act through those of its own people who want change. That means the Eaglemen. I want you to contact them and solicit their aid."

"Svyatog," Roark began, then stopped. *Where* to begin? He tried again. "Look, first of all, the Eaglemen want nothing to do with Gev-Harath, or any Lokaron."

"This is why it would be counterproductive for us to approach them directly, even if we knew how. We need you two, especially Katy. Her admission that she is a former Eagleman was what made me decide to go ahead with this plan. Her inside knowledge of the organization makes it feasible."

"But when they learn it's *your* plan, they'll reject it out of hand!"

"It will be up to you to persuade them of what you've come to understand, that Gev-Harath is their natural ally. You must play on the other pillar of their belief: the need to overthrow the EFP and restore the old American constitutional system—which, while hardly as idyllic as they like to believe, at least allowed for fruitful pluralism. The prospect of our support for such a restoration will at last bring it into the realm of the possible. And I believe their xenophobia can be overcome. They are American nationalists first and foremost, and their hatred of us is merely an inevitable reaction to a perceived threat to America's integrity. Once that fear can be laid to rest—"

"Maybe. But for now, that xenophobia is still firmly in place. And it extends to the two of us, for working for you. Damn it, Svyatog, the very reason we're here is that you couldn't keep us inside our whole skins on Earth, where the Eaglemen, manipulated by Havelock, were gunning for us! Even if they don't shoot us on sight—which they will!—they have no reason to listen to us."

"We can return you to Earth quietly. Before they become aware of your presence, *you* will have to go to *them*, armed with evidence that Havelock is working for Gev-Rogov. That should suffice to disillusion them with their leader and make them willing to listen to new alternatives."

"What evidence?"

"We'll go into that later . . . if you agree to help me. I can't deny that there is an element of danger for you." Svyatog looked from one of them to the other, and all at once he seemed even taller and more alien than he was. "I also can't deny that I'm acting out of self-interest . . . or, to be accurate, the interest of Gev-Harath. But it shouldn't be necessary for me to hypocritically pretend otherwise. Our interests coincide, for we have the same enemies: Gev-Rogov, the EFP, and Havelock. And we are never likely to have a better chance of attaining our common objective. Do you agree?"

Roark's eyes met Katy's for a moment. She nodded. He turned to the alien. "Tell us about this evidence, Svyatog."

CHAPTER ELEVEN

It was nighttime over Earth's western hemisphere when the interstellar ship slid ghostlike into its parking orbit. America's east coast lay under clear skies, and they could make out the well-remembered shoreline by the lights of cities.

Must be something in the air system I'm allergic to, Roark thought, blinking his eyes.

"There is the shuttle," said Svyatog, pointing. Sure enough, the craft occluded a wedge-shaped segment of the star-field as it approached its rendezvous. "On the basis of our observations of Rivera's routine, the time will be right later tonight to put our plan into effect—if you feel ready. If not, we can stay safely here in orbit until the next such opportunity arises."

The two humans shook their heads in unison. "No," Katy said. "We've had the trip to plan this out, and we're as ready as we're going to be. And we don't need to rest up." Once again, the ship had gradually shifted to the destination planet's diurnal period so they could adjust.

"Besides," Roark added, "we've got no time to waste. We don't know what Havelock's going to try next, or when he's going to try it. In fact, we're lucky it isn't already too late."

"Very well. We'll proceed to the Enclave as soon as the shuttle has docked."

Ada Rivera cursed as she almost stumbled. Fall was ending, and the carpet of dead leaves made the tree roots hard to see even in daylight. At night—even a cold clear night like this—the wooded fringe of the Enclave was downright hazardous. She steadied herself and continued on toward the accustomed hummock behind whose shelter she would use her flashlight to send a Morse-code signal to the observer waiting in the darkened woods beyond. It was typical of the communications techniques they used: so low-tech as to be undetectable. She only wished she could use the flashlight to illuminate her path, but to do so would risk observation.

She had almost reached the hummock when a figure stepped out from behind a tree into the moonlight and stood facing her.

Trained reflexes overrode startlement, and she fell into fighting stance. At first she didn't recognize the man, what with the darkness and the goggles he wore. But then he spoke.

"Good evening, Captain Rivera."

"Roark!" She started to gather herself for an attack. He raised his right hand. The sight of the weapon it held froze her.

"Don't, Captain. You're not as fast as this. Nobody is."

Rivera relaxed one muscle at a time, and spoke through a throat tightened by loathing. "Laser pistol. Lokaron make. Like those." She pointed at Roark's goggles, which she was certain were the kind of light-gathering opticals she'd been wishing she had, only far more compact than any human-made starlight scope. "Just the sort of stuff they'd issue to a loyal slave . . . or domestic animal." She sneered in the moonlight. "Go fetch, doggie!"

Roark didn't let himself be provoked. "I don't want to hurt you, Captain. But I have to insist that you come along quietly."

"So you can turn me over to your Lokaron owners, you mean? Why don't you just kill me now and get it over with?"

"Use your brain, Captain. The Lokaron have known about you for a while. They could have picked you up any time they wanted."

Rivera opened her mouth, then closed it before words could form. For a heartbeat, she was silent. Then she shook her head angrily, as though shaking off the thoughtful frown she'd worn and with it any doubts that had crept in. "To hell with that, you cocksucker—or *whatever* it is you do with the Lokaron! Why should I listen to anything from a goddamned traitor?"

"He's no traitor, Ada," came a quiet female voice from behind her. "Any more than I am."

Heedless of Roark's laser pistol, Rivera turned around. "Katy," she whispered. "So you *are* alive! I could hardly believe it when Havelock me. And I didn't *want* to believe it when he ordered me to send Pappas and Cantrell to do the two of you. I told myself he was wrong, that they'd really just be getting Roark. . . . " She blinked, then drew herself up and glared. "Why am I even talking to you? You're as much a Lokaron-loving Judas as Roark, or you wouldn't still be alive this long after you stopped reporting. Now go ahead and kill me. Surely, Katy, you at least have enough humanity left in you to give a fellow human a decent death, instead of delivering me to the Lokaron."

"We're not going to kill you, Ada . . . and we're not going to take you to the Lokaron. We're going *that* way." Katy pointed in the direction Rivera had been heading.

"That's right," Roark put in, gesturing with his free hand toward the darkened landscape outside the Enclave. "To a little place out there beyond the ridgeline. No Lokaron. Just us. All you're going to be required to do is hear us out. Afterwards, you'll be free to go."

"Just like that?"

"Just like that. Oh, of course you'll continue to be under Lokaron observation—you wouldn't believe me if I claimed otherwise. But you'll be no worse off than you are now."

Rivera's glare was back. "This is some kind of trick. But I don't suppose I have any choice." Shoulders slumped, walking in a dispirited shuffle, she started in the indicated direction.

Suddenly, with the lightning speed of which she was capable, she whipped out her flashlight and shone it full in Roark's face. At the same instant, she formed her free hand into a lethal weapon and sprang forward . . . only to halt in mid-lunge as she saw that Roark was only smiling, and that the laser pistol was still trained unwaveringly on her.

"Nice try, Captain. But these goggles have an automatic antiglare feature. You can't blind me that way, like you could if I was wearing U.S. Army passive night-viewing equipment. And now that we've gotten *that* out of the way, give me the flashlight and let's go."

"And while we're walking," Katy added, "you might use the time to contemplate the fact that you're still alive after that stunt—and what that fact implies about our intentions."

They proceeded. Rivera no longer made any effort to look defeated.

The abandoned farmhouse was far from the nearest human habitation. And if sheer isolation didn't assure security, a field generator did; any wandering kids or hunters who approached it found themselves experiencing a combination of headache and cramps that made them lose all interest in further exploration.

Outwardly, its weatherbeaten dilapidation had been left unaltered. Inside, it wasn't much more prepossessing . . . until one came to the inner chamber that Svyatog had had prepared before he'd departed for Harath-Asor, against this very contingency. The deserted rooms and corridors led around it in an endless loop, unless one knew the right closet door to use, and how to open the wall behind it.

In the light of its ceiling's illumination, that chamber was bare save for some chairs and a flat-topped device anyone familiar with the Enclave recognized at once as a small holo-projection display. It was also heated to a humanly comfortable temperature, to the relief of all of them—although Rivera carefully avoided showing it.

"Aren't you going to tie me to the chair or something?" she asked after Roark motioned her to sit down.

"We will if we have to," Katy said, removing her goggles. "But we'd rather not."

"Things like that tend to inhibit communication," Roark deadpanned. He continued to hold the laser pistol steady.

Rivera crossed her legs, folded her arms, and

looked from one of them to the other. "All right. So communicate with me. Why have you brought me here?"

Katy sat down on a chair facing her—outside Roark's line of fire—and began. "You're here because it was the only way we could get you to listen to us. And it's of vital importance that we convince you of a couple of things. The first is that we're not traitors, either to the United States or to the human race."

"That one," Rivera stated, clipping off each syllable, "will take some doing."

"Probably not as much as the second one." Katy drew a deep breath. "It concerns the Eaglemen— yes, Ben knows that I used to be one, and that you still are. We're also aware of Havelock's secret life as leader of the organization."

Their captive was all wide-eyed innocence. "What are you talking about? That's crazy."

"Cut the crap, Rivera," Roark growled wearily. "You're not Katy's cell leader anymore, concealing the identity of the big cheese. And even if we hadn't already known it, you spilled the beans earlier tonight, while you were still in shock over seeing her. You named Havelock as the one who'd told you she was still alive in the Enclave. She was always the *Eaglemen's* special source of information in there, not the Company's." Rivera's eyes narrowed to dark slits, and her mouth tightened into a thin line. "Now, this is going to take all night if you waste our time with a lot of bullshit. So just accept the fact that we know the truth, and don't worry about 'withholding confirmation' or any of the rest of that goddamned spook game-playing."

Rivera's armor cracked open a trifle, to reveal curiosity. "That last is an odd remark, coming from somebody in your line of business."

"Yeah, well, I suppose you could say I have a better right than most to be sick to death of it. And a slime mold like Havelock makes it even more sickening than it has to be."

Rivera's eyes narrowed even more, but not enough to hide the flame in them, and her features grew even more tightly controlled. Katy, observing her closely, smiled. "Why so indignant, Ada, if Havelock's just an operative of the government you want to overthrow? Why should you mind hearing Ben bad-mouthing him?"

"All right!" Rivera flared. "Since you seem to know everything—yes! He's our leader, as well as a high-ranking Company officer. And that silly cow Kinsella wonders why she's never been able to infiltrate us! He's deflected all her attempts, so neatly that she never knew they were being deflected. In the meantime, thanks to him, *we've* infiltrated the *Company*! And we know everything the Company knows!" She sat back and grinned at them. "There, I've confirmed it for you, whether you needed confirmation or not—for all the good it may do you and your Lokaron bosses! Which must not be much, or you would have used it already."

"We already told you, Ada, we don't need confirmation."

"Then what *is* the purpose of all this?"

"To make you aware that you're being duped." Rivera tried to speak, but Katy overrode her. "Havelock's using the Eaglemen the same way he's used the Company. Kinsella doesn't know he's one of you, but *you* don't know who his *real* masters are." She paused to draw a breath, but Rivera seemed too taken aback to fill the brief silence with anything more than an intense glare. "First of all, you need to understand that the Lokaron are divided into multiple sovereignties . . . nations, if you like—"

"We've had some inkling of that," Rivera acknowledged stiffly. "So what? They're all Lokaron."

"Maybe so, but if you think that means they're all alike, you're as wrong as some alien would be who said that you and an Iranian Shiite Muslim and a stone-age animist from the upper Amazon were 'all humans' and let it go at that. They're at least that different from each other—and they have different agendas. And some of those agendas are more in our interest than others."

"Horseshit!'" spat Rivera. "They're aliens! None of their 'agendas' can possibly mean anything good for us."

Katy leaned forward until she was, Roark thought, imprudently close to the Special Forces captain. "Let me ask you something, Ada. Do you seriously doubt that the Lokaron could have seared Earth clean of human civilization anytime they'd felt like it?"

"Of course they could have! But all they're interested in is profit. Havelock has explained it to us: they want a market to exploit, not a conquered wasteland."

"Yes, that's how most of them think—in particular, Gev-Harath, the dominant nation. They're the ones I work for."

"So!" Rivera bared her teeth. "You admit you work for them."

"Yes . . . and so does Havelock!" Katy hurried on, forestalling a reply that Rivera looked too stunned to make anyway. "But he and I don't work for the *same* Lokaron. His bosses belong to Gev-Rogov, the green ones. They don't think the way Gev-Harath does— the way you've been comfortably assuming all the Lokaron think. They *do* want a conquered wasteland!"

"You're out of your goddamned mind, you bitch!" Sheer fury had burned away Rivera's shock. "Havelock is human, for Christ's sake! Why would he want to work for aliens like these, uh, Gev-Rogov—"

"Actually, the plural is 'Rogovon,'" Katy corrected automatically.

"I don't give a flying fuck about the plural! The point is, if they're such monsters—"

"No, I wouldn't call them monsters. In fact, they're probably more like us humans than any of the other Lokaron. Think about that—and remember, from history, how humans have usually treated other cultures that were backward and helpless." Katy paused, and the fire subsided in Rivera's eyes as her look turned inward. Roark wondered if she was thinking of Cortez.

Katy smiled slightly and nodded. "So you see, there are worse things than money-grubbing, price-gouging merchants like the ones I work for. Especially when those merchants' interests coincide with ours. Gev-Harath is worried about the Rogovon too, and wants a counterweight to them. That means helping us modernize ourselves so we'll no longer *be* backward and helpless."

Something inside Rivera seemed to attempt a rally. "But Havelock wouldn't betray us! He's proven that he's committed to our cause. He's given us too much help—inarguable help!"

"Oh yes, I'm sure he's helped you whenever it's served his purposes. He's done as much for the Company. But he'll sell you out just as fast as he sold the Company out, and *would* sell the Rogovon out if he could find a buyer. In fact, he's *already* sold you out."

"Prove it! And while you're at it, explain to me what his motive is. According to you, Gev-Rogov has got it in for the whole human race. What's in it for him?"

"As a matter of fact, we *can* prove it." Katy took a remote out of her pocket and turned toward the holo stage. "We ourselves had no absolute proof before, although it was the only explanation that made sense. You see, Havelock has been keeping in touch with his Rogovon bosses via technology that's undetectable using anything humans have got. But once they knew what they were looking for, the Harathon security types were able to intercept his latest communication. It uses direct neural interfacing." Katy and Roark watched Rivera's expression harden at the mention of the forbidden technology. "But by means I won't explain—partly because there's no time, but mostly because I don't understand them myself—the Harathon were able to reproduce the shared virtual-reality environment they were using in holographic format, with the audio in English as Havelock was 'hearing' it."

Rivera sniffed. "Anything that can be produced can be faked."

"No doubt. Maybe they could even generate a bogus Lokaron that could fool another Lokaron. But do you really think they could do a *human*—a member of a race alien to them—that would fool another human? A human who knows the depicted individual personally, as you know Havelock? Watch him, and ask yourself if he's generated by an alien-programmed computer. And ask yourself something else: how did he obtain the information necessary to get your hit men into the private areas of that tower where Ben and I were living?"

Katy turned from the suddenly silent Rivera and fiddled with the remote. The recording had been made just before Svyatog had left Earth. He'd brought it to Harath-Asor, and the return trip had given them time to go over it. So they were no longer shocked when a miniature Henry Havelock appeared, seated across a table from a green-skinned Lokar.

"What have you to report?" demanded the Lokar without preamble.

"Nothing conclusive, lord." Rivera stiffened visibly at the way Havelock addressed the nonhuman. "The failure of our attempt to eliminate the two rogue agents—"

"*Our* attempt?"

"*My* attempt, lord," Havelock corrected himself. "At any rate, there is no indication that Gev-Rogov has been compromised in any way. The failure resulted from no new knowledge on Gev-Harath's part; it was due simply to—"

"—Typical human incompetence," the Lokar finished for him. Havelock was obsequiously silent. "I begin to wonder if you are the right choice to administer the Rogovon-occupied sector of Earth after all."

This time, Rivera's stiffening was convulsive, and a nonverbal sound at the low threshold of audibility rose from her throat.

The Havelock-image's head rose slightly. "Permit me to remind you, lord, that there will *be* no such 'sector' unless the political preconditions for the occupation are created. And for that, you need the resources I command. Only through me can you use the United States government and the Eaglemen as tools for building a Lokaron consensus behind a military solution."

Roark glanced at Rivera, who looked as though she was going to spring at the holo stage. But most of his attention was on the Rogovon figure. By now, he knew enough about Lokaron body language to recognize iron self-control. The translated voice's tone confirmed it.

"Very well. For now, I will permit you to continue with your plan—which, by the way, may now be free of the complicating factor Roark and Doyle represented, despite your failure."

The human holo image lifted one interrogative eyebrow in a way that would have removed anyone's last doubt that this was indeed Henry Havelock. "Lord?"

"We have been unable to pinpoint their location since the day after the attack on them. But our observers noted some suspicious activity in connection with a Hov-Korth shuttle launch. We believe it is possible, if not probable, that Svyatog has moved them off-planet."

Havelock frowned. "What could be the purpose of such a move? It would secure their safety, but also render them useless."

"Except as sources of background intelligence," the Lokar demurred. "At any rate—"

Katy jabbed with the remote, and the scene vanished. "There's more. But I think we've heard enough. Don't you?"

Rivera gave no indication of having heard her. She sat in a motionless silence that the other two left undisturbed—crowing would have been counterproductive even if they'd felt inclined to indulge in it, which they didn't. When she spoke, her words were as unexpected as the flat tone in which she said them: "So our people in the Caymans . . . ?"

"Oh, so those were Eaglemen?" Roark nodded, not really surprised. "Yes. I was there. It was Havelock who killed them."

Rivera nodded in turn. Finally, she looked up

and met their eyes. They met hers, and saw . . . murder.

Henry, old fellow, thought Roark, *you don't know it yet, but you're walking dead. And as for me, I think I'm going to make it a point to never get Ada Rivera seriously pissed at me.*

"All right," Rivera said, forcing each expressionless word past the barrier behind which she sheltered the dull hurt of betrayal. "So tell me why this Gev-Harath you're working for is any better."

"I already have, Ada. One thing I haven't mentioned, though: like you, they want the EFP regime overthrown."

"Why? Why should aliens give a shit about us primitives and our funny little governmental arrangements?"

"They *don't* see us that way! At least the far-sighted ones don't—like Svyatog'Korth, the one who counts. They want us to join them among the stars, as a trading partner and as an ally against Gev-Rogov. And they understand that in order to do that we have to free ourselves from the secular theocracy that's been holding us back in the name of slogans that were discredited before you and I were born! Svyatog will help. But we have to do it ourselves—which is what we've always dreamed of doing anyway."

Roark understood the import of Katy's *we.* He held his peace and watched these two women who'd once shared a communion of revolutionary commitment from which he was forever excluded, however reliable an ally he might prove to be.

"So that's why you took me tonight," Rivera said, nodding. "You want the help of the Eaglemen." She smiled a sad little smile. "So it's come to this. We're finally being offered a chance to fulfill our dream of restoring the Constitution . . . on behalf of aliens."

"No, Ada! We'll be doing it for ourselves, for our country. Our destiny is to take our place among the stars—and Gev-Harath wants to see us do it. That makes them our allies, but not our masters."

There was a long silence which Roark didn't dare break. Then Rivera nodded again. When she spoke, her tone was brisk and matter-of-fact. "Yes. And we *need* allies—all the allies we can get. The Eaglemen can't do it alone. We need the support of everybody in the U.S. government who's dissatisfied with the status quo."

"They may not all agree on what should replace it," Roark cautioned.

"Of course not," Rivera snapped, annoyed at him for stating the obvious. "But there'll be plenty of time to argue about that later. For now, we can't be choosy." She made a sound that was not a laugh. "Hell, if we're going to get in bed with Lokaron, who are we to turn up our noses at *human* allies whose motivations may not be exactly the same as ours?"

Roark kept to himself his relief that Rivera was seeing it that way. "Right. We're thinking of one in particular: Kinsella."

"*Kinsella?*" Rivera's scowl was back. Roark understood. It was a little like asking a chicken to seek the aid of Colonel Sanders.

"Yes, yes, I know," Katy said hastily. "She's not exactly a heroine to the Eaglemen. But her ambitions make her a natural enemy of the present power structure—one with connections in the Central Committee. If we can prove to her that Havelock has been betraying her, she's likely to react—"

"—The way I have tonight," Rivera finished for her. "All right. Let's prove it to her."

"That's the problem." Roark was glum. "How are

we even going to make contact with her, much less put our case to her?"

"Why not get her attention the same way you got mine?"

"Huh? You mean . . . ? But . . . how?"

"I think you'll be surprised at what the Eaglemen can do once we put our minds to it. I'll have to get in touch with Major Kovac, my cell leader, to set it up." The unhesitating way Rivera named that cell leader convinced Roark of her sincerity as nothing else had. "I'll have to make him aware of the facts, of course. But after I do . . . " She gave them a level regard, then held out her hand. "Are we agreed?"

Roark took the proffered hand. "I'll say this for you . . . Ada. When you decide to commit to something, you don't do it by halves." Katy placed her own hand over theirs and squeezed.

The three-way handclasp lasted a while, as each of them reflected on what they were setting in motion this night.

Roark finally broke the spell. "Let's drink to it." He reached into his jacket and brought forth a flask. "Appleton's rum—the best."

"I might have known!" sighed Katy.

CHAPTER TWELVE

Colleen Kinsella clutched her coat around her as she stepped out onto the top level of the Company parking garage—she hadn't buttoned it, forgetting the weather forecast. That forecast had proven out, as they often did (the Lokaron allowed weather satellites, any hidden capabilities of which they were quite able to detect); and in defiance of the lights of Washington a multitude of stars blazed in a sky whose crystal clarity, this time of year, portended unseasonable chill.

She recalled reading that, a century ago, before the advent of air conditioning, the British Foreign Service had classed Washington as a tropical post. That brought a smile on a night like this, although she could fully understand it in the summer. What she *couldn't* understand was how people had managed to survive the Washington summer in those days.

Of course, the summers weren't quite as hot then, she recalled as she walked briskly toward her car. The "global warming" of which the EFP's immediate forerunners had made so much was a fact, and had been since the Little Ice Age of 1300 to 1750 had ended. The average person hadn't known that, of course. When the opinion makers had unanimously told him it was the fault of recent industrial emissions, and that the free-market economy—and free speech on the subject—must die that Earth's biosphere might live, who was he to question it? After the media-induced hysteria had served its political purpose, it had been quietly dropped, and nowadays the facts were no longer suppressed. *What would be the point?* thought Kinsella. *Now that disagreement is outlawed, not merely demonized, there is no point. The rabble can be allowed to know how they've been manipulated. Why not? They're too stupid to understand it, and too slavish to resent it.*

She smiled with the wry self-knowledge of which she was sometimes capable. *Who am I to be looking down my snoot at "media-induced hysteria?" In an earlier generation, a certain imaginary "missile gap" got my family's first President elected—with the help of the Chicago machine's graveyard constituency! Who was it who said there really is an afterlife in Cook County?* The smile faded into a scowl of annoyance at the uninvited flash of irreverence, and she proceeded in a jerky quickstep. There was her car. . . .

Shock froze her larynx as the black hood went over her head, pulled down from behind. By the time she regained the ability to scream, and was gathering herself to do so, she smelled an odor she recognized all too well, and her voice refused to function as unconsciousness gathered her in.

Just before blackness closed over her, a panicky thought stabbed into her waning awareness—the fear government officials had been living with since the

Wainwright assassination. *Oh my God . . . the Eaglemen!*

"She's coming around," Rivera observed dispassionately.

"Did you really have to do it this way?" They'd been over it repeatedly, but Katy still didn't like it.

"We maybe should have sent her an engraved invitation?" Major Andrew Kovac, USAF, leader of the Eaglemen's command cell to which Rivera belonged, still wasn't happy with the conclusions to which the evidence had forced him, and his voice dripped his unhappiness. It wasn't that he was ambivalent—there'd been no ambivalence to his reaction on learning of Havelock's triple-dealing. But Havelock didn't happen to be present to take it out on, so the non-Eaglemen who *were* present would have to do.

"I only meant, Major, that these tactics aren't exactly going to predispose her to open-mindedness."

"Open-mindedness? *Her?* That—"

"Cut the goddamned bickering," Roark snapped. "She's awake."

Kinsella blinked away the cobwebs of unconsciousness as the stimulant they'd given her took hold. She straightened in the armchair where she sat unrestrained, and looked around the nondescript little room, distinguished only by its Lokaron holo equipment. Completing their survey, her eyes finally settled on the four people present. Roark hadn't known just what kind of reaction to expect, but the Director's coolness impressed him.

"I'm alive," she said, unnecessarily. "I suppose that must mean I'm to be held for ransom, or as a hostage, or something. Odd: I always thought the Eaglemen specialized in murder, not kidnaping."

Roark cleared his throat. "Actually, Director, we're

not all Eaglemen. I'm Ben Roark—you've probably heard of me."

Kinsella stared, openmouthed. Before she could speak, Katy stepped forward. "I also used to work for you, Director. But you probably don't remember me, as it's been a while. The name's Katy Doyle."

Kinsella looked blank at first, then her eyes grew even wider than they had at Roark's name. "Doyle! Yes, I remember now. But you were reported killed a long time ago."

"The rumor of my death was—"

"Yes, yes," Kinsella muttered impatiently. "But Havelock never said anything about you still being alive."

"You're going to be amazed at some of the things Havelock hasn't told you. Learning about them is, you might say, the reason you're here. But to continue . . . in addition to being a former Company agent I'm also a former member of the Eaglemen." Kinsella's face went absolutely expressionless. Katy continued as though she hadn't noticed. "I let that membership lapse some time ago. But the Eaglemen are, in fact, part of the alliance of which you're currently a . . . guest." She introduced Kovac and Rivera. Kinsella's stoniness cracked at Rivera's name, and Katy smiled. "Yes, that's right: the same Captain Rivera who is the Company's on-scene control inside the Enclave. That will make sense when you've learned more."

Kinsella addressed her through lips that barely moved. "So. Terrorists. A renegade." She jerked her chin in Roark's direction. "And . . . whatever it is you consider yourself to be. Does this 'alliance' have any other members?"

"Yes: Hov-Korth, a corporation—that term is close enough, and will have to do for now—belonging to the Lokaron nation, another convenience-label, of Gev-Harath. Mr. Roark and I are here as its representatives."

Kinsella's jaw sagged. Katy continued before she could regain the power of speech. "Yes, I know. The notion of the Eaglemen allying themselves with the Lokaron seems incredible. It will become less so when you've heard me out." She drew a deep breath and commenced.

It wasn't the same presentation she'd given Rivera, for this time it was necessary to establish Havelock's secret life as leader of the Eaglemen before even reaching the matter of his involvement with Gev-Rogov. So it took longer, and the Director interrupted with varying mixtures of incredulity, scorn and outrage more often than the Special Forces captain had. But she was easier to shut up; for all her self-possession, she couldn't forget where she was and who she was among. She'd never faced actual physical danger, nor received the kind of training that prepared one for it.

The *pièce de résistance* was the same, though: the holo projection of Havelock's interview with his Rogovon master.

After it was over, Katy resumed in a quiet voice that only seemed loud in the silence. "Now you can perhaps begin to see why we're all here. Havelock has betrayed the Eaglemen just as he's betrayed you—just as he's in the process of betraying the entire human race. And the Lokaron we represent—Hov-Korth, and by extension all of Gev-Harath—have no desire to see Gev-Rogov strengthened. They, too, are threatened by Havelock's treachery."

It wasn't certain how well—if at all—Katy's words were registering on Kinsella. But the Director was definitely emerging from shock. It started as an aguelike trembling, as though her rage was a seismic event. Then it climaxed with an eruption of extended profanity and obscenity that impressed even the military people present, finally subsiding as her breath ran out and her vocabulary settled into relative mildness—but only relative. "That lying, double-timing motherfucker! By the time I'm through with him he'll *wish* he'd been formally charged and brought to trial! He'll never see the outside of the Company's subcellar for the rest of what little remains of his miserable life! I'll—"

"No, Director! For the time being, it is very important that you not reveal any knowledge of Havelock's treason. You must continue to behave normally toward him."

"Why?" Kinsella's expression was ugly. "What exactly *is* you people's agenda, anyway? And why should I go along with it?"

Roark and Katy exchanged a brief eye contact. This was the crucial moment. They'd been over it before with the Eaglemen, but now push had come to shove and they could only hope Kovac and Rivera would be able to exercise the self-control the moment demanded of them. Without daring to glance at them, Katy spoke levelly to Kinsella.

"Our 'agenda' coincides with yours, Director. Gev-Harath cannot act openly against Gev-Rogov, backed by a Lokaron consensus, until there has been an overt act by the Rogovon. Therefore it is necessary that Havelock and his masters be strung along for now . . . until they go too far. Nor does this conflict with the Eaglemen's objectives. We've persuaded them that America's interests lie in getting a better deal out of Hov-Korth than the present treaties. But those treaties benefit the present American power structure. So before there can be any change we need a new leadership in the Central Committee. And you are the logical choice to supply that leadership."

Silence fell, and they watched carefully as Kinsella went poker-faced. Their analysis of her motivations was unambiguous. She had no interest in overthrowing the present regime; she only wanted to stop being its servant and become its master. She turned to the two Eaglemen. "Well, well," she sneered. "So much for all the idealistic slogans about kicking out the Lokaron and restoring the comedy show that passed for a government in this goddamned country back when it was pretending to take the Constitution seriously. Turns out that's just pablum for your constituency . . . just as phony as the bleeding-heart crap the EFP and its predecessors used to con the rubes. Why don't you admit it? You're no better than the rest of us!"

Roark and Katy held their breath and watched Rivera. But she kept silent under the provocation— hotheaded she might be, but she understood discipline. So she let Kovac respond. "We mean every word we've ever said. But we have to accommodate the political realities. Change is going to have to come gradually. And we're not going to get any change at all out of a Central Committee run by lard-assed bureaucrats like Morris and ideological necrophiliacs like Ziegler! We don't like you any better than you like us. But we're both opposed to the status quo. And we each hate Havelock even more than we do each other."

They watched carefully as Kinsella's head gave a small, unconscious nod. They'd agreed in advance on the response Kovac had just delivered. The Director would have laughed at a claim that the Eaglemen held her in any deep affection, and a seeming confession to her charge of power-seeking hypocrisy would have aroused her suspicions. But this contained just enough grains of truth to carry conviction.

"All right," Kinsella said, nodding more firmly. "So you're saying we can help each other. You're willing to help put me onto a new, reshuffled Central Committee if I'll go along with your plan to counter Havelock and the Rogovon, and then make the kind of deal you want with Hov-Korth afterwards, when I'm in power. Is that it?"

"An able summation, Director," Katy affirmed. "Except that there's one other thing we need from you: access to other highly placed people who, for whatever reason, want a change. We need all the allies we can get, especially strategically positioned ones. You must know such people . . . maybe even somebody on the Central Committee itself." From the dossiers the Eaglemen kept, they had a pretty good idea of who that somebody was. But they wanted Kinsella to think it was her own idea.

She didn't disappoint. "Hmm . . . Yes. I can think of one possibility. Earl Drummond."

"The President's cousin?" Roark hoped he was achieving the right tone of feigned surprise.

"Yes. He and I go back a long way. And he's the only one on the Central Committee who's had an original thought in the last thirty years. Hell, most of them *never* have!" Kinsella's face fell. "But he's always been a voice for the President's position: absolute opposition to all alien contact. Hell, Morrison thinks we should never have signed the treaties, although he's never explained how he thinks we could have avoided it!"

"Let that be our concern, Director," Katy soothed her. "If you can get us in to see him, we'll worry about convincing him of the necessity and rightness of what we're proposing."

"Well . . . I'll see what I can do."

"This wasn't exactly what I had in mind for a meeting place." Katy sounded jittery. Gazing out the car window at their destination, Roark sympathized.

"As I told you, he insisted on it." Kinsella was understandably defensive. "He said it was the only place he felt secure. Being family, he's practically at home here—everyone knows he's in and out a lot, so his presence won't even be noticed. And your faces aren't widely known . . . unlike mine, which is why he insisted that I not accompany you any further than this."

"I suppose," Roark drawled, "the same security concerns are why he only agreed to talk to Katy and me, with no Eaglemen present."

"Can you blame him? Ever since the Wainwright assassination . . . Well, it's time now. Go!"

Roark opened the car door, letting out the heated air and admitting a blast of midnight in which their breath frosted. He and Katy stepped out under the stars and proceeded southeast along Pennsylvania avenue, toward Seventeenth Street, where it simply stopped. The stretch of the avenue which had once separated Lafayette Square from the White House grounds had been obliterated a generation ago, lest someone park the same kind of cargo at the President's doorstep as had once been left outside the Oklahoma City federal building. They crossed Seventeenth Street and stood on the deserted sidewalk beside a wrought-iron fence, with the hideous old Executive Office Building to the right and their well-lit destination visible beyond.

An overcoated figure stepped from the shadows

between the streetlights. They tensed as he brought
up a hand, but it held only a Company ID card
whose lettering—luminous in the dark by virtue of
Lokaron imprinted circuitry—spelled the name
Kinsella had told them to expect. They produced
their own identification in turn. Without comment,
he gave them both a quick, impersonal frisking.

"This way," he said, and led the way a short
distance south along Seventeenth, to a small gateway.
A White House security cop opened it for them
wordlessly. *Following instructions received through
proper channels, or simply bribed?* wondered Roark.
Their taciturn guide led them around the north end
of the Executive Office Building and, abruptly, the
White House stood before them in all its enlarged
grandeur.

The enlargement had replaced the old Executive
Wing with one of the two harmonious extensions
Grover Cleveland had planned for James Hoban's
original mansion. Now the President's ceremonial
office—the only sort of office he needed anymore—
was located on the second floor, in the old Yellow
Oval Room. The First Family's private living quarters
were beyond that, in the new East Wing. They
approached an inconspicuous ground-floor door in
the new West Wing, which was devoted to whatever
business the President had to conduct under modern
conditions. A low, indirectly lit corridor with groined
arches overhead led to a double door. The Company
man gestured them inside, remaining on guard in
the corridor.

The room, low-ceilinged like everything else on
the ground floor, was like a very handsome traditional
library, with rich blond-mahogany paneling and a
blaze going in the fireplace. A man, dressed casually
in slacks and sweater, was tending the fire with a

poker. He turned as they entered, put away the poker and extended a hand. His face, somewhat darker than the paneling, formed a smile in his neat white beard. "Ms. Doyle. Mr. Roark. I'm Earl Drummond. Take off your coats, please. I've been looking forward to meeting you, having followed your . . . exploits with great interest for some time."

They shook hands with him, mumbling pleasantries. Katy was uncharacteristically tongue-tied, and Roark felt the same way. "It's a pleasure to meet you too, sir," he ventured. "Although it's hard not to feel a little intimidated by the, uh, venue you've chosen." *Could that possibly be intentional?* he didn't add.

Drummond smiled again and chuckled. His voice was a deeper shade than his skin. "Well, you know, there's something to be said for having a place to stay for free in Washington. Especially a place I'm pretty sure isn't bugged—not even by my old friend Colleen Kinsella."

Katy cleared her throat and stepped into the conversational opening. "Speaking of Director Kinsella, sir, I believe she has apprised you of what we want to discuss . . . and who we represent."

"She has," Drummond acknowledged, still affable but with an air of getting down to business. He indicated a semicircle of armchairs in front of the fireplace, and grew still more businesslike as they settled in. "Colleen has described Havelock's treason, in terms that—coming from her—compel my belief. She's also explained that you and the . . . shall we say *unexpected* combination of parties you speak for think we should let him continue undisturbed for now. I must say, that last part sticks in my craw."

"Nevertheless, sir, it's necessary. The Company could squash Havelock now, but he's merely a creature of the Rogovon, who are beyond the reach of any U.S. government sanctions. They'd just try something else . . . something that might work. In order for Gev-Harath to move decisively against them—"

"Yes, yes, Colleen has explained all this to me. I'm prepared to agree, provisionally."

"Thank you, sir." Katy let her relief show. "I understand why you find this course of action unpalatable."

"No, I don't think you do. It's not stringing Havelock along that bothers me. I'm quite familiar with the 'enough rope' approach to criminal investigation—which is really what we're doing here, on a rather grand scale. No, what bothers me is the fact that we're doing it this way because it's convenient for the Lokaron. The *good* Lokaron, of course . . . or so Colleen has assured me, although I'm damned if I can understand all the Gev-this and Gev-that business. But they're still aliens, and it's their show, and we're just supporting players." Drummond held up a hand as Katy started to speak. "But for now, let's move on to the other half of you people's agreement with Colleen: a shake-up in this country."

Roark and Katy glanced at each other. Not certain how much of the truth Drummond should be told at this stage, they had decided to give him the same version Kinsella had heard. Roark proceeded to do so. "Uh, yes, sir. It's our understanding that you would be agreeable to a new Central Committee, with Director Kinsella and yourself as the dominant figures."

"Well, you understand wrong!"

The same accelerated time sense that took hold of him in a firefight descended on Roark. He began a quick motion, stopped as he remembered he was unarmed . . . and then realized that Drummond was smiling again. "Better hear me out before you do anything drastic, Mr. Roark."

Roark made himself appear to relax. "So you were joking just now? Not funny."

"No, I wasn't joking. I have no intention of getting involved in this just to bring about a power realignment in the upper echelons of the EFP. No, sir. If I'm going to risk my hide, it'll have to be for something worth the risk: doing away with the EFP altogether! Not just changing its leadership or redirecting its priorities or otherwise 'reforming' it. I mean right between the eyes!"

Roark kept his mouth shut because he knew that if he opened it he would only blither.

Drummond smiled again, turned his head toward a recessed doorway, and put slightly more volume into his voice. "I don't think they believe me, John."

"No, I don't think they do." The owner of the new—and very familiar—voice emerged from the door.

Paralysis was no longer one of Roark's problems. He shot to his feet as though the armchair had been an ejector seat. Out of the corner of his eye, he saw that Katy had kept pace with him. And her vocal apparatus was a little ahead of his, though all it could do was stammer. "Ah . . . er . . . that is . . . Mr. President . . . "

John Morrison indulgently waved them back to their seats as he took one himself. He was even lighter in coloring than his cousin, with iron-gray hair cut too short to reveal its texture. He could easily have "passed" back in the last century when Americans of inconspicuously African descent had been wont to do so. The EFP had been noisily proud of itself for placing the first person of such background

in the White House . . . long after it had ceased to
matter much to everyone else. He'd outraged Vera
Ziegler and others of her ilk by letting himself be
overheard characterizing his ancestry as "pure house
servant." That bit of taboo violation had been far
from the last of his politically awkward public
utterances.

"Sorry I didn't introduce myself earlier," he said,
smiling, as Roark and Katy stiffly resumed their seats.
"But you must admit this entire meeting is a little
irregular, and I thought I ought to use Earl here as
a sounding board first. Oh, don't worry," he added,
seeing Roark's rapid eye-coverage of every corner of
the room. "We really *are* alone. You can speak
freely . . . as can Earl and I."

"Well, Mr. President," Roark temporized, "surely
you can see how it's a little disconcerting for us.
We've just heard Mr. Drummond—a member in
good standing of the Earth First Party's Central
Committee—declare himself, in effect, an Eagleman."

"Of course Earl's a Party member, as am I. Everybody in public life in this country is . . . by definition.
Just as Boris Yeltsin was a member of the Communist
Party of the Soviet Union, before he drove a stake
into its heart." Roark understood the reference,
though he'd been a preschooler when the polity to
which Morrison referred had dissolved. "So now you
know. If wanting to do away with the self-
perpetuating, brain-dead oligarchy that's been killing
this country the way ivy kills a tree makes one an
Eagleman, then, yes, Earl is one, and so am I. But
I *thought* the Eaglemen's agenda also included
getting the aliens off Earth. From what you've said
tonight, I gather it no longer does."

"We've explained to Director Kinsella that—"

"Yes, and she's explained it to Earl, and he's

explained it to me." Morrison sat back, hands resting on the arms of his chair, and his face took on a brooding expression. *Where have I seen that exact look before?* Roark wondered. Then, with a small shock, he remembered a giant stone figure that sat behind classical columns, in a monument within walking distance of this place.

Finally the President looked up and met his guests' eyes. "I may have been living a lie ever since I let the Party put me in this house to serve as its figurehead. But one thing hasn't been a lie: my opposition to the Lokaron treaties. That, at least, I could get away with saying publicly. What I *couldn't* say out loud was my real reason, which was the same as my reason for wanting to smash the EFP. I want America to be what it was before—what it was meant to be. In the last third of the last century it began to go tragically wrong. When the EFP gang came to power, they didn't kill freedom, they merely buried its corpse. We did that to ourselves. But then the Lokaron came. And now we have *two* alien entities controlling our lives and distorting our development—one a mutant birth from within our own national body, the other an interloper from outside. We've got to free ourselves from both of them if we want to reclaim our identity and realize our unique potential."

Gazing into those troubled dark eyes, Roark didn't trust himself to speak. Katy spoke for them, at first hesitantly, then with greater assurance. "I understand, Mr. President. Up to a point, I even agree. We can get rid of the EFP—in fact, that's been our real intent all along. And that's not all. We want you to take the lead in dismantling the American world hegemony and creating a global federal structure to replace it. Hov-Korth, the Lokaron faction we represent, wants to deal with this planet as a whole."

"This goes well beyond what you just told Mr. Drummond."

"Yes, sir. Out of caution, we told him what we'd previously told Director Kinsella, who isn't ready for the truth."

"No," Drummond put in with a smile. "I don't think she is."

Morrison wasn't smiling. "So America must submerge its identity in a world federation, which must then submerge *its* identity in a Lokaron galaxy."

"We can't return to what existed before, Mr. President. That's gone now. It's passed into memory, carrying all its good and evil with it. No, restoring political pluralism to this country won't recreate the past; it will enable us to adapt to the future—the future that the EFP has closed out."

Morrison looked stubborn. "America can only make a worthwhile contribution to that future by being itself."

"But what *is* 'itself,' Mr. President? Has the U.S. ever been a 'nation' in the traditional sense of one particular sort of people inhabiting, and being molded by, one particular landscape? You should know better than Ben and I that we've never been that. No, I like to think of America as a different kind of human association: a bridge from the past to the future, for the whole human race to cross freely. That's what we always were, before the EFP turned us into a museum of stale slogans. And it's what we can be again."

"What kind of future?" challenged Morrison. "A wholly owned subsidiary of this Lokaron corporation, Hov-Korth? Is the U.S. to be like some Caribbean island a century ago, run by United Fruit?"

"No. Our future is to take our own place among

the stars. Hov-Korth wants to see us do that, not
out of altruism but because they're farsighted enough
to see us as a counterweight to Gev-Rogov—which
wants to see us permanently primitive and exploit-
able. If we don't modernize ourselves, we'll always
be vulnerable to somebody like the Rogovon. Do you
really want our fate to depend on the ethics of
aliens?"

Morrison's eyes ceased to meet hers, and he
smiled a sad little smile. "No. Of course I don't.
What I want is . . . I want the old United States back.
And yet I've always known, deep down, what you're
telling me now. We can't turn back. We have to join
the universe that we now know exists out there. And
America can't do it alone." He paused and looked
around him. *Funny,* Roark thought, puzzled. *He's not
focusing on anything in the room. It's as though he's
watching something recede into the distance and
vanish, and silently bidding it farewell.* Finally, the
President met their eyes again, and spoke matter-
of-factly. "All right. What are you people proposing
in the way of a concrete plan?"

Roark spoke for them in his turn. "As Mr.
Drummond has doubtless told you, Havelock's plans
hinge on an attack upon the Enclave. The Central
Committee authorized the Company to mount such
an attack, but in fact the attacking force—like the
group on the inside, of which I was a member—
were heavily infiltrated by Eaglemen, put there by
Havelock. His real objective was to provide his
Rogovon employers with a *casus belli.* The attack
was aborted—"

"Yes, I understand you had something to do with
that."

"—but they haven't given up on the idea. By
keeping Havelock in the dark about the fact that the

Eaglemen—and now Director Kinsella—are on to him, we're encouraging him to try again. This time, we'll let it go just far enough to give Gev-Harath proof of Gev-Rogov's scheming, to place before the other Lokaron. Then we'll apprehend Havelock. At the same time, the Eaglemen will be in position to seize control of the nerve centers of the U.S. military. At that point, you'll make a broadcast to the nation and the world, laying bare what's been going on and declaring the restoration of the old constitutional system, abrogating everything that's been done since the EFP imposed its one-party regime."

"Including my own election as President?"

Roark's expression matched Morrison's wryness. "That is sort of awkward, isn't it? You'll just have to gloss over it, saying you're going to have to serve out your term as caretaker, after which *real* elections will be held. One of the things you'll declare null and void is the Lokaron trade treaties. Simultaneously, Gev-Harath, with Hov-Korth in the lead, will announce a willingness to negotiate new treaties. They'll also go public with their desire to do so with the new world federation you'll have just proposed."

Morrison was silent for a moment. "Well," he finally said, then paused as though letting it go at that. Then he straightened up. "I think we have some details to work out. Earl, would you order up some coffee for us? It looks like we're going to be pulling late hours."

CHAPTER THIRTEEN

Something wasn't quite right. Henry Havelock was certain of it as soon as he entered Kinsella's portrait-heavy private office and she looked up from her desk at him.

"You wanted to see me?" she inquired shortly, motioning him to a chair as though as an after-thought.

"Yes, Director. It's about the matter we discussed last week."

Kinsella's gaze sharpened. Her eyes looked a little bloodshot as they studied him. *Hung over?* he wondered. It might account for the little peculiarities in her behavior he was having so much trouble putting his finger on.

"You mean to say," she demanded, "that you're still trying to get me to authorize another attempt to attack the Enclave? After the way you landed me neck-deep in shit last time?"

Havelock thought he detected a note of calculation behind her irritability. He discounted it and met the objection head-on. "As you'll recall,

Director, the Central Committee okayed it in general terms."

"Yes—subject to a warning not to step on your dick again! And," she added venomously, "you haven't even been able to deal with that rogue agent—Roark, wasn't that his name?—inside the Enclave."

Havelock winced. The failure of the attempt on Roark and Doyle had been impossible to keep from Kinsella, although Rivera—wearing her Company-authorized hat—had at least had the presence of mind to conceal Doyle's presence on the hit list. "Yes and no, Director. Granted, we didn't succeed in terminating him. But our agents in the Enclave have reported no indication of his presence since then. The attempt must have alarmed the Lokaron into placing him in such deep security that he is effectively neutralized. In my considered judgment, he no longer represents an unacceptable wild card in the game."

"Oh?" Kinsella gave an arch look that Havelock found difficult to interpret. "But that still doesn't explain why, in your 'considered judgment,' we should try it again now."

"Why not, Director? The original idea—the *real* idea, of creating a crisis with the Lokaron that would bring down the present Central Committee—is still as sound as ever."

"But you thought an unsuccessful attempt would do that. And it didn't, did it?"

"I continue to maintain that it would have, had it actually occurred, even though the *abortive* attack admittedly fell short. But at all events, a successful one will surely suffice. And the time is ripe for that, given the apparent removal of Roark from the equation."

Kinsella appeared to cogitate. "All right. Draft a

proposal for me to submit to the Central
Committee."

"I suggest, Director, that we not bother the Central
Committee with things it doesn't need to know. At
any rate, there isn't time; the circumstances won't
remain optimal for much longer. We should simply
proceed on the strength of the earlier go-ahead we
received for the overall concept. In fact . . . " Havelock
made his eyebrows arch as though with the dawning
of an idea. "It occurs to me that we could maximize
the impact of our success."

"What do you mean?"

"Request a special emergency meeting of the
Central Committee at the time the attack is scheduled to commence. What could be more dramatic
than an announcement of success even as it is
occurring?"

"And what could be more embarrassing than a
pratfall with the full Central Committee watching?
Do you have any idea of the chance you're asking
me to take?"

"I'll attend as well, Director. That should tell you
something about my confidence that the plan will
succeed," Havelock said smoothly. "And in fact
you'll be running no risk at all. I'll give you, in
advance, a signed document accepting full responsibility in the event of failure. Not, to repeat, that
I expect failure. I anticipate a triumph that will
silence your critics. It will also magnify your stature
in the eyes of the existing power structure—a useful
insurance policy, in the event that same power
structure manages to survive the crisis we'll have
created with the Lokaron."

"Hmm . . . Yes, something to be said for covering
all bases. Very well. What date and time shall I give
them for this special meeting?"

Havelock didn't hesitate. "Three days from now, at twenty-two hundred hours."

"What? So soon?"

"All preliminary preparations have been made, Director. Certain last-minute personnel shifts will have to be made. But the time I've proposed will, I believe, be the optimum one."

"All right. Prepare a detailed operational plan—for *me* and not for the Central Committee."

"It's already prepared, Director. You'll have it later this afternoon."

As he departed, Havelock continued to puzzle over the curious oddities in Kinsella's behavior. *Time of the month, perhaps?* He dismissed the thought with contempt. *No time to worry about such trivia. Matters are coming to a head.* It was time to give Rivera her official instructions . . . and to transmit through Kovac, as head of the command cell, her real instructions. *And, at the same time, I'll be delivering the instructions that* really *matter.*

It was, he reflected, ironic. It never seemed to occur to the Eaglemen that the cell system they'd employed so successfully could be used to conceal a whole dimension of their organization from its own official command structure. *But, then, they trust me.* The concept of trust was too alien for him to fully understand; but he could analyze, from the outside, the way it affected other people's actions, and exploit the knowledge so gained. Thus he had done when he'd first set up his secret cell, composed of hard-case Eaglemen who firmly believed they were serving as a last-resort counterweight to a command cell whose members' commitment to the cause wasn't absolutely above suspicion. Not even the Rogovon knew about it.

It was a useful thing to have in reserve—so much

so that he'd held it back at the time of the first attempt to move against the Enclave. Now, though, the time had come to deploy it.

Isn't life fun? he thought with uncomplicated happiness, as he turned his mind to the problem of how he would employ the Rogovon to wipe out the secret cell after it had outlived its usefulness.

After the door closed behind Havelock, Colleen Kinsella took several deep breaths and brought herself under control. *That oily, two-timing bastard! I thought I was going to blow up in his smarmy face!* Tightly contained rage stabbed painfully at her abdomen. *The payoff for stringing him along had better be worth it!*

She forced herself to think calmly. What *had* he meant by that bogus afterthought about calling the Central Committee together to witness her triumph? *The obvious motive would be to make me look like a jackass when the attack fails. But since the attack is really just a provocation to let the Rogovon take direct action against Earth, what would be the point? And why would he have offered to provide me with a full-responsibility confession?*

She shook her head. It was like everything else about his scheme: unexceptionably logical. *Too bad the basic idea can't be salvaged somehow. . . .*

None of that! She bent down and began keying a combination of numbers into the electronic lock of one of her desk drawers. It opened, and she withdrew the small communicator Roark and Doyle had provided. It used neutrinos to send messages into which no equipment of Earthly manufacture could tap—and hopefully no Lokaron equipment would be positioned to do so, in the absence of any reason to anticipate such messages. The time had

come to use it, and let her new allies know that
things were in motion.

Roark responded to her call. He and Katy were
back in the Enclave, secreted on the uppermost
levels of the Hov-Korth tower. Svyatog had spirited
them there as part of a supply shipment—a disguise
that was, they hoped, as effective as it was uncomfortable. Fortunately, it would only be necessary to
keep the Rogovon in the dark for a short time.

Not, it seemed, short enough for Roark. "Why
three and a half days?" he demanded.

"He made some noise about 'last-minute personnel
shifts.' Anyway, what are you complaining about?
Surely there's a lot you can be doing before then."

"We can't do a damned thing but stew. Remember,
we can't risk tipping our hand until they actually
move."

"Well, then, you can keep one of you beside your
communicator at all times. I'm going to be calling
in with new developments as they break, and it won't
be any time to play telephone tag!" Kinsella broke
the connection irritably, and prepared to call Earl
Drummond . . . but then paused. She thought for a
moment, then completed the connection.

She gave him the same summary she'd given
Roark. "So," she concluded, "you'll be getting the
same invitation as everybody else on the Central
Committee. I'll be using the main conference room
at Company headquarters—it's the only room there
that's big enough. But, just in case, let me tell you
about the emergency egress route I had built into
it. . . ."

For Roark, the next three days stretched like a
wire drawn to the snapping point and twanged by
each little irritation.

At last, Kinsella called in—hurriedly, as she was already late for the emergency session of the Central Committee she herself had called—with the word that the attack was going in as scheduled. Roark slapped the disconnect button without even pausing to acknowledge, and whirled to face Katy. "It's time!" Then he spoke to the room in general. "Did you get that?"

"Yes," came the voice of Svyatog's translator. He and Huruva'Strigak waited in the ultrahigh-security precincts of the latter's office, where a hookup had enabled them to listen to Kinsella's message. "Our guards are even now taking up positions around the Gev-Rogov tower—too late, unfortunately, to stop a shuttle which just departed. They are also taking control of the human workers' quarters. You need to—"

"—Get there at once. We're on our way!" They sprinted for the door and continued at a dead run, out onto a landing flange where a little open-topped flitter waited under the cold winter stars. Lifting off under a powered-down version of the shuttles' drives, it circled around the tower's pinnacle and then arrowed downward, shoving them back into their seats with uncompensated g-forces. An equally extreme deceleration stopped them just short of the high-speed crash their senses had screamed was about to happen, and they descended to the low-lying human dormitory.

Entering, they walked into pandemonium. Tall blue-skinned Lokaron security guards with intimidatingly advanced-looking weapons were herding a crowd of vociferously angry but terrified humans into the cafeteria. Ignoring the looks he and Katy got, he approached the guard with the badge of rank on the chest of his black coverall. "Have you got them separated out?"

"Yes. One resisted and had to be stunned." The guards' carbine-sized laser weapons had a nonlethal setting, creating an ionized path for a high-voltage electric pulse that administered a temporarily incapacitating shock. "They are being held separately." The guard pointed to the far corner of the large room, where three men tended a fourth, unconscious one under the watchful eyes of two alien guards.

As Roark and Katy approached, the three looked up with varying expressions. One pretended—an instant too late—not to recognize them. "You!" snarled Pirelli, as Chen, wide-eyed, gasped, "Ben!"

"Yeah, Jerry, it's me. And this is Katy Doyle, whom you two probably don't know about, not being Eaglemen . . . unlike Stoner." He turned to the one with the bogus blank look.

"Huh?" Stoner's face was all innocence. "What are you talking about?"

Chen gaped. "Yeah, Ben—what do you mean, 'Eagleman'? Stoner, here, is one of our people. He's been here since before you were . . . turned." His voice died on the last word, as though he was still having trouble accepting what he'd been told.

"It's true, Jerry. He's an Eagleman—"

"Like me." Chen and Pirelli stared openmouthed as Rivera strode up. Stoner bared his teeth, all pretense gone, clearly restrained from springing for her only by the Lokaron lasers. She swept her eyes over all three of them. "Look, we don't have much time, so for now you're just going to have to shut up, listen, and follow orders. Chen, Pirelli: yes, I'm an Eagleman, one of several put into this operation by Havelock—who is the leader of the organization." She turned from their shock-marbled faces and faced the silently raging Stoner. "Jim, I've spilled all this because I've learned Havelock is a traitor—not just to the Eaglemen, not just to America, but to humanity. He's selling us out to a faction of the Lokaron. And he's making his move now. What we were told about tonight's attack was a crock."

"But," Stoner blurted, in defiance of Rivera's ban on speech, "if this is true, and you knew it, why did we go ahead and disable the security sensor system earlier tonight?"

"There's no time to give you the full story. Just take my word that in order for the Rogovon we're working with"—she indicated the guards—"to take action against the ones who've bought Havelock, we have to let the attack actually happen." She paused, gauging the expression that had come over Stoner's face at the words *the Lokaron we're working with*. "Yeah, Jim, I know. I've got a lot of explaining to do. But I don't have time to do it just now. I'll tell you one thing, though. In the process of stopping Havelock, we're going to do what we Eaglemen have always dreamed of doing: smash the EFP and restore the Constitution." She turned to Chen and Pirelli. "Yes, that's right. And even though you two aren't Eaglemen, I have a feeling it's what you want, too. And you'll hear about it later tonight—from the President himself." She allowed a brief pause, then put the whip-crack of command into her voice. "One thing hasn't changed, though: I'm still in charge of everybody here, Eaglemen and otherwise. So let's get moving! Take your orders from Roark and Doyle."

"First of all," Roark began, "we need to get these people here out of danger, in case things get fucked up and the attack proceeds further than we plan to let it. Jerry, coordinate with old Koebel and get some kind of organization going. Use your authority as a Federal agent—the time for secrecy is past. Assign

some people with first-aid training to take care of
him." He indicated the man who'd been stunned.
"Then join us. The rest of you, come on. We're going
to meet the attackers outside."

"Right," they chorused. Chen started to hurry
away, then paused and gave Roark's arm a squeeze.
"I never really believed you'd turned traitor. You may
be an asshole, but you're not that kind of asshole."

Before Roark could frame a response, the dull
crump! of a distant explosion brought the hubbub
in the cafeteria to a shocked silence. Then the
crackle of automatic fire mingled with the closer
sound of high-pitched Lokaron voices.

"The attack's started already!" barked Rivera.
"Move!"

The hubbub in the Company's main conference
room subsided as Henry Havelock entered. He
surveyed the Central Committee members, milling
about in confused tension, and saw thirty years'
accumulation of intellectual constipation. *More than
that, actually,* he corrected himself. After all, the
average age of the room was well over sixty, and few
of them had exhibited any detectable neural activity
since leaving college—nor even before that, except
at the very low level required to parrot long-
discredited but still-orthodox collectivist dogmas. *And
since then . . . well, kissing the ass of whoever's above
you on the ladder while simultaneously stepping on
the face of whoever's below doesn't even take much
physical coordination.*

Something bothered him, though—something not
quite right. Before he could put his finger on it, Vera
Ziegler separated herself from the crowd and strode
forward, pointing her finger in a way she doubtless
thought suggested a cry of *J'accuse!* "There you are!

Perhaps you can provide an explanation, since Director Kinsella has vanished."

"Vanished?" Havelock frowned. This was unplanned-for.

"Yes! She was here when we arrived, but no one's seen her for several minutes. I warn you, this treatment of those of us who form the vanguard of enlightened, progressive thought will not be tolerated! There will be a full investigation of this latest outrage by the military-industrial complex and its intelligence apparatus. . . . " Ziegler's honking trailed off as two men in light combat dress, carrying minimacs, emerged from the door Havelock had used and deployed left and right along the wall behind him. Two more men followed, struggling under the weight of what Ziegler, had it not been for the ignorance of military matters in which she took such simple pride, might have recognized as a 5.57mm caseless assault chaingun. The feet of the support weapon's tripod crashed solidly down onto the floor, and its ammunition cassette was clicked into place—sounds which seemed louder than they were in the uncomprehending hush that had descended.

The noise seemed to break Ziegler's uncharacteristic verbal paralysis. "Havelock, what is the meaning of this? I demand—"

"Oh, shut up," Havelock told her, fulfilling a wish of years' standing. Her mouth formed a circle of speechless shock. At the same instant, he reached into his coat, withdrew a small autopistol, and fired point-blank.

There was no visible entry wound, for the bullet went through her wide-open mouth. *She died just as she lived,* Havelock thought with an inward chuckle. But the soft-nosed slug blew out the back of her head. In the stunned silence, Havelock

observed the dark reddish-oozing mass that lay on
the floor a few yards behind her collapsed form. *So
she did have something in there after all!* Then he
turned, stepped aside, and nodded to the chaingun
crew, while hastily inserting a pair of earplugs.

It was well that he did so, for the chaingun
crashed into a continuous explosion that was, in this
enclosed space, ear-shattering—a din in which the
screams were inaudible. The sleet of lead swept back
and forth across the crowd like a scythe, ripping
limbs from trunks, blasting through bodies and
sending great gouts of blood and ruined internal
organs flying into the faces of those behind, who had
mere fractional seconds of horrified awareness left
before they, too, were blown apart. Then, abruptly,
the chaingun ceased firing, and the only sound was
a weak moaning that arose from a few still-alive
throats, mostly belonging to people half-buried under
heaps of shattered bodies. The two men with minimacs advanced across the room, their bootsoles
making little splashing sounds in the blood and other
fluids. There were a few stutters of autoburst fire,
and then silence.

Well, thought Havelock, looking through the acrid
haze of smoke at the abattoir that had been the
Central Committee of the Earth First Party, *the
country ought to put up a statue of me for that.
Come to think of it, I will put one up.*

And yet, something still nagged at him—a sense
that something was missing. Something . . . or somebody.

Oh, yes; Ziegler did mention that Kinsella had left.
Too bad, but not crucial.

Still . . . isn't there somebody else missing as well?

He dismissed the matter and gestured to his men.
They departed, moving through the deserted

corridors of a building whose few occupants at this time of night had already been dealt with. They emerged on the top deck of the parking facility, in time to see a Lokaron shuttle descending in a blaze of running lights and the bluish-white glow of its drive's dissipated waste heat. Havelock could hear numerous sirens in the distance—the sound of D.C. officialdom's response to the blatant violation of its airspace. But such things had now ceased to matter, though the bureaucracy didn't know it yet.

The shuttle touched down with scarcely a bump. *Love to know how the Lokaron do it,* Havelock thought as he advanced across the deck. The shuttle's ramp lowered with a whine and a frost of escaping steam in the chill night air. A Lokaron figure descended, silhouetted against the interior lights.

"Your instructions have been carried out, lord," Havelock murmured. Those instructions—to decapitate the EFP—had been given at his own suggestion, but stressing that fact would serve no useful purpose at the moment.

"Good. And the data we require?" Valtu'Trovon extended a six-digited hand.

"Here, lord." Havelock handed over a disc containing the kind of detailed information on Cheyenne Mountain's subterranean layout necessary to plan a precision strike.

"Good," Valtu repeated. Without another word, he turned back toward the ramp. Havelock started to follow him as per their agreement. Then, reaching the ramp, Valtu gestured to someone inside.

Hmm . . . Havelock frowned. *He's acting oddly. I'll be able to handle him, of course. Still, can't hurt to—*

Valtu hurried up the ramp. Above, atop the shuttle's nose, a recessed turret extruded itself with a low hum and began to swivel, revealing what looked like the mouth of a weapon.

Wait a minute! This isn't right—

It was Havelock's last thought, as the plasma weapon turned his private universe into something indistinguishable from the surface of a sun.

The turret tracked back and forth, spitting plasma bolts in a rapid-fire crackle. Of Havelock and his men, not even ashes remained.

Inside the shuttle, Wersov'Vrahn spoke diffidently to Valtu. "Shall we destroy this building as we depart?"

"No. There's no point. And we must proceed without delay to meet *Krondathu*." The Rogovon *Rogusharath*-class strike cruiser was already on its way Earthward, and Valtu, no space navigator and therefore irritably dependent on those who were, wanted nothing to jeopardize his rendezvous with it. "Besides, I just got a disturbing report from our people still in the Enclave. There have been some odd movements of Harathon security personnel. It appears that the attack may have been compromised."

"But . . . how?"

"I don't know. It's probably nothing. Still, we'll take no chances. Lift off at once. And while enroute, download the contents of this disc to *Krondathu*."

"At once, sir." Wersov passed the order to the shuttle pilot.

Peering cautiously from underneath the barely raised cover of the air vent, their eyes still half dazzled by the blinding plasma bolts, the two humans watched the Rogovon shuttle lift off, swing its nose around, and plunge into the night sky at a seemingly impossible acceleration. It was soon lost among the stars.

They looked at each other, then glanced at where Havelock had stood before being consumed by starfire, then looked at each other again.

"What the hell is *really* going on here?" breathed Colleen Kinsella. Her face was slick with sweat, and not just from the bloom of heated air that had rushed outward from the plasma weapon.

"Damned if I know," Earl Drummond grunted. "But we'd better get on that fancy communicator in your office and let our people inside the Enclave know what's happened."

"Yeah. I think you're right."

They closed the cover and descended, retracing the route through the ventilation system that had taken them from the main conference room just before it had been turned into a slaughterhouse.

The attackers advanced through grounds landscaped in accordance with unnervingly alien aesthetic precepts, and they occasionally exchanged nervous glances. The lack of opposition was eerie.

Despite their nervousness, they didn't open fire immediately when a line of five figures stepped out and deployed across their path. The figures were, after all, human.

A moment of silent uncertainty passed. Then a figure—female, small—stepped out from the skirmish line of new arrivals and saluted the attacking force's leader. "Everything's secured in here, Andy."

"Good job, Ada." Andrew Kovac turned and faced the mass of stunned incomprehension behind him. "All right, people, stand down. As of now, the attack is terminated. Some of you know why." He didn't say, *the Eaglemen among you*. One shock at a time was enough. "As for everybody else, all you need to know for now is that this whole operation was motivated by high-level treason, and that we had to go through the motions of penetrating the Enclave in order to prove it. Now you can be told the whole truth . . . and the President is about to tell it to you!"

The combat-dressed men gaped at each other, slowly lowering their weapons, and the words *the President* rose repeatedly above the hushed murmur. Kovac smiled and raised his voice. "That's right: the President himself! In fact, we're a few minutes behind schedule, so his address to the nation should have begun already." He reached inside his camo fatigues and pulled out a small portable radio. He switched it on and turned up the volume as far as it would go. "Gather around and listen. This thing doesn't have much of a speaker."

A voice that was not one of the regular announcers of any of the nearby D.C. stations was just finishing a stammering introduction. Then came the unmistakable voice of John Morrison, thin and tinny in the outdoor air.

> *"My fellow Americans: even as I speak to you tonight, a drama is already unfolding. A drama of dark treason and frightening danger, but one whose conclusion is a new beginning for our nation . . . a new dawn of the—"*

The roar of an assault-rifle shattered the night, drowning out the thin voice. Kovac's combat dress stopped the first few slugs, but their force sent him staggering backward. Then the tracery of automatic fire reached his unprotected face, which exploded in blood. As he toppled over, half a dozen of the men he had commanded sprang forward and leveled their weapons, some at their own fellows and some at Rivera and her companions. The killer stepped between the two groups. "I am Captain Terence Fannin, and I am assuming command by authority of the ultimate high command of the Eaglemen. Yes, that's right," he continued, raising his voice over the sudden hubbub. "Major Kovac was an Eagleman too—but a traitor, along with the rest of the command cell. The rest of you can join us now, and we'll finish cleaning out this nest of alien monsters!"

He paused expectantly, leaving the alternative to joining unstated. Into the silence came the President's voice, from Kovac's radio where it lay on the ground.

"—and thus the treason of Henry Havelock has been exposed, thanks to the vigilance and patriotism of various people—including members of the Eaglemen, of which organization he was the clandestine leader, but which he betrayed just as he betrayed everyone with whom he ever dealt—"

Fannin snarled and raised a booted foot to smash the radio into silence. . . .

From behind Rivera and her fellows came the noise and glare of alien weaponry. A ragged line of Harathon security guards backed into the scene, firing back at advancing Rogovon. Fannin froze, as stunned as all the other humans.

It was all Rivera needed.

Launching herself into a flying side-kick from her deceptively passive stance, she made her body into a projectile that struck Fannin and sent him reeling back, toppling over Kovac's corpse. Then she was atop him, pulling his combat helmet back so that its chin strap choked him and then yanking it savagely sideways. The snapping sound was audible even above the alien firefight.

"Take them!" she yelled to Kovac's former command.

The spell broke and everyone present exploded into action. Three members of Havelock's clandestine cell went down in a spray of blood, chewed up by automatic fire whose volume overcame their body armor. Of the other three, Chen and Roark took on one each while they were still too stunned to use their weapons. The third cut Pirelli down with a short-range burst, then brought his assault-rifle around—slowly, or so it seemed to Roark—to bear on Rivera.

"Ada!" he yelled. At appreciably the same instant, he finished off his opponent with a chop to the Adam's apple and plunged forward.

He was almost in time.

The assault-rifle barked. Rivera wasn't wearing body armor. The slug plowed unimpeded through her upper right chest.

Roark crashed into the man who'd fired, getting him in a headlock from behind. Then Katy was there too, facing Rivera's immobilized killer, with a combat knife she'd scooped up from the fallen Fannin. She brought the knife swiftly in, low, and then up. Roark didn't consider himself inordinately impressionable, but he knew he'd be a while forgetting the man's scream.

He didn't let himself pause. He dropped the thrashing form and whirled to face the other humans. "Move, damn it! Reinforce these Lokaron!" He indicated the steadying Harathon line. After a barely perceptible hesitation, the humans obeyed. But they were rolling now, and they launched a counterattack that the Harathon could only follow.

The Rogovon fell back in disarray, and the sounds of firing diminished.

Roark turned back and knelt on the ground where Katy sat beside the now-avenged Kovac, cradling a smaller female form in her arms. A few feet away, the radio lay unheeding. As the sounds of battle died away, John Morrison's voice could be heard again.

> "—further declare the Earth First Party dissolved. It is a dead hand that has gripped our nation's heart for too long. As soon as the current state of emergency is over, I will call for a constitutional convention for the purpose of repealing all amendments that have been illegally passed by that party since its seizure of extra-constitutional power. Thus we reclaim our heritage and rekindle the flame of liberty. That flame will be a torch that lights our way into a future of vast changes but infinite promise—"

Rivera stirred. Blood bubbled on her lips as she spoke. "Hey, Katy. . . . "

"Yes, Ada?" Katy brought her tear-streaked face close, to hear the weak voice.

"That future he's talking about. . . . You and Ben make it a good one, will you? Make it worth this." Rivera coughed, and blood gushed. She convulsed and then lay still.

After a time, Roark felt a hand grasp his shoulder. It was Chen, limping but alive. "Ben, look." A tall alien form, flanked by guards, was approaching through the floodlit night.

Roark got to his feet. "What's the word, Svyatog?"

"The Eaglemen have seized the American miltary and communications nerve centers as planned—this was why your President was able to broadcast his address. And, with the help of your people, we've killed or captured the Rogovon who attempted to break out of their tower. But . . . "

"But what?"

"Remember the Rogovon shuttle that departed before the attack? We now know that Valtu'Trovon was aboard. And we know where it went. Havelock and his men massacred the Central Committee—"

"*What?*"

"—leaving Kinsella and Drummond as the only survivors. We know this because they just contacted us. They watched the Rogovon shuttle arrive, make contact with Havelock . . . and kill him, departing afterwards."

Too much was happening. Roark shook his head sluggishly. "Svyatog . . . what the hell's going on?"

"Kinsella and Drummond asked me the same question. I don't know—at least not in detail. But this much is clear: we can no longer rely on the intelligence we obtained by intercepting Havelock's conversations with Valtu. Actually, we never could. It's clear that the Rogovon have their own plan, which they found necessary to conceal from Havelock . . . presumably because it would have been unacceptable even to him And now they've eliminated him, indicating that he is no longer useful to them—which suggests in turn that the plan is about to go into effect."

"But now that the human attack on the Enclave has laid an egg, they won't have the 'political climate' you've always said they needed. Won't that make them call it off?"

"Indications are otherwise. If anything, events may have stampeded them into throwing caution to the winds and proceeding with their plan, trusting on sheer audacity."

"What is this . . . plan?" Even as he asked the question, Roark knew perfectly well that Svyatog couldn't answer it. But he needed to ask it anyway, to make a human sound against a night that had suddenly gotten colder and darker.

"Unknown. We're trying to find out by interrogating the Rogovon prisoners. But they're only underlings. And besides, there isn't time. Valtu's shuttle has departed, to rendezvous with a Rogovon strike cruiser."

"With a . . . what?"

Svyatog hesitated. "It's a warship. Very formidable even by our standards. By *your* standards, it . . . well, it could . . . " The translator mercilessly tracked Svyatog's voice as it trailed off into a miserable silence. The Lokaron straightened with an obvious effort. "At any rate, I have no more time. The Harathon cruiser *Boranthyr* is in low orbit, and it represents our only hope for countering the Rogovon. I am leaving now to join it." The alien eyes held Roark's. "You have done your part. But now I must do mine. Your world is in greater danger than you can comprehend. Farewell." Svyatog turned abruptly and strode off in the direction of the Harathon landing field.

Katy lowered that which had been Ada Rivera to the ground and stood up. The tear tracks on her cheeks were dry, and her voice was steady. "I'm going."

"Huh?" At first, Roark didn't understand. The his eyes widened. "You mean go with Svyatog? Katy, we're talking about a battle straight out of space opera! Let the Lokaron handle it. What could you do except get in the way?"

"I'm going," she repeated, with nothing in her voice to suggest that his words had even raised a ripple in her consciousness. She gave the body at her feet a last look. "I have to. I hope you'll come too, Ben. But whether you do or not, I'm going." Then, all at once, she was off at a dead run, following Svyatog's retreating form.

Roark watched her go, and his mind leaped back to another night of fire and blood, when he'd seen her for what he'd believed to be the last time.

Never again! he thought desperately. And he bounded after her, with Chen's plaintive yell receding behind him.

He'd almost caught up to Katy when they rounded the corner of a shed and saw the lean shape of Svyatog's shuttle ahead, brightly lit and humming with the noise of rising energies. Svyatog was boarding, silhouetted against a rectangle of light that was a hatch.

"Svyatog!" screamed Katy with the last of her wind, against the whine of alien machinery.

It was hard to tell, but for an instant it seemed as though Svyatog might have heard her. But then the hatch slid shut, and he was gone.

Katy staggered to a dejected, gasping halt. Roark grasped her shoulders and held her as the noise rose in pitch and the shuttle's landing jacks began to lift slowly from the concrete, actuated by its drive.

Then the hatch was open again, and a figure they could recognize despite its alienness stood against the interior light, beckoning urgently.

Without pausing for thought, they sprinted for the hatch, Katy a couple of feet in the lead.

At the last moment, with Katy reaching frantically for the outstretched Lokaron hands, Roark thought they were too late after all. But then, Svyatog and his underlings grasped her forearms and lifted her up and into the hatch, more easily than they ought to have done. Roark forced an ultimate effort out of his bursting lungs and agonized leg muscles, and covered the remaining distance just as the shuttle rose too high for the Lokaron to get a decent grip. *Yeah, too late . . .*

With a sensation that could be most nearly compared to static electricity, a force that negated weight took hold of him as he passed the barriers of an invisible field that surrounded the rising shuttle. His final, desperate leap sent him high enough to grasp a slender Lokaron hand. At that instant the shuttle began to accelerate, and he was almost snatched away into the wind. But Katy added her grip to the Lokaron's, and together they hauled him through the hatch just before automatic safety overrides slammed it shut.

The shuttle screamed off toward the cold stars.

CHAPTER FOURTEEN

An immense five-sided building in Arlington, Virginia, had once housed the U.S. armed forces' supreme headquarters. To those who had eventually formed the Earth First Party, that building had been a focus for their national self-loathing, its very name a byword for everything to which they deemed themselves morally superior. So after taking power the Party had made a great public show of demolishing it, to the accompaniment of speeches replete with mold-encrusted antimilitary boilerplate and announcements that a New Age had dawned. At the same time, with no show at all, the old Air Force facility under Cheyenne Mountain had been vastly enlarged to accommodate a high command that was more top-heavy than ever.

It was there that a gaggle of the generals and admirals who constituted that top-heaviness now stood under the leveled guns of hard-faced, combat-dressed young junior officers. They stood on the balcony of the command center, their backs to the railing that overlooked an auditoriumlike expanse of consoles,

241

whose operators had continued without a hiccup to function under the new command structure.

General Hardin attempted bluster, with a vigor that set his belly jiggling. "For the last time, Lieutenant Cady, I order you and your people to lay down your arms and place yourselves under arrest, by the authority vested in me as chairman of the Joint Chiefs of Staff!"

The Navy SEAL's face revealed no emotion, not even contempt. "You no longer hold that post, General. You have been relieved by the President."

"The President?"

"Yes, General: the President. He is, as you may recall, the commander in chief of the armed forces, under Article II, Section 2 of the Constitution—which has never been officially abrogated."

"Well, er, no ... but ... "

"But for almost thirty years the office has been held by people who exercised their authority only at the behest of the Central Committee. Well, that's over now. President Morrison has appointed a new JCS, with General Kruger as its chairman."

"Kruger?" blurted the six-star Commandant of the Marine Corps, to which Kruger belonged. "But he's only a brigadier general!" It was the highest rank to which a nonpolitical officer had been able to aspire for a generation.

"Not anymore. He's had a rather abrupt promotion to full general. You see, we're going back to the normal rank structure, in which four stars are as high as it gets in peacetime." Cady finally let his disdain show as he surveyed the absurd constellations of stars on the shoulders of these Party hacks.

Hardin turned to wheedling. "Look, Lieutenant, let's be sensible about this. We're all, uh, patriots, of course. But we can't forget to put number one first, can we? After this has all blown over and things get back to normal, I can be a help to your career. A *big* help. So let's just . . . I mean, why don't we . . . ?" His voice died a slow death, killed by what he saw in Cady's eyes.

Before the SEAL lieutenant could speak, a voice rang out from one of the consoles below, charged with urgency. "Lieutenant, the early warning system is picking up something odd. In fact . . . Oh my *God*!"

The strike cruiser *Krondathu* had approached undetected even by Lokaron instrumentation, by the simple expedient of killing its orbital velocity and letting Earth's gravity pull it inward. Now, nearing the planet and with the time for concealment past, it deployed a weapon it had spent its time at Luna's leading-Trojan point preparing in secret.

From fore to aft along the great ship's ventral spine, a series of superconducting magnetic coils had been rigged—the physical manifestation of a colossal mass driver, most of which lay in domains of pure force. At the instant *Krondathu* reached a computer-decreed point in its trajectory, titanic banks of superconductor loops released their hoarded energy. A carefully reshaped nickel-iron asteroid flashed along that line of coils, accelerated to a velocity which, piled atop *Krondathu*'s, sent it curving down toward Earth. Presently, it entered the outer reaches of the atmosphere and began to glow from the friction that would burn most of it away. Most . . . but not all.

"Do something!" screamed General Hardin.

But it was already apparent that nothing could be done. That projectile's preposterous velocity made it impossible for America's antiballistic defenses—all surface-based, of course—to even try to stop it or deflect it. Indeed, there had just barely been time for the computers to project its impact point.

"Shut up!" Cady snapped, dropping all pretense of respect for Hardin's rank. "That uniform you're wearing is supposed to mean you're prepared to die in the defense of your country. Well, you're about to get the opportunity to be worthy of it. Maybe no one will ever know how you died—but try to do it right!"

It was all he had time to say. And it may be that, in the instant they had left, Hardin met his eyes silently and stood a little straighter.

To an outside observer—had any such observer lived to tell about it—a solid bar of light, eye-hurtingly intense in the predawn darkness, speared the Earth at Cheyenne Mountain. But there would have been barely enough time for that image to register, before the eye that had seen it was burned out forever by a fireball of inconceivable energy-exchange. Then the fireball itself was only a rapidly fading glow inside a cloud of dust that boiled outward and mushroomed upward.

In short, that hypothetical observer might well have thought himself in the presence of a nuclear detonation. But Cheyenne Mountain was designed to withstand nukes—it might even have survived one placed with the precision of Lokaron computers programmed with the data Henry Havelock had supplied. This multiton mass of metal and rock smashed through the Earth's crust, shattering by concussion those portions of the base it didn't obliterate outright, and releasing a flow of magma which erased all evidence that there had ever been any work of Man in this place.

❖   ❖   ❖

Too stunned for nausea, Roark and Katy stared at a screen displaying the image—downloaded from a satellite in low orbit—of America's central Rocky Mountains region. Infrared enhancement stripped away the veil of night, revealing the violation of their world.

"A deep-penetrator kinetic weapon," Svyatog's translated voice explained from behind them. "Useful for taking out hardened targets whose location is precisely known."

They barely heard him as they watched the expanding ring of dust move rapidly outward from the glowing ember where Cheyenne Mountain had been, like a ripple from a pebble hurled into a pond.

"First the dinosaurs," Katy whispered, "and now us."

"Scarcely." The translator reproduced Svyatog's attempt at a reassuring tone. "As I indicated, this is a precision weapon, depending on its extreme velocity rather than its mass. It is not to be compared to the kind of ecologically catastrophic asteroid impact that occurred sixty-five million of your years ago."

From the bottom of a well of nightmare, Roark heard his own mechanical voice. "Still, I'll bet a bunch of them could create something just like nuclear winter."

"Undeniably. But I am confident that the Rogovon don't intend to employ them in such numbers. It would be a singularly inefficient approach, when it would be much simpler to . . . " Svyatog stopped awkwardly. He looked uncannily similar to a human who realized he'd put his foot in it.

The cruiser's captain provided a merciful interruption. "Factor, *Krondathu* and the Rogovon shuttle are making rendezvous."

Svyatog gave the equivalent of a curt nod. The

Lokaron lacked the naval tradition that made a ship's captain its absolute despot. And although the military was the province of the gevahon pseudogovernments, there was no question in anybody's mind as to who was in charge when a hovah bigwig like Svyatog was aboard—especially when the hovah in question was Hov-Korth. "Come," he said, leading the two humans to the holo tank.

The control room they crossed wasn't too large. *Boranthyr* was, Roark thought, probably the equivalent of a light cruiser in human wet-navy parlance, though she was the largest Harathon warship in the Solar System. But her navigational holo tank was quite up to displaying the situation in which they found themselves.

In the center of the circular well hung a small blue marble representing Earth. Near the outer rim, at twelve o'clock (Roark automatically superimposed a clock face on the display) and creeping slowly counterclockwise was a smaller bone-white one: Luna. Sixty degrees "ahead" of it, at ten o'clock, a purple symbol denoted the leading-Trojan point from which *Krondathu* had departed. A trail of little green dots marked the strike cruiser's course, curving inward toward the center and terminating with the green arrowhead of *Krondathu*'s current position, at about six thirty and halfway in. A red arrowhead marked their own ship, accompanied by two little diamonds of the same color that denoted the Harathon picket vessels that had been available in orbit—capable of obliterating any merchant ship, but useless in a clash of real warships. Their course, commencing in a low orbit around the blue Earth symbol at eleven o'clock and sweeping outward around the planet to the left, had now brought them to a position at about the same bearing from

Earth as *Krondathu* but well inward. Ahead of the two ships, little hollow circles of green and red showed their projected courses. Those courses converged.

The important thing to remember, Roark told himself, was that the Lokaron space-drive wasn't magic. It cheated Newton and enabled ships to accelerate for lengths of time undreamed-of by human spacecraft designers, but it didn't exempt them from gravity and inertia. They had to follow trajectories (albeit breathtakingly fast ones) subject to the same basic laws . . . like the one along which *Boranthyr* was now boosting.

They'd rendezvoused with her after their manic departure from the Enclave, and then immediately accelerated outward into an orbit intended to intersect the incoming *Krondathu*'s course. The Rogovon shuttle had followed such an orbit earlier, and now they watched the shuttle's very small green dot mate with the larger arrowhead of the same color, and vanish.

"Captain," Svyatog ordered, "have communications raise *Krondathu*. I want to speak to Valtu'Trovon as soon as he's available."

It seemed longer than the couple of minutes it actually took before Valtu's green face appeared on the com screen. Roark and Katy stood aside from the pickup and listened as Svyatog's translator pendant interpreted Valtu's side of the conversation for them as well as his own.

"Ah, Svyatog," Valtu began. He looked rushed, as though he'd hastened from his just-docked shuttle to answer the unexpected hail, but he attempted urbanity. "I can't tell you how happy I am that you got away from the Enclave in time! I myself was fortunate in having departed on routine business shortly before the natives attacked. Appalling! As soon as I heard the news I ordered *Krondathu* to Earth to help with rescue operations and . . . whatever else seems indicated."

Against his will, Roark found himself admiring Valtu's sheer chutzpah. Even more impressive was Svyatog's smooth reply. "Thank you for your concern, Commissioner. But no rescue will be necessary. The situation at the Enclave is now under control—due in no small part, I believe, to the Gev-Rogov security personnel, whose response to the crisis was remarkable. Indeed, anyone who didn't know better would have thought they'd had forewarning."

It took about one-third of a second for the radio waves to wing their way from *Boranthyr* to *Krondathu* and back. Valtu's pause was just a trifle longer than that could account for. "Ah. Well. As you are aware, we Rogovon have for some time taken the potential threat from these natives more seriously than have certain others."

"Like Gev-Harath?"

"I was thinking more in terms of decadent Gev-Lokarath and infantile Gev-Tizath. But . . . well, admit it, Svyatog: events have proven us right, and you wrong! These humans, like all natives, are nothing more than dangerous animals! Their relative technological sophistication doesn't change this—it merely makes them more dangerous. We of Gev-Rogov recognize this reality, and have the means at hand to deal with the crisis your fatuity has created."

"Such as the kinetic weapon you've just used on the military headquarters of the principal human power?"

"Yes! The American government is obviously implicated in what has occurred, and must therefore be regarded as an enemy. We have prevented it from coordinating any military action against us—an entirely legitimate precaution." Valtu inflated himself in a vaguely toadlike way, and it occurred to Roark that this was the first time he'd seen Lokaron sanctimoniousness. "We feel we're acting on behalf of all Lokaron, not just ourselves."

Svyatog gave to the clicking sound of Lokaron laughter a harshness Roark had never heard before. "Enough of this farce! We're well aware that you engineered the attack on the Enclave through your human agent Havelock, precisely for the purpose of justifying the coup you've now set in motion. But the attack has failed, thanks to two humans in my service." He motioned Roark and Katy forward into the pickup. "All the resident commissioners now recognize the truth. They will support Gev-Harath in demanding sanctions for this attempt to monopolize the human market in violation of intergevahon agreements. Gev-Rogov will stand alone."

For a moment, Roark thought Valtu was still trying to brazen it out . . . but it was only the communications delay. At first the alien face merely went expressionless. Then its green skin began to darken, and the almost nonexistent lips drew back to reveal the serrated ridges which chewed meat. And Roark, who'd fancied that he had gotten used to the Lokaron, felt a chill slide along his back.

"So be it, Svyatog." All pretense was gone from the strangely metallic Rogovon voice. "As for Gev-Rogov standing alone, when has it ever been otherwise? But I must tell you that you're wrong about a couple of other things. First of all, our aim isn't to 'monopolize' this world. We're not interested in it as a market, which is how your limited mind has always seen it, but as a *colony*. The rest of you have never really appreciated Earth's potential. We do, because it's like our world, only better. You might say it's like our world *should* have been. It's a simple matter of—" (the translator, for the first time in Roark's experience, simply went silent for the space of a couple of words, defeated) "—as anyone with any perceptiveness can intuitively grasp. Earth is the natural second home of the Rogovon subspecies, the living space where we can grow to our full potential and assume the primacy to which—" (the same two Rogovon words, and the same brief silence from the translator) "—entitles us."

"The present inhabitants might disagree." Beneath Svyatog's dryness, Roark could tell he was shaken. *I keep forgetting how different the various Lokaron subspecies are from each other. Maybe the Rogovon concept—religious, philosophical, whatever—that stopped the Harathon-programmed translator cold is as alien to him as it is to me.*

Valtu gave the two humans a look whose contempt transcended cultures and worlds. "Earth is wasted on these vermin. Actually, the entire ecology of which they are a part is merely a bothersome irrelevance to this world's true destiny. After this ship assumes low orbit, we will neutron-bomb the planet down to about a meter's depth. Later, it will be seeded, using biological packages from the Rogovon homeworld."

"You're mad! The gevahon you've already antagonized will never stand for this. We're dealing with a living world—a cosmic rarity, as we all know—and, what's even rarer, a sentient race!"

"I've never understood why you're so attached to them, Svyatog. Perhaps you could use these two as breeding stock to reestablish their species somewhere else . . . except, of course, for the *second* thing you were wrong about. You see, there will be no coalition to demand sanctions against us, because there will be no witnesses. All the gevahon will be saddened to learn that the humans struck so cleverly as to destroy all Lokaron on the planet and in orbit, leaving only *Krondathu* to exact vengeance."

"You *are* insane, Valtu! No one will believe this story!" Svyatog's translated voice held a new dimension of alarm. *Yeah*, Roark thought, *this is different. We're talking Lokaron lives now.* But his sardonicism lasted only an instant. *Come on, can you really blame him? Especially when one of those Lokaron lives happens to be his own?*

"Oh, they'll suspect. But will anyone go to war over a suspicion? I doubt it."

"It will be more than mere suspicion! This ship will bear the word that you've murdered all the Lokaron in this system."

"If you examine the relative vectors of your ship and ours, you will find that there is no way you can escape. My computer analysis assures me of this; otherwise . . . well, surely you don't imagine I would have told you all this. And in the time I've kept you talking, it has grown even less possible." Once again, Valtu's face wore that disturbingly predatory look. Like the Cheshire cat's smile, it seemed to linger after he broke the connection and the screen went blank.

The two humans stared at Svyatog, waiting for him to say something that would awaken them from this evil dream. He showed no sign of noticing. His aspect was one which they'd never seen before, and which discouraged any inclination they might have felt to interrupt his introspection. Finally, he straightened up and addressed the captain. His words were as decisive as ever, but even the translator conveyed a certain hollowness in his tone. "Captain, calculate a course

change which will take us far enough from this
system's sun to engage our transition engine. Assume
the highest acceleration endurable by personnel, and
ignore all other considerations."

"Yes, sir. But . . . " The captain's eyes went to the
holo tank, where *Krondathu*'s dark-green arrowhead
pursued its Earthward course.

"*All* other considerations, Captain!"

"Yes, sir." The captain busied himself, and presently the ululation of a high-gee warning reverberated through the ship.

"Uh, Svyatog," Roark ventured as they all strapped
themselves into acceleration couches. "What, exactly,
is happening?"

"Our one advantage," Svyatog began, speaking as
much to himself as to the humans, "is that this is
a military ship, with its own integral transition
engine—the only such ship in this system other
than *Krondathu*. Thus we need not shape a course
for Gev-Harath's transition gate; we can enter
overspace anywhere beyond a certain distance from
the local sun. So we are, of necessity, Valtu's first
priority—"

Conversation ceased as the g-forces pressed them
down into their couches.

Aboard *Krondathu*, Valtu'Trovon was paralleling
Svyatog's thoughts closely as he watched *Boranthyr*'s
course change in his own holo tank.

"So," he rumbled, "they're actually trying it." He
didn't deign to notice the look that Wersov'Vrahn
doubtless thought was surreptitious. He knew the
underling wouldn't dare criticize him openly for
telling Svyatog his real aim. *Nor should he*, came
the defensive thought. *It was a harmless bit of
self-indulgence on my part*. "Wersov," he said

aloud, "tell the captain to alter course to overhaul
Boranthyr."

"Yes, sir." Wersov passed the order on instantly.
Then, as they lay in their acceleration couches, he
spoke in tones of diffident inquiry. "Ah, sir, this will
draw us away from Earth, greatly delaying the
commencement of—"

"Of course, you idiot! That can wait. Nobody still
in the Enclave is going anywhere. They'll still be
there when we finally execute the bombardment."
One of whose neutron bombs, Valtu reminded
himself, was due to burst directly above the Enclave.
"And all the merchant ships and pickets can only get
out through the transition gates, which are now
guarded by *our* pickets. *Boranthyr* is our only worry.
Svyatog knows that, and he's using it in a desperate
attempt to draw us after him, in hope of a miracle."

Valtu studied the holographically projected miniature of the tank's display that floated before his eyes.
Boranthyr's boost was resulting in a new trajectory,
no longer curving outward from Earth to meet *Krondathu* but lining outward in a flat hyperbola. *Krondathu* was now following an equally flat intercept
course.

What, he wondered, *does Svyatog hope to gain?*
It was as he'd told Wersov: they could deal with
Earth, including the Enclave, at their leisure after
disposing of *Boranthyr*.

As we will *dispose of it! That ship couldn't get
away even if it could match our acceleration.* The
chief limitation on both ships' ability to pull sustained
gees was crew endurance . . . which was less limiting
for the Rogovon, bred for a planet of very nearly
Earthlike gravity. *And their firepower is inferior to
ours, even counting those two pathetic pickets
Svyatog has with him.*

So, Valtu asked himself once more, *what does he hope to gain?*

Roark was wondering much the same thing as he lay on his acceleration couch in *Boranthyr's* control room. He turned his head—carefully but without undue hazard under an acceleration of 1.44 G—to face Svyatog. "Why are we keeping the pickets with us? They don't mount transition engines, do they?"

Svyatog replied with some difficulty. This was twice his normal gees for him, and he wasn't a trained military spacer. Only the time he'd spent adjusting to Earth's gravity enabled him to endure it on an extended basis. "No. The pickets, like civilian ships, have to use the transition gate. But it's pointless to send them there. The Rogovon must have it covered, to keep everyone bottled in this system."

"But why not detach them as decoys to get *Krondathu* off our backs?"

"It wouldn't work. Valtu knows as well as I do that they can't escape. Only this ship can. So he'll pursue us until he catches us . . . which he will. And then we'll need every quantum of advantage we can possibly muster."

"But Svyatog," Katy protested, "you keep talking as though this ship was hopelessly outmatched. Surely that can't be so! I mean . . . well . . . " She gave a vague gesture that encompassed the control room around them and the ship around it. Roark understood. He, too, had stared through the shuttle's viewports, openmouthed, as they'd rendezvoused with the apotheosis of transcendent engineering that was *Boranthyr.*

Svyatog also understood. With great caution, he turned his head around on a neck that had much the same vulnerabilities as a human one, until he

could meet Katy's eyes. "You must understand that
this ship, while a perfectly well-designed and up-to-
date example of its class, is nothing special as
warships go. In point of fact, it is the smallest class
that mounts transition engines for independent
operations. There's never been any need for anything
larger in this system, where we never expected to
have to fight any real battles. It was only stationed
here to . . . to . . . "

"Show the flag?" suggested Roark.

"Yes," agreed Svyatog after a brief pause. He
activated a holographically projected display in front
of them. They recognized its outlines from what
they'd glimpsed through the shuttle's ports. "This is
a schematic of *Boranthyr.*" Another glowing display
joined the first in midair. "And this is *Krondathu.*"

"Uh . . . are these to the same scale?" Katy sounded
faintly ill.

"Svyatog," Roark began hesitantly, "I know there
isn't time to cover all the technical details, but can
you give us some notion of how a space battle is
fought? It's a little outside our experience. Are we
talking about kinetic-kill weapons like the one the
Rogovon just used on . . . " His voice trailed off, and
he gestured "down" toward the receding Earth.

"No. Those are for fixed planetary targets. For
interspacecraft combat, nothing that strikes more
slowly than light will serve." As the Lokar spoke,
color-coded indicators awoke within the three-
dimensional displays at his mental command, denoting the weapon systems of which he spoke—more
of them, and often larger ones, in *Krondathu.* "The
basic offensive weapons are lasers. For longer-range
engagement, missiles are used. But—"

The Lokaron equivalent of "general quarters"
sounded, reverberating through *Boranthyr's* hull. In

the tactical display, tiny green dots separated themselves from *Krondathu* and raced ahead.

"It appears," Svyatog said calmly, "that we're now within range of the missiles I was just discussing. Their drives are overpowered, quickly burning themselves out to produce extreme accelerations."

"You ain't just whistlin' Dixie," Roark murmured. With alarming speed, the green dots closed the range on the red icon that symbolized, among other things, his and Katy's bodies. But Svyatog remained composed. Then a series of commands rang out, indicator lights flashed like Christmas decorations . . . and, fractional seconds later, the green dots began going out.

"It is a tactical truism," Svyatog resumed, "that shipboard laser installations, using artificial gravity-based techniques to enhance their range, can engage missiles before those missiles' bomb-pumped X-ray lasers can be employed."

But one dot kept homing in relentlessly. Roark began to see in Svyatog what he'd come to recognize as the signs of fraying calm. When the dot burst into a cascade of green, he didn't bother to ask what it meant.

Alarms sounded, more indicator lights flashed . . . and everything was as before save for a palpable air of relief in the control room. The two humans gave Svyatog questioning looks.

"The deflection shields held," the Lokar explained. "They, too, depend on the space-distorting properties of artificial gravity. Unless overloaded by an overwhelming attack, they make precise targeting solutions difficult. For that reason, ships try to close to shorter ranges. They also employ fighter craft that seek to get closer still and perform precision strikes." Rows of launching cradles appeared in the holograms. As usual,

there were more in *Krondathu* than in *Boranthyr.*
"These fighters also have high-powered, short-duration
drives—though not as extreme in either respect as the
missiles. They have crews of two, as well as the highly
sophisticated navigation computers necessary for
piloting at extreme speeds over relatively short
distances. Indeed, the living crew members' functions
are largely concerned with weapons delivery."

"How can the crews—especially Harathon crews—
stand that kind of high acceleration?" asked Katy.

"They are specially picked and trained people. But
you have correctly pinpointed a limiting factor.
Crewless, fully computer-controlled fighters have
been tried, with unsatisfactory results."

"Doesn't that give the Rogovon an advantage?"

"To a certain extent. But our defensive fire-control
computers take into account the g-forces the Rogovon
can stand—as theirs do those that *our* personnel can
stand. It's not so much a matter of the absolute
accelerations involved as it is of the element of
surprise, or lack of it."

There seemed nothing more to be said as the
clocks crept inexorably on and *Krondathu* drew
abreast of its prey. *Boranthyr*'s captain tried a salvo
of missiles, but to no one's surprise they perished
without effect. Next he tried evasive course changes,
but *Krondathu*'s computer matched them effortlessly.
Svyatog grew more and more visibly tense. *He's not
a military officer,* Roark reminded himself. *Still, a
little of the old stiff upper lip, or whatever, would
do wonders for my morale.*

Then, abruptly, things began to happen. Alarms
gave tongue, the light show resumed on the readout
boards, and the tactical display became more crowded as the ships' icons gave birth to litters of smaller
ones: fighters and then missiles.

Roark and Katy made eye contact. No words were needed. They were united in their helplessness, unable to do anything but represent, in some fashion, the now-distant blue world whose fate was being decided by aliens.

They watched as the ships poured laser energy into each other's deflection shields, which shed it. They watched as the two pickets peeled off and flung themselves at the Brobdingnagian strike cruiser, only to be contemptuously speared by lasers which killed one and sent the other limping off. They watched as the fighters worked their way inward, some dying and others avoiding the defensive laser fire by maneuvers and boost variations the tactical display was too large-scale to show.

Then *Boranthyr*'s deflection shields began to flicker and fail, the ship began to take physical hits, and the battle was no longer just an extremely high-tech video game with colored lights crawling prettily around the holo tank.

Boranthyr shuddered and bucked like an abused animal as segments of hull vaporized explosively. They'd felt sickening tugs and shifts from the evasive maneuvers; these now paled in comparison to the shock waves that flung them against the restraints of their crash couches.

The control room, buried deep in the ship's bowels, wasn't hit. But the incalculable tons of metal and composites wrapped around it couldn't keep out the noise, and acrid smoke began to seep in through the vents.

Until I get to hell, thought Roark, stunned and nauseated, *this will do.* He spared a glance for the schematic of the ship. His training as an employee in the Enclave enabled him to take a stab at reading the legends that accompanied all those stroboscopically flashing scarlet indicators. Much of the vocabulary and symbology was beyond him. But he had a pretty good idea he was watching *Boranthyr* die.

The worst of it was the sense of passive uselessness. *These aliens are defending my world, and there's not a damned thing I can do—except, I suppose, die with them, which it looks like I'll be doing soon enough. I'm not even as uncomfortable as they are, because I can handle g-forces better—*

The idea exploded in his brain.

"Svyatog!" he yelled above the cacophony, not pausing to think it through because there was no time. He pointed at the schematic, indicating a row of the launch cradle symbols. "Those fighters haven't been launched."

"No. It is established tactical doctrine to hold some of them in reserve . . . although, in this case, the captain considered launching the ship's entire complement at the outset, due to—"

"Never mind that!" He couldn't read the Lokar's expression, but Katy looked shocked at the brusque interruption. "Listen: let me take one of them out!"

"What did you say?" Katy's voice rose to an incredulous squawk.

"But you don't know how!" Svyatog's words came out in a less flabbergasted way than his body language suggested they should have. Roark suspected a case of translator overload. "You have no training!"

"No, but I was an employee in the Enclave, which means I'm familiar with your neural induction headbands. I'll bet the fighter pilots use them, to interface directly with the controls."

"But surely you remember, from that very experience, the inherent limitations of the technology."

"That's right!" Katy's voice held an urgency just

short of panic. "It won't magically turn you into some kind of top gun fighter pilot!"

"It won't have to. You heard Svyatog: a fighter practically flies itself. The so-called pilot and copilot are there to give it general directives—and, once it's gotten in close enough, to ram the weapons down the enemy's throat and cut loose." Roark turned back to the stupefied-looking Lokar. "Svyatog, I may not be a space pilot, but I *do* know weapons. All right—not *these* weapons. But I've got the trained reflexes, the . . . mind-set. That ought to provide a foundation for the neurally fed information to build on. Anyway, that was how old Koebel explained it to us."

Svyatog seemed to pull himself together. He took advantage of a lull in the noise to give Roark a steady regard. "Even assuming that you could do this, we already have fighter pilots. Professional ones. What would be the purpose of this exercise in quixotry?"

"You said it yourself: fighter-versus-ship combat is a guessing game in which the ships have the advantage of knowing how much acceleration the fighter pilots can handle. The Rogovon fire-control computers are programmed with the figures for Harathon pilots. But I can throw a monkey wrench into the works! I can gun a fighter faster than they think is possible, without passing out. I'll have a better chance than your professionals of living long enough to get in close."

Svyatog opened his mouth, but then closed it, and nothing came from the translator. He tried again, and this time his words held anger. "No! This is ludicrous! What about command-and-control? How will you be able to understand orders from this ship's fighter-coordination center? No, I cannot permit—"

The din of tearing metal bellowed through the ship, followed closely by a concussion that flung them sideways, and the telltale boards went wild. A new alarm began whooping, and Roark recognized the "abandon ship" signal.

He met the slit-pupiled alien eyes and spoke as quietly as conditions permitted. "I don't think you have anything to lose, Svyatog. And as for command-and-control . . . it looks like this ship's fighters are going to be on their own pretty soon."

Their eye contact held for a moment longer, as the control room crew hastily departed after turning their functions over to the computers that could, unaided, continue to fight the ship for a little while. They were almost the only ones left when Svyatog finally spoke briskly. "Come! We must get to the lifeboats." He pointed to the still-functioning sche-matic, indicating their assigned life craft and the flashing dotted route that led to it.

That route led past the reserve fighters' launch cradles, which blinked their readiness.

They hurried along the passageways, past Lokaron crew members too rushed to spare Roark and Katy more than a passing glance. Presently they were abreast the fighter bays.

"This way," said Svyatog, gesturing them down a side corridor.

They found themselves on a kind of mezzanine, overlooking a row of cradled fighters. Their entry created a double sensation among the personnel crewing the control consoles—first at the sight of the humans, and second (and more profoundly) at the recognition of Svyatog. There was a quick, hushed colloquy between Svyatog and the individual in charge. Then Svyatog addressed Roark.

"I didn't even bother asking the captain, knowing

what his response would be. But the fighter-control officer here is descended from a long line of Hov-Korth retainers. He has accepted my authority in this matter. He will get you secured in a fighter."

"What about you?" asked Katy in a small voice—the first sound she'd made in a while.

"You and I will continue on to the lifeboat."

"What's the use? Where will it go?"

"Remember, one of our picket craft still survives. It will retrieve this ship's survivors."

"After which *Krondathu* will vaporize it!"

"Perhaps. Or perhaps simply leave it to wander this system until its life-support is exhausted, knowing it can't escape through the transition gate. But what other choice have we? And we won't even have that choice if we don't hurry. Come!"

"No. I'm going with Ben."

"*What?!*" Svyatog's translator and Roark's voicebox formed the word in unison.

"The fighters have a crew of two, and I assume there must be a reason for it. Ben will need a copilot—one with human acceleration tolerance, or the whole thing is pointless. And I'm precisely as qualified as he is: zero equals zero."

"But . . . but . . . " The translator managed a highly creditable stammer.

"Forget it, Svyatog," Roark said resignedly. "Her mind's made up. Believe me—I know."

"You humans are mad." The slit-pupiled eyes flicked from one of them to the other and back again, and they held an expression that neither of them had ever seen in Lokaron eyes. "Simply mad," Svyatog repeated. Then he was off, leading the way down a ladder to the level where the fighters waited.

A technician got them situated, as Svyatog's

pendant provided translation. The side-by-side acceleration couches were, as usual, not to human proportions; but they were designed ergonomically to adjust to occupants varying through the entire Lokaron range. Likewise the headbands were flexible enough to adjust, more or less, to human crania. There was the usual lack of perceptible sensation when those headbands were activated.

The technician finished his hurried instructions and departed. Svyatog lingered. "As soon as I've left, give a mental signal and the controller will launch you. After that . . . "

The ship shuddered under them. "Get your blue butt out of here, Svyatog!" Roark started to utter some bravado of the "see you later" variety, but thought better of it. Svyatog also seemed to stop himself short of saying something. He turned away and was gone. The cockpit clamshelled shut around them, and they were alone in a world of deceptively simple-looking alien technology.

"Svyatog's right, you know," Roark grumbled. "We're out of our fucking minds." Even as he spoke, he thought a command. The curving canopy that had closed over them became a receiver for outside visual pickups, and seemed to vanish. Their eyes told them they were sitting in an open cockpit, gazing down the launch tunnel at a small circle of star-studded blackness.

At Roark's next thought, they were pressed back into their cushioned seats. The tunnel's walls flashed past in a blur and the fighter shot out into infinity. Astern, *Boranthyr* was a toy damaged by a petulant child, dwindling into the distance.

Valtu glared at the icon of *Boranthyr*. That ship had done more damage than it should have. But now

it was blinking in the holo tank, indicating a ship
clearly abandoned and under computer control.

"Tell the captain to finish it," he grated.

The command was superfluous. Even as he and
Wersov watched, the icon flickered and went out.
Krondathu's was the sole cruiser-sized icon in a
display consisting otherwise of the damaged Harathon
picket and the midgelike swarms of fighters.

"Recover our fighters." It was another order that
Wersov quietly did not pass on. He was a former
military officer, an area of expertise which helped
make him valuable to Valtu, and he knew the captain
would have found the command's obviousness insult-
ing. At any rate, *Krondathu*'s fighters were already
on the way back to their mother ship. There was
nothing more for them to do. The English word the
translator programs had assigned to them was actually
somewhat deceptive; they weren't intended to fight
others of their own class. Instead, their targeting
systems were designed with large ships in mind. The
surviving enemy fighters would be taken care of by
the ship's defensive lasers, or else to left to lifesystem
failure.

Wersov was about to suggest the latter, but the
final squadron *Boranthyr* had launched continued,
irritatingly and irrationally, to press the attack.

"Kill those insects," Valtu ordered.

This time Wersov did transmit the command. But
then he paused, studied the display, and made a
suggestion. "If you'll note, sir, the last fighter they
launched, shortly before *Boranthyr*'s destruction, is
behaving a little oddly . . . hesitantly, one might say,
as though there's something wrong with its flight
controls. I suggest we concentrate on the others, as
that one probably presents the least threat."

"Very well," Valtu acceded. This was, after all,

Wersov's field. The order was passed, and the fighters began to die.

Valtu turned away from the display, bored. "I'm going to my quarters. Tell the captain there's no hurry after we finish the fighters; we'll let the picket finish hauling in the survivors before obliterating it. Then we'll return to Earth and get on with the main business."

A little display screen to Roark's left showed the position of the fighter and its squadron mates. Only two of those blips—their own and one other—still flew.

They were still well behind the other fighter. Partly this was because Roark's mental commands, despite the training he'd received in the Enclave, still had an awkward and tentative quality. But mostly it was intentional.

"Can't we apply some more thrust?" asked Katy, who had watched in horror as the rest of the squadron had perished. So far, they were quite comfortable. "Take some of the heat off that last fighter?"

"No." Roark struggled to hold his mental concentration as he spoke. "Remember what we decided. Our ability to pour on more boost than they think is possible is our only advantage. We've got to hold it in reserve until the decisive moment."

As he spoke, the other blip went out. They were alone in the squadron display.

"I think that moment is here, Ben."

They spared the time to meet each other's eyes. Then Roark settled into his acceleration couch as comfortably as possible. "Okay. Hang on tight."

Using all the mental discipline he'd learned, he commanded the fighter to accelerate to seven Harath-Asor gravities. He remembered to repeat for verification, thus overriding the automatic safety cutouts.

The fighter plunged ahead.

Wersov stared in horror as the holo tank reported impossibility.

"Get Valtu back up here!" he yelled. "And kill that fighter!"

Krondathu's defensive systems tried to obey. Lasers stabbed through empty space where computer analysis told them a Harathon-crewed fighter was supposed to be.

Roark and Katy had agreed on the maximum acceleration under which they could function, based on things they'd read. Now, Roark wasn't so sure. *You're not a young hotshot anymore,* he gibed at himself as he felt the flesh of his face sag sideways. *Actually . . . was I ever a young hotshot?*

But, he told himself firmly, five Earth gravities were perfectly acceptable for a fairly extended period, if one was in good health. Miserably uncomfortable as he was, he wouldn't pass out.

He stole a glance at Katy. She seemed to be doing all right. He recalled reading that women held up well under high g-forces. Still . . . *If she can do it, I can do it!* Idiotic though it was, the thought was useful.

He dragged his eyeballs away to study the two displays that, for now, made up the sum total of his existence: the tactical one that showed their approach to *Krondathu;* and the schematic of the enemy ship which, while less detailed than the one they'd studied in *Boranthyr's* now-vaporized control room, showed the crucial points which were the targets for close-in fighter attacks.

"What is this?" bellowed Valtu as he strode, disheveled, up to the holo tank.

"That enemy fighter, sir—the one we decided to leave for last," Wersov explained, his usual equanimity in abeyance. "We're experiencing difficulty stopping it because—"

"Well, use all laser armament against it, including the ship-to-ship ones. Yes, I know, it's not what they're designed for. But there's such a thing as a lucky hit." He looked at the display, but lacked the background to interpret everything in it. All he saw was the one fighter icon left, pathetic in its aloneness. "What was I called up here for, Wersov? Does a strike cruiser need my personal supervision to deal with one miserable fighter? One which *you* suggested we ignore?"

"Our targeting solutions have been thrown off by this fighter's accelerations, sir. Our data indicate that Harathon crews should have lost consciousness, at least."

"Then something is obviously wrong with your computer models! Tell the captain to—" Valtu stopped as, belatedly, Wersov's precise wording registered: *Harathon crews*. And he recalled the two humans who'd stood beside Svyatog in *Boranthyr*'s control room.

"No," he said, too low for Wersov to hear, and stared at that onward-hurtling blip. "It isn't possible."

Krondathu wasn't visible to the naked eye, of course. But when Roark willed the sensors to light amplification, a little gleam of reflected sun shone dead ahead.

He'd told the fighter to attempt a random set of evasive maneuvers, and the variable g-forces were sickening. But, he told himself, it wouldn't last. Soon they'd begin their attack run.

"Katy," he said with difficulty, "at the last ten seconds I'm going to pile on a couple more G's. Do you think you can take it?"

"Sure," she replied with more confidence than she felt. "Question is, will you have enough blood in your brain to do the targeting?"

"I think so. The computer does most of it. I just tell it where I want the stuff delivered. And I've pretty much got that worked out. So—"

It was only a glancing, fleeting brush by a laser pulse from *Krondathu*. But Roark's console exploded in a shower of electric sparks as the fighter lurched to starboard, buffeting them against their enclosing harness. Then a secondary explosion shook the little craft.

Katy shook her head to clear it, then looked at Roark. He wasn't moving, and the flesh of face and right hand she could see were blackened.

She forcibly emptied her mind of all save its neuroelectronic communion with the fighter, letting that fighter become her body and forgetting she had another one—a body of vulnerable flesh and pain-transmitting nerves. She ran a diagnostic check: the drive still functioned, as did her controls and most of the weapon systems. It was enough. She commanded more thrust, and the universe began to darken around the periphery of her vision. It was so hard to concentrate. . . .

Yes! *Krondathu* was a visible spark of reflected sunlight up ahead. It grew with impossible rapidity, hurtling at her.

The computer knew the details, the precise targets Roark had programmed onto the schematic. She had only to think the command at the precise time, a command that boiled down to *kill*.

A trio of small missiles leaped ahead, their tiny drives destroying themselves to produce a brief acceleration of space-distorting intensity and a velocity that was a significant fraction of light's.

Only then did Katy let an extraneous thought enter her mind: the dying face of Ada Rivera. She sent that thought out with the missiles, on wings of vengeance.

A defensive laser managed to catch one of those missiles, blasting it off course. The deflection shields sent another veering away. But the third impacted at the precise ninety-degree angle at which the shields were useless.

The warhead was small, and vacuum does not transmit shock waves. But this was, in effect, a contact nuclear explosion.

In Katy's fading vision, the oncoming *Krondathu* vanished in a universe-filling fireball that blew out the visual pickups and left her in darkness before her eyesight could be permanently destroyed.

Then the expanding wave front of gas, dust and occasional chunks of debris reached the fighter, sending it into a mad tumble and flinging its occupants about with a violence that was beyond the crash couches' ability to protect them. Katy's consciousness mercifully fled. Roark's was already gone.

Curving metal segments slid up from the deck and down from the overhead and clamped together, enclosing the two badly damaged humans in escape pods which the dying fighter ejected into space as its final act.

Those pods' homing beacons were still feebly broadcasting, and their lifesystems still barely functioning, when the Harathon picket finally found them. The search would have long since been terminated, save that a certain very high Hov-Korth executive would not permit it.

EPILOGUE

Svyatog'Korth had been to Earth a number of times over the years, but this was his first visit in a while—he wasn't getting any younger, and he no longer traveled as much on hovah business. And even in his salad days he'd never seen this particular part of the planet, unless one counted the virtual tours of it that he'd always enjoyed so much.

But that had been before the Cheyenne Mountain strike. For a long time thereafter he'd shied away from viewing that which his species—to which the Rogovon did, after all, belong—had wrought. But by now this part of North America had recovered, and the snow-capped peaks of the Rockies shone in the sun over lower slopes clothed in pine forests over which hawks circled, seemingly undisturbed by his air-car. He had been honest when he'd given his evaluation of the strike's ecological impact to the pair he was now going to visit. Besides, this region— *Colorado* was the name of the political subdivision— wasn't in the immediate neighborhood of the stricken area.

A stunning valley opened out below the air-car, reigned over by a lordly peak and graced by a gleaming upland lake, while in the distance a town could be glimpsed. His implanted data-retrieval resources spoke of *Maroon Bells/Snowmass Wilderness Area* and *Aspen*. The air-car left them behind and began to lose altitude as it approached its destination.

Svyatog, with little to do in the way of piloting the craft, continued to examine his memories. *Yes, this hemisphere was in autumn then, too—thirty-seven autumns ago, when it all began.* But that had been a very different autumn, on this continent's eastern edge, where the leaves turned fire-colored as they died. Here, the trees that had given their name to the town wore soft gold raiment.

There were many of those trees clustered at the feet of the mountain he was approaching, with snow-dusted pines above them, and rough-hewn crags piled above those. It was the kind of mountain Harath-Asor hadn't known since aeons before it had felt its first Lokaron foot. *But this is a younger world,* Svyatog reminded himself. The air-car descended onto one of the aspen-clothed lower slopes where a low, rambling house, built of native stone and timber, seemed a natural and proper part of the landscape.

Svyatog emerged, pulling his old-fashioned sleeveless robe more tightly around himself against the brisk air. He'd barely started up the graveled walkway when two humans emerged from the house—first the female and then, a little more slowly, the transmitter. *No,* Svyatog corrected himself, *the primary male. . . . No, simply the* male! *Must remember that.*

"Svyatog!" Katy Doyle-Roark's voice, at least, hadn't changed much. Otherwise . . . well, he knew how to read the signs of aging in humans. She wasn't showing them nearly as much as her parents had at her age, before the new biotechnology had been widely available on this world. But she had already been past her youth when she first had access to those techniques, and Svyatog could read the tale of gray hair and wrinkled skin. The same was even more true of Ben Roark; he was (Svyatog doggedly did the mental arithmetic without cybernetic assistance) seventy-nine local years old, a greater age than the average member of his species had once expected to attain. His hair was grayer than Katy's, and he'd lost most of it . . . rather an improvement, in Lokaron eyes. All things considered, he didn't look bad.

His voice was still recognizable, too. "Hey," he said after the pleasantries were done, "let's get inside and have a drink! We haven't got any voleg, but I'll bet you can make do with brandy."

No, thought Svyatog, *nothing has really changed.* He remembered those two faces as he'd seen them—or what was left of them—in the picket craft's rudimentary little sick bay. Lokaron technology had once repaired even worse damage to Katy's body—but it had been immediately available then. The picket had only had emergency life-support units, and even those had required jury-rigging to accommodate humans. And the trip back to Earth had been prolonged by the need to hold the g-forces down. It was just short of a miracle that Katy had survived to reach the Enclave and its state-of-the-art medical facilities, and not at all short of one that Roark had. But they'd made it, and under the circumstances wonders had been worked. Ever since, Katy had moved almost as well as she had before; and regenerated flesh had taken hold over most of Roark's body, leaving only limited areas of the shiny smoothness that grew to cover burn tissue. Little visible trace remained of what they'd once given for the life of their world.

They entered—Svyatog dipping his head carefully at the human-proportioned doors—and seated themselves with their drinks in a cathedral-ceilinged room. Logs burned brightly in a massive stone fireplace, and wide windows overlooked distant mountains and the westering sun. They spent a moment in companionable silence, with each other and their memories.

"You know, Svyatog," Katy finally said, with the smile that age had been as powerless as the ravages of war to dim, "I've never forgiven you for having been conscious when we got back to Earth."

"That's right," Roark agreed. "You got to experience all that was going on then, while we were stuck in regrowth vats!"

"*You've* never forgiven *me*?" Svyatog hoped the translator conveyed his righteous indignation to the full. "I'm the one who was left to deal with your American politicians without your help. Believe me, I would gladly have joined you in the vats!"

"Yeah, I can imagine." The reconstruction of Roark's face had made his nasty grin even nastier, and age had improved it still further. "I understand Colleen Kinsella, in particular, was ricocheting off the walls."

"Indeed. She felt—with some justice, perhaps—that she'd been misled."

"I'll bet! After she found out Morrison was abolishing the Central Committee she'd been angling for years to get onto . . . !"

"Her old friend Drummond managed to reconcile her to the new order of things. Still, it probably didn't hurt that she was no longer in a position to make trouble. She finally found herself face-to-face with the fact that she had no real power base outside the Earth First Party—which vanished like a bad dream when Morrison declared it dissolved, because it commanded no more popular affection than any other decayed, outworn theocracy."

"A theocracy which lacked even the excuse of religion." Katy nodded. "Like the Soviet system forty-some years earlier. It sort of makes you wonder. Could the whole thing have been avoided if, back around the turn of the century, enough people had *dared to disagree?*"

Roark nodded emphatically. "All they had to do was stand up on their hind legs and say out loud that the emperor was butt-naked."

"I recall the fable to which you allude. It illustrates the problem. Never underestimate the strength of the herd mentality—especially when the herd in question is newly under the influence of the mass communications media, and the adherents of a single viewpoint have a stranglehold on those media." Svyatog tactfully omitted the qualifier *among your species*. It was unkind . . . and, he admitted to himself, unfair. *There, but for a fortuitous accident of history, go we.* Odd, he reflected, how often he fell unconsciously into the cadences he'd picked up from his browsings in this world's religious literature.

"At any rate," he resumed, changing the subject, "you also missed President Morrison's next proclamation, which was his call for the formation of what was to become the Confederated Nations of Earth."

"I've never gotten over being amazed at how smoothly that went," said Katy.

"It surprised all of us. In retrospect, it probably shouldn't have. After the nightmare era of totalitarian states and their wars and genocides, this world was ripe for a loose global federalism based on individual liberty. Actually, it had been for decades. The EFP was merely a rear-guard action by those unwilling to relinquish their accustomed secular religion of statism."

"There were other comparable holdouts elsewhere," Katy recalled. "Islamic militants, unreconstructed Communists in the Russian and Chinese successor states. . . . "

"There were problems," Svyatog acknowledged. "But President Morrison was able to overcome them, even though the Cheyenne Mountain strike had left the United States less capable of enforcing its will militarily. Ironically, that may have helped by making the plan less threatening. The CNE didn't look quite as much like a disguised American empire as it once would have."

"So the Rogovon actually did some good in spite of themselves," Katy mused. She fell into a silence that neither of the others broke, as they all thought of the dead. Kinsella, now forgotten . . . Drummond, remembered fondly by some . . . the Eaglemen, so many of whom had died at the Enclave or Cheyenne Mountain . . . John Morrison, whose colossal statue on the Washington Mall gazed aloft and pointed to a distant goal.

After a while, Katy smiled and spoke again. "Anyway, Svyatog, we're glad you could come here. We understood why you thought you weren't going to be able to. But now, with the war over—"

"Practically over," Svyatog corrected. "The peace conference is still grinding on. But there can be no doubt of the outcome, except in details. So it's no longer necessary for Gev-Harath to minimize contacts here—if, indeed, it ever was. Personally, I always thought we were going a little overboard in being scrupulous about our neutrality. But I was in the minority, and in the end Hov-Korth went along with the other hovahon. They felt that our gevah needed to overcompensate a bit, given its long-standing special relationship with Earth."

"That much is true," Roark opined. "Hov-Korth, in particular, practically underwrote the Confederated Nations' success by dealing with Earth through it. You led the way in that."

"Which is precisely why so many felt that our hovah needed to lean over backwards, as your saying has it. Hypocrisy, really. Everyone in Gev-Harath was secretly cheering for you in your war with Gev-Rogov. And the outcome left us all delighted."

"Astonished, you mean," Roark said drily.

There had been no Lokaron war over the attempted coup in the solar system. It would have been bad for business. Gev-Rogov had quietly paid reparations to the gevahon involved, and that had been that. And the now-unified human race had begun to modernize itself, now that Hov-Korth (through Svyatog) and, subsequently, all of Gev-Harath had entered into a genuine trading relationship with it. Before many years had passed, it had begun to expand along the lines Svyatog had proposed, into Sagittarius and Lupus toward the galactic core.

Then, a decade ago, that expansion had begun to run afoul of Gev-Rogov's.

The CNE had been prepared, in the name of realpolitik, to forget what the Rogovon had once sought to do to Earth. It had proposed a parceling out of the contested planets—the kind of compromise the various gevahon routinely made. But those were compromises among *Lokaron*. The idea of dealing with natives on the same basis was without precedent. Gev-Rogov hadn't even thought it worth the courtesy of a formal refusal.

Eventually, the Rogovon encroachments had grown intolerable. The CNE had declared war a year ago because the alternative was for the human race to slink, beaten, back to its home system. The resigned sighs of Gev-Harath and the other friendly gevahon had been almost audible, for it was in the nature of things that a war between Lokaron and non-Lokaron could have but one outcome.

Like many others, Svyatog was still trying to adjust his reality structure to accommodate what had happened. . . .

"Have you heard from Andrew lately?" he asked.

"Oh, yes! Just last week." At the sound of her son's name, decades slid from Katy's face, dissolved in joy. She and Roark had conceived a child in the teeth of medical advice, for her body hadn't really been all that young even before taking the damage that Lokaron bioscience had only imperfectly repaired. That one experience of childbearing had been enough to bring them around to the doctors' viewpoint, and they hadn't repeated it. But mother and son had both lived, and they'd never regretted it. "He's the executive officer of a battlecruiser, you know. We hadn't heard from him since before the Battle of Upsilon Lupus, and we knew his ship would almost certainly be engaged. So we were worried—"

"Naturally," Svyatog commiserated.

"But unnecessarily, as it turned out," Roark grinned.

"Yes. Your fleet's losses were minimal, weren't they?" Svyatog's polite smile was a mask for complex emotions. *What's the matter with me? Why should I feel ambivalent? I ought to be overjoyed for my friends. After all, they* are *my friends, and the CNE is an ally of Gev-Harath and a lucrative market for Hov-Korth. And I've never had any use for the*

Rogovon—they're enemies, and they don't even belong to my subspecies.

And yet . . . they're Lokaron! And for the first time in history, Lokaron have been defeated by natives— by an alien race, I mean.

Nor had it been mere defeat. Gev-Rogov's battle fleet had been *annihilated* at Upsilon Lupus. The military experts were still analyzing the details of that battle, but the main outlines were clear enough.

The desperation ploy Roark and Katy had used thirty-seven years before had been the kind of trick that only works once. Knowing who they were fighting, the Rogovon had simply reprogrammed human acceleration tolerances into their targeting computers. So there had been no tactical surprises. But the Rogovon fleet had ignored any number of elementary precautions it would have followed as a matter of course had it been going into action against *real* opponents—meaning Lokaron ones. Perhaps even more importantly, the human fleet had been built from the ground up over the past decade or two, with all the Lokaron civilization's military experience to study with preconception-free eyes, and all its mistakes to learn from without embarrassment. That fleet had been crewed by the heirs of a history of total war—not just the safely remote frontier spats of the gevahon. And those crews had grown up on tales of what had almost happened to their world at the hands of Gev-Rogov. . . .

"I've heard reports," Svyatog said mildly, "that there were unexplained delays in accepting the surrender signals from some of the Rogovon ships."

"Yeah, so I understand. Well . . . " Roark took a pull on his drink and let his expression finish the sentence for him.

"Anyway," Katy piped up, a little too brightly, "the

fighting's over now. Andy and all the rest of Admiral Arnstein's people will be returning home soon. All that's left now is the peace talks."

"Yes. And those shouldn't take much longer. The news from Tizath-Asor is positive." With their planetside forces in the contested region at the mercy of Arnstein's unchallenged battle fleet, the Rogovon had been left with no alternative to the unthinkable. They'd sued for peace, asking Gev-Tizath to serve as broker. So now, for the first time in history, Lokaron negotiators (*Rogovon ones, at any rate,* Svyatog mentally hedged) sat across a table from counterparts of another species and had terms dictated to them. The other Lokaron powers wouldn't allow those terms to be too severe. Still . . .

Yes, he decided with bleak honesty, *it may take a while before I decide just how I'm supposed to feel about this.*

Outwardly, he smiled a Lokaron smile and raised his drink. "In accordance with your culture's custom, I propose a toast: to Lieutenant Commander Andrew Roark and all his brave comrades."

"Hear, hear!" Katy clinked brandy snifters with him.

"I'll drink to that." Roark hoisted the rum he'd chosen at the price of a patently ritualistic glare from his wife.

Now she glared again, with just as little conviction. "You'll drink to anything!" And the last of whatever undercurrents the room had held dissipated in the general laughter.

"Hey, I'm starving!" protested Roark. "Svyatog, we've stocked up on some items you like—or, at least, that you sell to the other Lokaron."

"That's right," Katy affirmed. "And you can stay the night, can't you? I'm sure you've been here long enough, this trip, to adapt to Earth's diurnal cycle. And we've got a state-of-the-art reconfigurable guest bed that can adapt to *you*."

"Certainly. But I must get an early start in the morning. My shuttle departs from Front Range Spaceport before noon."

They went in to dinner as the setting sun vanished behind the Rockies. The rest of the evening passed in a convivial exchange of shared memories, in the warmth of flaming logs and the glow of good booze. And the bed they offered him was everything Katy had said it was. He couldn't blame that for the fitfulness of his sleep.

The next morning, all was pleasantries as they bade him farewell. But after he'd gotten into his air-car and was preparing for departure, Roark stepped forward. His eyes held ghosts of what had briefly passed between them the previous night, and he spoke with unwonted seriousness—almost with urgency.

"Svyatog, I want you to remember something. Aside from all you've done for us personally, the human race will always owe Gev-Harath one. We'll never forget that. Whatever happens, whatever the future holds, there'll always be that special relationship you spoke of." And then the canopy closed between them. The air-car lifted, and the two alien figures dwindled in the distance.

Svyatog set in a southeasterly course, and the canopy automatically polarized against the rising sun ahead. He marveled as always at the dramatic quality of this landscape: the rough-hewn, almost brutal quality of the raw stone that thrust upward in titanic masses. *But there's been no time for wind and rain to wear those masses down, smoothing and rounding them into what I remember from Harath-Asor*, he reminded himself. *This is a far younger world.*

For some obscure reason, the thought made him recall Roark's last, uncharacteristic words. *Whatever did he mean? He was so very earnest. It was almost as though he thought I needed reassurance. Could it have been what we were saying last night?*

Of course not! he chided himself. He'd dismissed his misgivings during the night, attributing them to the unaccustomed setting and its subliminal psychological effects. *Preposterous! Remember, we're talking about Gev-Rogov—technologically rather backward, socially archaic. Oh, all right: they* are, *I suppose, Lokaron. But they were ineptly led and stupidly overconfident, blundering along as usual under their inflexible centralized system. It's not as though this had happened to one of the mainstream Lokaron polities.*

No. Of course not. What I did, years ago, was merely a move in the established, familiar game of Lokaron power politics. Nothing has really changed.

Has it?

He flew on into the morning.